**Rick heard a series
of irregular clicks . . .**

He dragged his mouth from Lexie's, lifting his
eyes instinctively to the source of the irritating
sound. It took only a split second for his brain
to register what was happening and not much
more than that for his reflexes to kick in. He
thrust Lexie against the wall and shoved her to
her knees.

"Oh, my God . . . !" She breathed the exclamation
in a barely audible whisper, then ducked even
lower as the horrible creaking filled the air.

The solid black mass of the elevator car was
rolling down the narrow shaft, its descent
labored and sluggish—but relentless. It kept
coming, sinking lower and lower on its time-
worn runners and ancient cables. The advancing
monster was less than two meters above them
now and still dropping.

There was nothing they could do to stop it.

ABOUT THE AUTHOR

As far back as she can remember, Jenna Ryan has been dreaming up stories, everything from fairy tales to romantic mysteries. She now employs her vivid imagination spinning yarns for Harlequin Intrigue, her favorite romance series. A resident of Victoria, British Columbia, Jenna has been a model, an airline reservation agent, a tour escort and a lingerie salesperson. She now writes full-time.

Books by Jenna Ryan

HARLEQUIN INTRIGUE
88–CAST IN WAX
99–SUSPENDED ANIMATION
118–CLOAK AND DAGGER

Don't miss any of our special offers. Write to us at the following address for information on our newest releases.

Harlequin Reader Service
901 Fuhrmann Blvd., P.O. Box 1397, Buffalo, NY 14240
Canadian address: P.O. Box 603,
Fort Erie, Ont. L2A 5X3

Carnival
Jenna Ryan

Harlequin Books

TORONTO • NEW YORK • LONDON
AMSTERDAM • PARIS • SYDNEY • HAMBURG
STOCKHOLM • ATHENS • TOKYO • MILAN

Harlequin Intrigue edition published May 1990

ISBN 0-373-22138-X

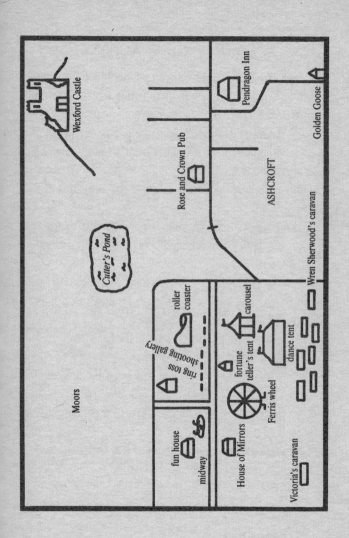

Wexford Castle

Cutter's Pond

Moors

roller coaster

ring toss
shooting gallery

fun house

midway

House of Mirrors

Victoria's caravan

fortune teller's tent

Ferris wheel

dance tent

carousel

Wren Sherwood's caravan

Rose and Crown Pub

Pendragon Inn

ASHCROFT

Golden Goose

CAST OF CHARACTERS

Lexie Hudson—She came to London to practice law—but school never taught her how to find a murderer....

Rick Matheson—He went undercover as a roustabout, but would this be his last assignment?

Diana Beroni—Lexie's client—did she murder her lover?

Wren Sherwood/Glen Barrie—He went under an alias and knew every con...until he met with death.

Victoria Farraday—She seemed aristocratic— what was she doing running a struggling carny troupe?

P. J. Fitzwilly—Once a petty thief...now Scotland Yard's eyes and ears.

Gwendolyn Sykes—What did her piercing eyes see in that crystal ball?

Charles Gideon—Was his bungling manner just a cover?

Leonard Skelton—He fancied his fun-house puppets more than he did people.

Prologue

Aidan O'Brien...

Wren Sherwood, known to his fellow carnies as Glen Barrie, turned his late partner's name over and over in his mind. Yes, Aidan was dead, no doubt about it. If any man knew that for a fact, Wren did. He should have known; he'd been the one to torch Aidan's dingy Soho flat.

Irritably, Wren paced the floor of his caravan. Much as he would have liked to indulge himself, he had no time to waste on memories. There were several more urgent thoughts. First and foremost, he had to move the Saxony jewels to a new and safer location. He hadn't stolen them two years ago to lose them now. And of course, it went without saying that he had to eliminate the threat to his own existence.

There should be no problem in either area, he decided with a quick glance at his watch. The carnival had put down its usual summer roots outside the tiny English village of Ashcroft in Devon. The nearby hills were heavily wooded, the rivers deep, the moors mist shrouded and vast. A body could be disposed of quite readily in any of those places. He had only to select one of them, hide the Saxony jewels in a different spot and all would be well once more.

Maybe things would be even better, he mused, absently wiping a smudge of dirt from the caravan's side window. If he handled this situation properly, he might just be able to eke out another two years in his newfound home. By then the heat would surely have subsided sufficiently for him to fence the jewels and take up residence in Monte Carlo.

He stole another look at his watch. It was 10:07. The carnival had closed down for the night, and many of the workers would be heading for their trailers. Soon enough he'd have his chance.

In an effort to fill the minutes between thought and action, Wren collected two used teacups from his kitchen table and turned for the sink. He was halfway there when the door to his caravan gave a tiny squeak.

Now that was odd, he reflected, setting the cups down on the counter. Diana couldn't possibly have returned from her walk yet, and no one else was likely to venture in here unannounced. Not unless...

His fingers twined themselves instinctively around the handle of the cutlery drawer, then locked in place as a bitter voice suddenly broke the stillness of the muggy air.

"Don't waste your time, Glen," it advised from the doorway. "I know what you're planning to do, just as I know who you really are. The great Wren Sherwood, alias Glen Barrie. Murderer, thief and undoubtedly any number of other vile things."

Wren yanked open the drawer, but a raw chuckle from the direction of the table told him, as did his groping fingers, that the gun he habitually kept there was missing.

"I see you take me for an utter fool," the voice continued, closer now than before. "I'm disappointed in you. You place a gun where any bumbling idiot can find it, then expect it to be there when you need it most. And you do need it, don't you, Wren? You planned to use it this very night. You were going to kill me as you have so many others over the years."

Wren straightened from the drawer. Turning slowly, he inquired, "What would you have done in my place?"

He heard the hammer of a gun—his gun—being cocked. "Exactly the same thing," he was informed in a chilly tone. "Goodbye, old friend. I'm sure there's a nice warm spot reserved for you—in hell!"

GLEN'S CARAVAN was as black as pitch when Diana Beroni returned to the carnival site after her walk. It took several long seconds for her eyes to adjust to the murky interior, but then she didn't really have to see to find her way around. Glen kept the place as neat as a pin. She could cross the floor blindfolded and not bump into a single piece of furniture.

Shivering slightly beneath her raincoat, she called out "Glen, are you here?"

There was no response, and with a shrug she turned on the light. Lowering her head, she began fumbling with the belt of her raincoat, then she paused as her eyes landed on a pair of feet jutting out from behind the counter.

"Glen?" she repeated in a puzzled tone. "Oh, for heaven's sake, what are you doing now?" Her lips curved into an amused smile. "Surely you wouldn't be polishing the sink pipes at ten thirty in the evening. Honestly, you and your bizarre penchant for cleanliness. Can't you give it a rest for even one night?"

When no reply—sarcastic or otherwise—was forthcoming, Diana rounded the counter, stepping over a throw cushion and giving his foot a gentle nudge with her toe.

"You really are the most exasperating man," she teased. "Why don't you—"

The question halted abruptly as she focused on Glen's motionless body, on the trail of blood that had spilled from the hole in his throat.

"Dear God, no," she whispered, pressing a hand to her stomach. "No! This can't be! Glen! Glen, wake up! Wake up!"

Her voice rose with every word, until she was screaming his name out loud. She dropped to her knees, afraid to touch him, afraid to do anything except stare. "Glen!" she screeched. "Glen, please, get up! You can't be dead! You just can't be!"

She was still screaming his name when she spied the gun next to his arm. It was the sight of the weapon more than the sight of her lover's body that made her recoil in horror. With a strangled sob, she crawled away from the counter and kept crawling until she ran into the legs of the table. She would have crawled right out of the caravan if she hadn't glimpsed the shadow that passed soundlessly by the side window.

A dozen different emotions battled inside her. But it was fear that swiftly won out. Fear that the shadow might be someone who'd seen her come in here. Someone who might intend to harm her.

She scrambled to her feet and made a desperate dive for the gun. She had no choice but to pick it up, no choice at all. The shadow was drawing closer. She could hear the person who'd cast it on the outer steps, could see the door being pushed open.

Turning her head to one side, she held the gun in front of her with both hands. Her finger wrapped around the trigger. Then, choking on a cry of terror, she squeezed off a single resounding shot that shattered the glass of the window and threw her back against the wall.

"What in the world— Diana, have you lost your mind?" The carnival owner, Victoria Farraday, cringed as she flung open the door and lurched inside. "First you scream, then you take a blind shot at me. What on earth has gotten into you?"

Too shocked to respond, Diana let the gun clatter to the floor at her feet. "It's Glen," she whispered not moving from where she stood. "He's—he's dead!"

THE CROWD OF ONLOOKERS that gathered outside Glen
Barrie's caravan watched in appalled silence as Victoria
ushered Diana through the door and into their midst. Only
one person on the grounds knew what had really happened
there that night. And as the fear of discovery gradually began to fade, that person risked a small inward smile.

Maybe, just maybe, things would work out after all.

Chapter One

Medieval, quaint and charming.

Those three words sprang to mind as Lexie Hudson angled her Jaguar along the shrub-lined road that wound down toward the River Ashburn. It was an old and lovely section of the country, far from the madding crowds of London and the legal firm of Bardsley, Sutcliffe and Townsend. Unfortunately for Lexie, it was also an unfamiliar section of the country. Already she'd taken a few wrong turns and been forced to stop and ask directions from a stoop-shouldered farmer whose slurred local dialect had all but stumped her.

A steady drizzle made the track before her slick and difficult to navigate. The temperature was in the low sixties, the humidity high, the smell of lilacs and wild roses heavy in the air. But even those things weren't enough to keep her from thinking about her firm's newest client.

Diana Beroni, a carnival dancer who until six months ago had been working at a nightclub in Potenza, Italy, stood accused of murder. And what a murder, Lexis reflected, shaking her golden-brown hair from her eyes. Not only had the deceased, Glen Barrie, better known as Wren Sherwood, been Diana's lover, but he'd also been a thief and murderer himself.

Three years before, he'd reportedly botched an armed bank robbery, killing a teller and two security guards in the process. Eleven months later, he and his partner, Aidan O'Brian, had made off with a collection of jewels belonging to Sir Desmond and Lady Saxony. Then less than two weeks after the heist his partner's Soho flat had been gutted in a fire, leaving Aidan dead and no sign of either Wren Sherwood or the stolen jewels.

That the man had finally received his just deserts was an issue Lexie chose not to debate. That the fate of her firm's client might very well hinge on whatever evidence she could dig up at the carnival was her primary reason for driving to Devon and the only thing that mattered.

Lexie had come to London four years earlier from Cambridge, Massachusetts, fresh out of law school and eager to ply her trade. The magic of England had gripped her the moment she'd stepped off the plane; a three-week visit with her sister in York had made her long to stay on this side of the Atlantic. But staying, to her mind, meant proving herself in areas more impressive than the minor assault-and-battery cases she'd dealt with since passing the British bar exams.

Thankfully her relationship with Rodney made it possible for her to devote the bulk of her energy to her career. Dear, steady, reliable, uncomplicated Rodney Boggs, a junior partner at the rival firm of Watson and Moresby and her soon-to-be-fiancé. If all went well, she'd be wearing his engagement ring by Christmas—or so he kept insisting.

If his plans had a rather prosaic ring to them, she managed to ignore it. She was very fond of Rodney, perhaps not passionately so, but they did have a great deal in common. And certainly no one could deny that he was a wonderful man, an understanding man who would never throw her life into an emotional tailspin. All things considered, they'd make an ideal couple.

Smiling wryly to herself, Lexie eased her car around a cluster of gray thatched cottages. The road broadened slightly once she reached the village. Banishing the image of

Rodney's familiar features, she turned her attention to the row of shops and stores that rose crookedly on either side of her.

Ashcroft, she'd been informed by her associates, was a quiet little community. Very peaceful, but not entirely isolated. A photographer's delight, it sat nestled in a combe at the base of a densely forested hill not far from the River Ashburn. Moorlands stretched out to the west, and to the north she could just make out the crumbling peak of an ancient castle.

It wasn't until she passed the Rose and Crown Pub on the far side of the village that she heard the distant strains of carnival music. Though the sound should have seemed incongruous, it didn't strike her that way. Possibly because her wonderfully outrageous Grandfather McLaren had once been a carny in Yorkshire. Carnivals and countryside just naturally went hand in hand to her.

She stopped her car where the road more or less ended, peering through the drizzle at a long grassy path that meandered down to a flat plot of land covered with a collection of tents, booths, rides and no less than thirty brightly colored trailers. She was busy pawing under the front seat for her umbrella when she heard a sharp tap on her window.

"Miss Hudson?" The person who spoke was dressed in black denim pants, boots and a leather jacket that more properly befit a member of a motorcycle gang than a regal-looking woman of sixty with silver white hair and a thin, wiry build.

At Lexie's nod, the woman pulled open the car door and offered her hand. "I'm Victoria Farraday. I own the carnival. Mr. Sutcliffe told Diana you'd be arriving this afternoon. I thought it best to come up and meet you."

Abandoning her search for the elusive umbrella, Lexie stepped from the car. "It's Lexie," she said automatically, accepting the firm handshake. "I'm very glad to meet you.

I was told that you put up the money for Ms. Beroni's defense, as well as her bail.''

"A portion of it," the woman said, smiling. "In truth, several of Diana's friends contributed to the cause. You see, none of us believes she was capable of killing Glen. Or perhaps," she amended with a grimace, "I should call him Wren."

"That was his real name," Lexie agreed. She tugged at the collar of her raincoat and tried to keep the heels of her pumps from sinking into the muddy pool of earth and water beneath her. "I understand that Wren Sherwood had been with you for two years prior to his death."

"Yes." Sighing, Victoria led the way along the path to the carnival. "I'm afraid I'm not one for checking references as closely as I should," she confessed. "My nephew owned the carnival originally. After his death a few years back, I was forced to take over the entire operation. When the man I knew as Glen Barrie showed up as we were in the midst of a rather poor season, my only prerequisite was that he be willing to work long hours in whatever capacity he might be needed."

"So you knew nothing about him."

"Not a thing."

At that vehement denial, Lexie spared the woman a curious glance. Victoria Farraday's handsome features bore the telltale traces of a hard life. Yet despite that, her bearing was proud and aristocratic. Her blue eyes, too, seemed particularly assessing, though perhaps she wasn't quite as shrewd as she appeared. Wren Sherwood had obviously fooled her, and by all reports the man had been something less than a masterful con artist.

Lips pursed, Victoria indicated a long red caravan three hundred yards to her left. "Glen's home," she stated flatly. "He and Diana lived there for just over five months. I'm sure you're aware that the police have already come and gone."

Lexie managed a nod as she tugged on the belt of her sopping raincoat. She'd been thoroughly briefed before leaving London. Not unexpectedly, the police had found Diana's prints all over Wren Sherwood's trailer. Nevertheless, that wasn't the real problem here. It was the gunpowder residue on her hands that had ultimately landed her in jail.

Taking one final look at the dead man's caravan, Lexie forgot her own discomfort and glanced over at Victoria. "I understand Diana fired a shot through the window just as you were about to enter."

"Yes, she did," Victoria admitted slowly. "Whoever killed Glen left the gun on the floor beside him. After Diana discovered his body she must have seen me pass by the window and not realized who it was. In her panic she grabbed the gun and fired."

"She thought you were the murderer."

"I'm afraid so."

Lexie considered asking Victoria exactly what she'd been doing prowling around outside the trailer that night, then decided against it. The carnival owner's statement was a matter of record. She'd been in the process of checking the fair grounds, heard Diana scream and run over to Wren Sherwood's caravan to see what was wrong. It was a perfectly plausible explanation, and until she talked with Diana, Lexie sensed it might be wiser to withhold any further questions.

Rain continued to drizzle from the cloud-swollen skies. Lexie could feel the moisture seeping through the protective layers of her clothing. For the life of her, she couldn't imagine anyone preferring even the lure of an outdoor carnival to a game of darts in some warm, dry pub on such an inclement day.

She squinted through the mist at the striped tents and colorful facades of the arcade games. There were lineups everywhere and few umbrellas in sight. Unlike her, the peo-

ple here seemed to have grown accustomed to adverse
weather conditions.

She wondered briefly if all the publicity connected with
Wren Sherwood's death could be partly responsible for the
high attendance figures. The murder had taken place only
ten days ago. The police might be long gone, but that didn't
necessarily mean that public interest in the case had waned.

Drawing her to one side, Victoria whisked her through the
outer gate and into the carnival. "Diana is staying with
Gwendolyn Sykes," she said, motioning toward the top of
a bright yellow trailer visible on the far side of the meadow.
"Gwendolyn's one of our very best fortune tellers, though
not, I confess, one of Diana's closest friends."

Lexie digested that tidbit of information in silence, but
her gaze was riveted on a group of wary observers who were
watching her from the end of the midway. Although there
couldn't have been more than seven or eight of them, judg-
ing from the shuttered expressions on their faces, she suspected her work would be cut out for her during the next
week or so. Her grandfather had told her long ago that carnies were notoriously tight-knit and closemouthed. She had
a strong hunch they wouldn't be too inclined to talk to a
stranger, no matter how noble her intentions might be.

Resolutely, Lexie dragged her gaze from the brooding
group and let it stray over the caterpillar ride to a distant rise
on the far side of the meadow. Through the deepening mist
she spied the remnants of a structure much older than any
of the castles and abbeys she'd seen during her drive from
London.

"Algernon's workshop," a male voice informed her.

Surprised by the cryptic remark, Lexie whipped her head
around just in time to see the man who'd made it duck
lithely under an angled support rail. He was tall and blond
with a lean, rangy build and had about the most arresting
features she'd ever seen. However, while his look was that

of a Nordic athlete, his accent definitely wasn't European. Actually, it sounded like a blend of Australian and Midwestern American. Interesting—and oddly appealing.

His beautiful blue eyes flicked to hers and he motioned idly toward the ancient obelisk she'd been staring at. "It's an old Roman fortress supposedly inhabited by the ghost of a French alchemist named Algernon."

As Lexie returned her dubious gaze to the barely visible structure, the man smiled slightly, turning his attention to Victoria. "Jamie says to tell you there's a big problem in one of the food tents."

Victoria let her breath out in an exasperated rush. "With the freezer, no doubt." Her expression was apologetic when she looked at Lexie. "I'll have to go down and see how serious this problem really is. If you don't mind, I'll have Rick show you to Diana's caravan." She motioned from one to the other. "Rick, this is Lexie Hudson. Her firm is handling Diana's legal affairs. Lexie, Rick Matheson, one of our handier roustabouts."

A roustabout? Lexie regarded the man as covertly as possible, taking note of his rather long hair, worn work boots and faded jeans that emphasized the length of his smoothly muscled legs. Well, maybe he made his living rigging tents and setting up carnival rides, but that wouldn't have been her first guess.

"Now, if you need anything at all," Victoria continued, "my caravan's at the far end of the row. I'll be there most of the evening working on the books, assuming, of course, that the leak in my roof has been repaired."

The latter, more of a question than a statement, was directed at Rick whose striking blue eyes, Lexie suddenly realized, were surveying her in an unobtrusive albeit thorough fashion.

"All done," he said, wrapping his fingers around her arm and propelling her in the direction of the trailers. "You won't be taking any more unexpected showers in the middle of the night.''

With a laugh, Victoria moved away and was quickly swallowed up in the crowd.

If she'd had the foresight to wear hiking boots instead of Italian leather pumps, Lexie might have entertained a second thought or two about being left alone in Rick's company. Certainly, she would have considered pulling free of his steadying grasp. While she seldom fell prey to outward appearances, she sensed something in this man that went far beyond his Elysian features, something she was certain she'd do well not to examine too closely. Not with Rodney up in London, patiently awaiting her return.

"So you're a lawyer, are you?" Rick inquired, his lips curving into a slow smile. At Lexie's distracted nod, he sent her a speculative look. "Since you're here, I take it you don't think Scotland Yard unearthed everything they could about Wren Sherwood's death."

Once across the midway, the ground was somewhat firmer and she risked a quick upward glance. "I don't know what to think yet," she replied truthfully.

His smile broadened, and she fervently wished he would release his hold on her arm. It might upset her balance, but at least she'd be able to put a few discreet inches between them.

"Don't most legal firms send out private detectives to do their digging?" he asked, his tone only mildly curious.

She shrugged. "Not always. It depends on the circumstances, on how much danger is likely to be involved."

An inscrutable light entered his eyes. "Any murder investigation can be dangerous, Lexie."

It was on the tip of her tongue to ask him how he'd reached that sage conclusion. Unfortunately, the chance for any further conversation between them was lost when a dark-haired woman in her early thirties appeared at the door of the yellow caravan. Her eyes were deep brown, her features patrician and pale, her expression hesitant.

"You must be Lexie Hudson," she said, opening the door a bit wider and offering Rick a wan smile of greeting.

Nodding, Lexie slipped under the wide awning that sheltered the stoop. In the back of her mind she registered the fact that Rick's hand had dropped back to his side. Strangely, though, she could still feel the imprint of his fingers on her arm....

Drawing herself as erect as she could with the mud still squishing beneath her feet, she shoved the odd sensation away, and ventured an encouraging, "Malcolm Sutcliffe sent me down to do some investigative work on your case, Ms. Beroni."

"Diana," the woman murmured, standing aside. "Please come in. I've just made a pot of tea. Perhaps you'd join me."

Lexie stole a furtive look at Rick's impassive features. She couldn't read his expression, but she got the distinct feeling that he wasn't quite as far removed from this situation as his position at the carnival would have her believe. She should have questioned him when she'd had the chance, she realized belatedly. Roustabouts tended to be jacks-of-many-trades. This man and his carny cohorts might turn out to be veritable gold mines of information. At least they might if she could maintain a professional attitude long enough to do her job.

Sighing inwardly, Lexie thanked Rick, then at Diana's bidding stepped into the caravan, resisting the urge to look back at the disturbing blue eyes that followed her inside. And once inside, she didn't dare look back at anything or anyone.

There were piles of colorful clothes and jewel-studded costumes everywhere she turned. A profusion of scarves, stockings, bras and briefs spilled from three open trunks. The counters were crammed with make-up pots and mirrors, the shelves heaped with hats, stuffed animals, kewpie dolls and multihued tinsel wigs. The place was a disaster area with only the round kitchen table devoid of exotic paraphernalia.

"You'll have to excuse the mess," Diana said, removing a fringed green shawl from the back of a chair. "I'm not much of a housekeeper and neither is Gwendolyn. We, uh, make a habit of avoiding each other whenever possible, so we haven't really worked out any systems of organization yet."

"I take it you don't get along with your new roommate," Lexie noted, recalling the statement Victoria had made on their walk from the village.

Diana lowered her eyes. "No, we don't, but it's not important."

Lexie wasn't so sure, but she didn't press the matter. After removing her sodden raincoat and muddy shoes, she took a seat at the kitchen table, watching as Diana brought out a tray of tea and cream-filled biscuits. The woman was understandably distraught over the events of the past several days, and because of that, Lexie forced herself not to jump headlong into a clinical interrogation. Instead, she bit her tongue and waited for her client to open the conversation.

Thankfully, Diana did just that, albeit in a rather abrupt and agitated manner.

"I didn't do it," she blurted out as if appealing to a ruthless judge. "I didn't kill him, and I swear to you I had no idea who he really was."

Lexie groped for the right words. Tact wasn't always her strong suit, especially when she was looking for answers. "I know you didn't" was the best she could come up with. She pushed several strands of damp hair from her cheeks and tried again. "I'm sorry, Diana. I realize how upsetting this must be for you, but you have to understand the severity of the charges against you. I believe you didn't kill Wren

Sherwood. Unfortunately, my belief isn't enough here. The police found your fingerprints on the murder weapon, powder residue on your hands and several witnesses in the village who heard you and Wren arguing volubly two days before he was shot.''

"Yes, but I wasn't arguing with anyone named Wren Sherwood," Diana insisted. "To me he was Glen Barrie, and what those village people heard was nothing more than a minor spat. Glen was angry because he thought I'd been flirting with a young man in the audience that night.''

"Someone who works at the carnival?" Lexie asked hopefully.

"No, just a tourist. I'd never seen him before, and I haven't since. He was a stranger to me. Glen was jealous, that's all. He got angry, but he got over it. We made up later that same night. You can ask just about anyone who works here.''

That sounded reasonable enough. Lexie made a mental note to corroborate the story, then inquired, "What about the night he died? Did you see or hear anything at all that you didn't mention to the police or Malcolm Sutcliffe?''

Giving her head a weary shake, Diana began pouring out the tea. "There isn't really much to see on the moors at night," she admitted. "When the carnival closed at ten o'clock, I left the grounds like I always do and took a walk past Algernon's workshop—that's the old Roman fortress—across the moor to Cutter's Pond, then around it to the edge of the village.''

"And you didn't notice anything out of the ordinary?''

"No. Everything was the same as usual. Very quiet, except for the pub. It's always crowded in there. I cut down the lane beside the Rose and Crown, stopped to pat Burt Drury's basset hound, then went back to the carnival. I didn't run into anyone.''

"But some of your co-workers did see you leave the carnival after your last show.''

"Several, but I gather from what the police told me that that doesn't prove much of anything."

"No, I'm afraid it doesn't." Lexie sat back in her chair, stifling a sigh. "All right," she said after a moment's pause. "What happened once you got back?"

Diana took a sip of her tea and lowered her eyes. "That's when I found him. I went into the caravan, turned on the lights and called to him. At first I thought he wasn't there, but then I saw him, lying behind the counter. I—I didn't touch him, but I could see he wasn't…breathing. There was a cushion, too," she added. "From the sofa. I should have known something was wrong the minute I spotted it on the floor. Glen was a fanatic about neatness. He couldn't stand to have a single thing out of place either in his caravan or in his game booth."

"He ran the shooting gallery, didn't he?" Lexie asked.

"Yes. Fitz will show it to you if you want to see it."

"Fitz?"

"P. J. Fitzwilly. He has the adjacent booth. The ring toss. The two of them used to play Scrabble during the lulls. At the end of each day Glen would collect the money from all the arcade booths and take it to Victoria." Diana took another sip of her tea. "Anyway, to get back on topic, I don't remember much after I found Glen's body. I know I saw someone moving past the side window, and I guess I picked up the gun that was lying beside his arm. But I don't really remember firing it. I must have, though, because I heard the glass shatter, and I do recall bumping into the wall and dropping the gun on the floor just as Victoria came in. That's why my fingerprints were on it." Her voice trembled, and she stopped speaking to draw a shaky breath. "It looks bad for me, doesn't it?" she ventured tremulously. "I can't prove I didn't kill him, and neither can you."

"Well, not yet," Lexie returned. "But something will turn up."

"You sound awfully sure of yourself."

Yes, she did, Lexie thought. In fact, she sounded down-right positive. Why, she wasn't sure. After all, this was hardly a routine case for her. True, she'd done any number of background checks before, and at the request of her rather sedentary employers, she'd even done a little snooping in the field. But she was no Miss Marple. She was just Alexandra Hudson, philosophy student turned lawyer. And for all her studies of Socrates and Plato, she could scarcely begin to understand the nature of a murderer's thoughts.

Of course, second-guessing a killer would be a foolish undertaking. She'd have to attack this case from a more logical angle. That meant asking a lot of questions and greatly sharpening her powers of investigation. And that meant going over Diana's story until every last detail of it was firmly ingrained in her mind—including the less than palatable aspects of the woman's relationship with Wren Sherwood.

On that distasteful note, Lexie took a deep breath and looked across at her client. "Okay, Diana," she said calmly. "We'd better start at the beginning. I need to hear about your first meeting with the man you knew as Glen Barrie and how you came to be involved with him."

OUTSIDE THE YELLOW CARAVAN, the drizzle had turned to a steady rain. Rick Matheson eyed the unpromising clouds and for a moment half-wished he were back in Melbourne or Chicago. Or even Vienna or Maracaibo. The location didn't really matter. He was no stranger to travel. Over the course of his lifetime, he'd lived in close to fifty different cities, towns and villages in seventeen different countries. If he'd been smart, he would have followed in his father's footsteps and become a free-lance photographer. But no, he'd chosen to sail for England nine years ago. He'd traded in a promising career as a globe-trotting photojournalist for a flat off the Tower Bridge Road in London and a job with Scotland Yard. As a result, instead of sweating out a trip down the Amazon, he was standing in the rain in Devon, listening at trailer windows and pretending to be a carnival roustabout. So much for the prestigious life of a plain-clothes inspector.

An inspector with an assignment to carry out, he re-minded himself. For the past two years, Scotland Yard had been hunting for the elusive Wren Sherwood, not to men-tion the stolen Saxony jewels. While the man might be dead, the jewels still hadn't been recovered. Until they were, Rick would continue to work at the carnival just as he'd been doing for the past week.

Shifting his weight on the muddy ground, he shoved his hands into the pockets of his jacket. Through the thin glass, he heard Diana's voice droning on.

"I was a dancer in Potenza," she told Lexie. "When the carnival came to town, I decided to go and see it. I hap-pened to bump into Victoria, and we started talking. The next thing I knew, she was telling me about an opening she had in the Viking dance show. She said I'd fill the bill per-fectly if I didn't mind a lot of traveling."

"What about the jewels?" Rick muttered under his breath, aware of the rain seeping through his jeans, soak-ing him to the skin.

Whether Lexie had any intention of delving into that subject quickly became a moot point. Three carnies had wandered off the midway and were heading in his direc-tion. Pushing himself away from the caravan, he stepped into the growing shadows—and right into the path of a squat little man of fifty with narrow features, darting eyes and a thinning cap of brown hair beneath his battered barker's derby.

"Afternoon, Rick," P. J. Fitzwilly greeted him, his thick Cornish accent infused with just a hint of cockney. "Found yourself any buried treasure, have you?"

Rick held back a grin. Fitz had been a petty thief and pickpocket when they'd first met some five years before in

London. Though Rick didn't exactly trust the man, he'd been a helpful snitch in the past, and he did know his way around a carnival.

"Keep it down, Fitz. I'm undercover, remember?"

"Eight bloody days worth and counting," Fitz mourned. Chuckling, he stuck a soggy cigar stub in the side of his mouth, then opened his baggy jacket for inspection. "I'm still clean, mate. Nothing but me own wallet and pocket watch under these old rags."

"Yeah, well, just make sure you keep it that way."

"I'll keep me ears open and me mouth shut," Fitz countered, evading any firm promises. "Speaking of which, you might be interested to know that I saw Skelly paying a mite more attention than usual to Wren Sherwood's caravan this morning. Looked to me like he was just itching to try out the lock."

Rick glanced down the row at the unoccupied trailer, then over at the fun house where Leonard Skelton worked. A former undertaker, Skelly, as he was better known, had joined the carnival just over eighteen months ago. For the most part he kept to himself, although during the eight days Rick had been on the grounds, Rick had spotted the man in Gwendolyn Sykes's company more than once.

He considered taking a walk to the fortune teller's tent, then thought better of it. The workers here had been extremely reticent with the police assigned to investigate Wren Sherwood's death. If they suspected his connection to Scotland Yard, Rick knew he could kiss this assignment goodbye.

Turning up the collar of his jacket, he regarded an expectant Fitz. "I'll keep an eye on him," he said.

"Might be worth your while," Fitz noted shrewdly. "Because if there's one person at this carny who truly had it in for our Glen Barrie, that person would be Skelly."

Eyes sparkling, the little man cocked a knowing brow and scuttled off toward his booth, leaving Rick to wonder just how much Percival J. Fitzwilly knew about Wren Sherwood's death that he wasn't telling.

TWO FADED Royal Albert teacups. They looked so very innocent, yet they said so very much. Perhaps they would ultimately tell a story of death....

And then again, perhaps they wouldn't.

A trembling hand reached out to lock the cups away where they wouldn't be seen. This story must remain untold. Let Diana Beroni take the blame for her lover's murder. Surely she deserved to be convicted.

But would she? Or would the woman who'd been spotted in her company today find a way to get the charges against her dropped?

No! That wouldn't do at all. Diana's attorney must never learn the truth.

The hand stopped trembling as the seed of an idea began to sprout. A warning, that's what was needed. Surely she would get the message then. And if she didn't— Well, there was more than one way to snuff out a problem. Oh, yes, in a carnival where death had so recently cast its blackened shadow, there were any number of ways.

Chapter Two

"I swear these reports will haunt me in the great beyond," Rick's partner complained. "Here I am posing as a bon-bon salesman who stopped to visit a carnival on his way home to Exeter, and I'm still typing out blasted reports."

With one skinny finger, Charles Gideon stabbed at the keys of his portable typewriter while his free hand dug into a generous helping of newspaper-wrapped fish and chips.

Rick leaned against the dresser in his partner's room at the Pendragon Inn, munching absently on a piece of fried cod. "It could be worse, Charles. You could be typing reports back at the home office."

"And listening to the chief superintendent's complaints about his lumbago. No need to remind me, Rick. I'm not quite so daft that I'd chuck this assignment for such a dreary alternative. Nevertheless, the fact remains that I was on holiday over in Dartmeet, angling for trout, when the boys caught up with me. I don't know as you'd be turning handsprings if you'd suddenly had your time off stripped from you like so much excess baggage."

No, he probably wouldn't, Rick conceded, not believing Charles's fish story for a minute. Beneath that slick but prosaic surface, the good sergeant fancied himself to be a true ladies' man. A modern day Don Juan, from the tips of his brown Oxfords to his currently grease-splattered tie. He might have been angling for something in nearby Dart-meet, but Rick doubted it was for trout.

Charles tapped out the last word in his report, then added the sheet to the skimpy pile of papers beside him on the bed. "Finished at last," he stated, patting his pencil-thin mustache with a napkin. "Now I suppose you'll be wanting me to pay another visit to the carnival site."

Rick stretched his sore shoulder muscles and in the back of his mind wished he'd been assigned a more amiable partner. Charles Gideon possessed the personality of a floor lamp and a rather lackluster one at that. "It's your turn to watch Diana do her Freda the Viking goddess act," he said at length. "I've fixed everything I can in that particular tent."

"I'm sure you have." Charles fiddled with an imaginary crease in his pants. "You realize, don't you, that we might just be chasing a wild goose by focusing our attention so strongly on Diana Beroni? After all, there's no proof that she had the Saxony jewels in her possession. Maybe she simply murdered Sherwood to free herself up for someone else."

And maybe she didn't murder him at all, Rick thought grimly. Ignoring his partner's patronizing tone, he shrugged. "I've thought of several possibilities, Charles. At the moment our best bet would seem to be keeping one eye on Diana and the other on those few people Sherwood was known to spend time with."

"Such as?"

"The fortune-teller, Gwendolyn Sykes." Rick slid away from the dresser. "Before you buy a ticket for the Viking dance show tonight, you might want to have your palm read. Word has it that Sherwood was a superstitious man. He never did anything unless all the occult signs were working in his favor."

"Marvelous," Charles muttered, clearly unenthused. "And what will you be doing in the meantime?"

"Hunting for buried treasure." Rick kept his response purposely vague. Circumstances might have forced him into Charles's company, but that didn't mean he had to explain his every move to the man. "I'll check in with you tomorrow night," he added, pulling the door open.

"Buried treasure, indeed," he heard Charles snort as he left. "Probably has some bird tucked away in one of those seedy carnival caravans."

Rick let the remark slide, closing the door behind him with a firm click. He'd learned a long time ago that there was nothing to be gained from sparring with someone who'd been passed over for promotion one too many times. At forty-six, Charles had gone as far as he was ever likely to go in Scotland Yard. He'd either have to accept that fact or start looking elsewhere for employment.

The inn's meager reception area was deserted when Rick reached it. Even the front desk was unattended. Near the door, a coal fire burned in the blackened grate, but the flames did a poor job of staving off the chill that had crept in from the moors. Rick zipped up his jacket and was making his way across the carpeted lobby when he saw Lexie Hudson step into the building, a designer suitcase in one hand and a leather valise in the other.

In spite of himself, he couldn't prevent the warm rush of blood that swept through him at the sight of her. That she was a distraction he really didn't need made no difference. Something about her fascinated him. Whether it was the curious look she'd given him outside Diana's caravan or the defiant gleam in her eyes when she'd noticed that hostile group of workers staring at her from the midway, he couldn't say. He only knew that she was one of the most intriguing women he'd ever met—not to mention one of the loveliest.

Her features were strong yet delicate, her skin fair without being pale. Her wide-set eyes hovered somewhere between hazel and brown, and the layers of golden brown hair that framed her face, while currently rain soaked and tangled, would, he suspected, fall quite sleekly into place around her shoulders when dry. All in all, she had a very fresh look about her—and a stubborn set to her jaw that he found incredibly appealing.

With a firm shake of his head, he closed the distance between them and took the suitcase from her unresisting fingers.

"Thanks," she murmured, shoving her wet hair back with her free hand. "It's heavier than I remembered."

"You're obviously not a light traveler," he remarked, aware of the burgeoning mistrust in her eyes. "Have you checked in yet?"

"No, but I have a reservation."

"Then you'd be Alexandra Hudson," a woman's soft voice interceded. A pretty blonde came out of the dining room, wiping her hands on her apron. "My name is Kate, Miss Hudson," she said at Lexie's silent affirmation. "I tend bar. If you'll just sign the register, I'll have Robbie take your bag upstairs. Hello, Rick," she added invitingly. "Stopped by for a pint, have you?"

Lexie glanced at him from beneath her lashes, and Rick had no choice but to nod. What other reason could a carnival roustabout have for being at the Pendragon Inn?

"Just a half," he said. "I have to get back to work."

"It'll be waiting for you," Kate promised. Smiling, she handed Lexie a key from the latticework of pigeonholes behind the desk. "Oh, and you've a telephone message as well," she disclosed, her smile widening. "From a Rodney Boggs in London. He said you should call him at home this evening as the chess match at his club has been canceled."

Rick arched an inquisitive brow. "Rodney?"

"He's a...friend," Lexie said after the briefest of pauses. She seemed to be on the verge of adding something else, but changed her mind and glanced at the telephone on the desk.

Rick bit back a grin. Unless he missed his guess, this Rodney person didn't have much of a hold on her heart. For some strange reason, the observation pleased him, though why it should was beyond him. She was lovely, yes, but he didn't dare risk blowing his cover simply because he had an affinity for headstrong brunettes.

"Yours is room nine at the top of the stairs to the left," Kate was saying in her pleasant way. "The bathroom's at the far end of the hall. Dinner's at eight and the bar is open until eleven. Now, if you'll excuse me," she apologized, "I really must get back inside. Mrs. Pendragon and her husband have gone to the cinema over in Tavistock, and I'm filling in for them."

She departed with a cheery wave and a swish of her long muslin skirt, leaving Rick to face Lexie's openly curious gaze.

"Have you worked at the carnival long?" she asked, still regarding him somewhat circumspectly.

He lifted an offhand shoulder. "Not long, no. I was passing through town just over a week ago, heading for the coast, when I ran out of money."

"So you went to work for Victoria."

He hid another smile. Her mutable expressions said more than words ever could. She looked adorable standing beside the desk, staring up at him with that semiaccusing look in her eyes, her hair hanging in long, wet rats' tails over her drenched raincoat. He could tell that the coincidence of his arrival at the carnival on the heels of Wren Sherwood's death didn't sit well with her.

"Something like that," he agreed before she could pin him down further. From the corner of his eye he saw a gangly youth step out of the creaking lift and scoop up Lexie's bag. Taking his cue from the young man, Rick moved reluctantly away from the desk. "Don't let me keep you from calling Rodney," he said, his tone deceptively bland. "I'll see you tomorrow."

Her only response was a slight nod that pretty much confirmed his suspicions. She wasn't carrying any torches for Rodney Boggs—and she definitely didn't trust carnival roustabouts.

As he turned for the bar, it occurred to him that he'd have to watch himself very closely where this woman was concerned. One false step and his cover could all too easily be blown. Evidence notwithstanding, Rick wasn't entirely convinced of Diana's guilt. And if by some chance she was innocent, if there *was* a murderer still lurking around the carnival site, the situation could prove to be highly dangerous—for him and for Lexie.

WREN SHERWOOD'S MURDERER smiled a slow, wicked little smile as the carnival finally prepared to close down for the night. One mistake and for a time the entire setup had been in jeopardy. But mistakes could be rectified, given sufficient thought, not to mention a healthy dose of good fortune.

"'Tis the luck of the Irish, I possess," the murderer proclaimed in a low whisper. A tiny sliver of light caused the Saxony jewels to sparkle. "You're mine now, all mine. You're everything I've worked for these past two years, and all I have to do to keep you is sit back and wait. And watch. And thank my lucky Irish stars for all the uneasiness that exists around me."

Full lips curled into a vengeful smile. The deadly waiting game had begun. Time would dictate the next move. Time and the findings of Diana Beroni's London attorney.

"CUT THE JUICE, Norman!" a grease-covered man shouted. "Victoria wants these carousel horses to glide smoothly, not shake their riders' ruddy teeth out."

Lexie looked back at the malfunctioning merry-go-round as she forged a path through the carnival. Though unnerving, it came as no great surprise to find the operator's eyes trained on her rather than on the machinery before him.

Suppressing a sigh, she continued to trudge across the wet ground toward the fortune-teller's tent. The rain had stopped during the night, leaving behind only a misty overcast. It was just after 8:00 a.m., and the carnival wouldn't be open for another hour yet. It was the perfect time to begin her digging.

Though Diana's trial wasn't scheduled to begin for another three weeks, the carnival would be pulling up stakes in seven days. With the evidence against her now, that would surely spell disaster for Diana Beroni.

"You Lexie Hudson?"

Lexie started at the raspy voice behind her. Careful not to step into the puddle she'd just avoided, she turned to regard the female speaker.

There seemed little doubt that she was a fortune-teller. Her head was wrapped in a canary-yellow turban; her strawberry-blond hair hung in frizzy curls down to her shoulders. Though she was only fractionally taller than Lexie's five feet six inches, her bone structure was much larger. She looked strong and capable, and the gleam in her slitted eyes spoke more of challenge than friendliness.

"Gwendolyn Sykes," the woman introduced herself roughly. "I read tea leaves, palms and tarot cards. For a price, I'll gaze into my crystal ball to see what the future holds. I keep my nose out of other people's business, I don't squeal on friends or enemies, and I haven't got an alibi for the night Wren Sherwood was killed. Anything else you want to know?"

It took Lexie only a split second to recover from Gwendolyn's verbal assault. "Yes." She lied without batting an eyelash. "Could you tell me where I might find P. J. Fitzwilly."

"Fitz?" Gwendolyn's heavily made-up eyes narrowed. "You mean you weren't looking for me?"

"Should I be?"

"I don't know. Depends what you're after."

"I'd have thought that would be obvious," Lexie replied calmly. "I'm after the truth."

Gwendolyn laughed. "About Wren, or the jewels he's supposed to have stashed here?"

"About a murder."

A sour smile tugged at the fortune-teller's lips. "In that case, maybe we ought to have a chat, you and me."

Spinning on her heel, she marched through the puddle without a care, soaking the hem of her multicolored skirt and leaving her companion with no choice but to follow. Thankfully, Lexie had traded in her skirt suit and leather pumps for a pair of faded blue jeans and ancient Reeboks. Rodney wouldn't approve of her casual attire, but that was his problem. She had a job to do. Maybe if she didn't look as if she'd just stepped off the Strand, she'd stand a chance of making some headway with these people.

"In here," Gwendolyn announced, pushing her way into the cluttered tent.

On the threshold, Lexie stopped in her tracks, holding the flap up with her hand and staring at the trappings of the poorly lit chamber. It was weird, to say nothing of gaudy. A huge, burgundy tapestry adorned with charcoal outlines of snakes and birds, stars and crescent moons hung from the rear wall. Honeysuckle incense smoldered in a collection of small black pots. The floor was covered with straw, and thick, green candles burned low in a cluster of ornate silver sconces. Dozens of colorful cushions were piled high next to a wide folding screen, a padlocked trunk resided along the third wall, and in the center of the tent sat a cloth-covered table upon which stood a strangely opaque crystal ball.

With a grunt, Gwendolyn plopped herself down onto a speckled toadstool ottoman and glared at Lexie. "Well, what are you waiting for? An invitation from royalty? Get in here and take a load off. I haven't got all day, you know."

After a second's hesitation, Lexie complied, dragging a fat, tasseled pillow over to the table and sitting cross-legged on it.

Eyes glued to the crystal ball, Gwendolyn demanded, "You want to know how long I've been at the carny, right?"

"Right," Lexie agreed, regarding the orb and the woman behind it with more than a few misgivings. Somehow she hadn't expected this. "How long?"

Gwendolyn waved a distracted hand and peered deeper into the crystal ball. "Four years, off and on. I like to come and go from time to time. Danny didn't mind and neither does Victoria."

"Who's Danny?"

"Victoria's nephew."

"The one who died and left her the carnival?"

"The very same."

"What about Wren Sherwood?" Lexie pressed. "How well did you know him?"

It was the wrong thing to ask. Gwendolyn's expression grew cold; her lips thinned to a tight line.

"None of your business," she snapped. "Glen—Wren—whatever you want to call him, he was a prince the whole time he was here. That's all you need to know." Scowling, she returned her gaze to the crystal ball.

Wren Sherwood, a prince? Lexie fought a disgusted shudder. Of course he might have picked up a few pointers from his late partner. Aidan O'Brien had apparently been quite the rake before his death two years ago.

"You don't think she killed him, do you?" Gwendolyn barked, still peering intently into the crystal. Crossing her palms, she passed them slowly across the ball. "In that case, let's just see what a bout of scrying turns up, hmm?"

"Bout of what?"

"Scrying—gazing at a reflection of the future." With the tips of her fingers Gwendolyn caressed the orb. "First the mist, then the blackness, then the images," she whispered in a husky tone that had Lexie looking around distrustfully. As far as she could tell, the ball was clear, not an image in sight.

"What do you see?" she questioned warily.

Gwendolyn pointed to the center of the crystal. "I see the meadow. It's empty now except for a few wrappers and some glitter. The carnival's gone, the people have moved on. All but two, that is." She drew a cross on the glass. "I'd say it's rather unlikely that they'll be moving anywhere ever again."

Lexie refused to acknowledge the creeping sensation down her spine. No one could predict the future. "Which two?" she managed in a reasonably constrained voice.

Gwendolyn ran her nail down the front of the crystal. "It's hard to say, but I should think— Yes, it's becoming much clearer now. I believe one of them is Wren Sherwood. As for the other..." She lifted guileless brown eyes to Lexie's. "I could be wrong, of course. The future is a roil of uncertainty. However, the other one appears to be a woman."

In the silence that followed Gwendolyn's thinly veiled warning, Lexie swore she could actually hear the loud thudding of her heart. She was positive that the smoke from the candles suddenly grew thicker, the smell of honeysuckle more powerful. Deliberately wiping her clammy palms on the legs of her jeans, she forced herself to inquire, "I don't suppose you'd care to identify this woman, would you?"

The fortune teller regarded her with no particular expression. "No, but take my advice, Lexie. Build your defense back in London. This is a carnival, and we here don't take kindly to—"

Her sentence broke off as the tent flap rustled and a tall, thin skeleton of a man appeared. Before Lexie could get a good look at him, he muttered a thickly accented, "'Scuse me. I didn't know you had company," and hastily stepped back out of sight.

"One of the workers," Gwendolyn revealed as the flap dropped into place. "Pay him no mind. Where was I?"

Lexie dragged her gaze from the heavy flap. "You were telling me about the dangers of snooping around a carnival."

"Did I mention the word *danger*?" Gwendolyn's smile was distant. "I don't think so, but just as long as we understand each other."

Oh, they understood each other all right, Lexie thought, forcing a civilized smile to her lips. The woman was a fraud who obviously had something to hide.

"Thanks for the advice," she said, standing. "I'll keep it in mind." And aware of Gwendolyn Sykes's piercing eyes on her back, she left the tent.

"Do come and see me again before you leave," the fortune-teller called after her. "I promise I'll give you a palm reading you'll never forget."

A raw burst of laughter punctuated that menacing statement, and for one rash moment, Lexie was tempted to stomp back inside and give Gwendolyn a black eye she'd never forget. She might have done it, too, if she hadn't happened to spot Rick lounging against an arcade booth on the far side of the midway, looking far too rumpled and sexy for her peace of mind. Like everyone else she'd passed that morning, he was watching her. Closely. And so was the smaller man inside the booth.

"I bet that stung," Rick drawled, grinning. "Someone should have warned you not to tangle with Gwendolyn before breakfast."

"Sleeps with her claws out, that one does," the other man added, tipping his derby. "Her fortunes can be a mite wicked. Best to avoid her until she's had her palm crossed with a few silver coins."

"Thanks for the belated warning," Lexie said, joining them with a reluctance that surprised her. Sexy or not, Rick posed no threat to her. At least no emotional threat. She was an almost engaged woman. Surely no man could turn her head when she had someone as wonderful as Rodney waiting for her in London. She looked up. "Is there anyone else I should avoid?"

Rick shrugged. "Just Fitz here. He claims to be a reformed pickpocket, but some of us have our doubts about his sincerity."

Lexie stared at Rick's companion. "You're P. J. Fitzwilly?"

"At your service," Fitz said with a cheery wink. "But you needn't worry your pretty head about me sincerity. I'm well and truly reformed these days. Haven't snatched me so much as a halfpenny in three and half long years."

"What about that other man?" she asked.

Fitz seemed perplexed. "Other man?"

"Skelly," Rick informed him, making no attempt to deny the fact that he'd obviously been watching Gwendolyn's tent for quite some time. He kept his eyes on Lexie's face. "What do you want to know?"

For a newly hired roustabout, he seemed awfully familiar with his co-workers. Lexie met his steady gaze. "Who is he? What does he do here? How long has he worked at the carnival?"

"He's Leonard Skelton. He runs the fun house, and he's worked here for eighteen months."

"Will he talk to me?"

"I wouldn't count on it."

"Why not?"

"He's not one for talking, miss," Fitz inserted. "Used to be an undertaker, our Skelly did. Fancies his fun house puppets more than most humans hereabouts."

"And that includes curious lawyers," Rick added, his tone faintly humorous. "You'll find he's not alone there, Lexie."

"You mean to tell me that all carnival people are secretive about their pasts?"

Rick pushed himself away from the ring toss booth, moving just a little too close for her comfort. "Some are," he replied, staring down at her through those hypnotic blue eyes of his. "It depends on what they're hiding."

She didn't back away. "What about you, Rick? Are you hiding something?"

His answering chuckle held no trace of concern. "If I were, I'd be a fool to have signed on in the middle of a police investigation."

She couldn't argue with him there. And yet, she couldn't quite bring herself to trust him, either. It made no difference that he was the most attractive man she'd ever come across. Attractive men could still be criminals.

At the subtle twist of amusement on Rick's lips, she had the sudden, uneasy feeling that he was reading her mind. Hastily, she stepped away from him. "I, ah, I'd better leave you to your work," she mumbled. "Could you tell me which caravan belongs to Victoria?"

He gestured toward the end of the midway. "The green one. You can't miss it. It's set apart from the others."

Nodding her thanks, Lexie started for the carnival's perimeter. She didn't know where Rick Matheson fitted into this jumbled puzzle, but her intuition told her that he did. She only hoped his involvement wouldn't turn out to be more than her traitorous defenses could handle.

"YES, I SAW Diana leave the carnival..."

"No, I didn't see her return..."

"Yes, I did see her return..."

"I don't recall seeing anything..."

After four solid hours of curt, uninformative answers to her questions, Lexie was ready to pound her head against the nearest stone wall. How could so many people see so little? Didn't anyone look out windows anymore?

Gradually, the din from the midway penetrated her frustrated thoughts. Barkers squawked loudly through their patched megaphones. Calliope music blared from the now-functioning carousel. Encouraging shouts burst forth from the arcade. Bells clanged, children shrieked and everywhere Lexie looked, she saw splashes of color and movement.

She had to relax, she decided as the festive mood of the crowd began to weave its magical spell around her. So she hadn't made a major breakthrough that morning. At least she'd corroborated a few important facts. In keeping with her statement to the police, Diana had been seen leaving the carnival grounds at closing time. She'd also been seen returning to the site at ten-thirty.

Had she ever displayed any violent tendencies? Her co-workers said no. Had she made up with Wren Sherwood after their spat two nights prior to his death? Yes. Did anyone besides Diana know that Wren Sherwood kept a gun in his caravan? Another yes, grudgingly offered in most instances, but a yes nonetheless.

"Ah, there you are, Lexie." Victoria detached herself from a swarm of carnival-goers outside one of the larger food stalls. "I hear you came looking for me earlier this morning. I must have forgotten to tell you, my day begins at six, rain or shine."

"That's all right. I managed to fill the time." Lexie motioned at the milling crowd. "You seem to be doing very well."

Victoria nodded. "It appears that sensationalism is an attraction unto itself. It's just a shame that a man had to die in order for our fortunes to improve."

"Yes, it is." She paused to study the carnival owner who was surveying the midway crush with a most satisfied expression. Was it possible...?

No, of course it wasn't. Victoria wouldn't murder someone simply to attract attention to her carnival.

No, the more she thought about it, the more Lexie was convinced that whoever had killed Wren Sherwood had somehow discovered his true identity and his connection to the Saxony jewels. Find them, and she'd likely find the person responsible for Wren's death.

Out of the corner of her eye, Lexie saw Victoria lift an acknowledging hand. "Keep it brief, Skelly!" she shouted above the swell of music and noise. "I want you back at the fun house in case anything should break down."

Skelly? Lexie snatched her head up, managing to catch a fleeting glimpse of the man she'd spied earlier in Gwendolyn's tent. "Where's he going?"

"Oh, up to Wexford Castle I should think. He drives there every day for lunch." Victoria made a dismissing motion with her arm. "I wouldn't concern myself too much with that one, Lexie. You'll get nothing out of him."

Wouldn't she? Lexie kept her gaze riveted on the skeletal man. "I'd better be going," she said, inching away. "I still have a lot of people to talk to. If you're free later today, I'd like to take a look inside Wren Sherwood's caravan. I understand you have the key."

"I will have come teatime," Victoria corrected. "I'm told that it's being sent down by courier from Scotland Yard, at the request of your firm."

That was news to Lexie. "It can wait till then," she said, trying desperately not to lose sight of Leonard Skelton.

She was halfway across the sprawling fair before she remembered Victoria's words. Skelly drove, not walked, up to the old castle every day.

Since he wasn't likely to offer her a ride after making such a determined effort to avoid her that morning, Lexie was forced to backtrack to the village and retrieve her car. Although she wasn't sure she wanted to subject her pricey Jaguar to the abuse of a bumpy country track that couldn't by any stretch of the imagination be called a road, she eased it into gear and crawled through the cobbled streets of Ashcroft until she spotted the turnoff that led her beyond the outskirts of the village—to the ancient and highly treacherous walls of the ruin that was Wexford Castle.

Chapter Three

A ghostly white veil of fog curled in wispy tendrils about the walls of the sullen castle. Though it was now little more than a shell, Lexie knew it would have been a spectacular sight in the late fifteenth century, back before Cromwell's brutal armies had plundered every fortress in their path.

She parked her car next to an overgrown thicket and let her eyes slide upward to the decrepit tower. Rodney would have loved this place. Dark and gloomy and filled with shadows, it reminded her of his town house in Chelsea.

Mortar fire had destroyed much of the ancient structure, but not so badly that she couldn't make the distinction between what had once been an impressive manor house and the fortifications that had obviously been added at a later date. While a number of turrets still stood, the stonework had been allowed to fall into a sad state of disrepair. Only a portion of the arched gateway remained intact, the majority of it having long since lost the battle against the ravages of time and nature. Moss clung to the fractured boulders, and around the foundations an impossible tangle of thorny vines had forced their way inward through the gaping cracks.

Even at a distance, Lexie noticed the smell of decay, of moldering earth and vegetation and wood. Rotting beams protruded from the castle's worn battlements; arrow-slit windows showed only darkness beyond; and the fog, that insidious cloak of white that had rolled in from the moors, made the entire building seem like something out of a sinister fairy tale.

The silence was pervasive so high up on the hill. She suspected that the view of the village below would be lovely on a clear day, but at the moment there was nothing to see except mist.

Lexie huddled deeper into the folds of her baggy black sweater, forcing her feet to carry her through the gateway to the rutted lane that led to the old castle. Up close, the ruin looked even more imposing and infinitely more dangerous. Where the outer bulwark had caved in, the rubble lay in broken heaps, permitting large shafts of light to enter. She spied the remnants of a narrow stone staircase, another shattered wall and several precariously balanced slabs of stone that seemed on the verge of toppling over.

In spite of herself, she couldn't keep her imagination at bay as she once again beheld the buttresses of the lopsided tower. Could this have been a Camelot of sorts in its heyday? Had a knight in shining armor lived here once? Had some marauding warrior been locked away in that dark tower?

Smiling, Lexie shook aside her whimsical fantasies. She'd come here to find Skelly, not to entertain notions of medieval derring-do.

On the far side of the clearing, she could just make out the shape of a green van. She recalled seeing vehicles of that type around the carnival. Skelly probably was here, she reasoned, but where? Unless he was a fool, he wouldn't set foot inside Wexford Castle.

From the gloomy reaches of the manor house, Lexie picked up on a peculiar shuffling sound. Indistinct but unmistakable. Whether the source was human or rodent, she couldn't be sure. She only knew that every ounce of common sense she possessed was screaming at her not to enter the place.

Coward, she accused herself in an effort to bolster her floundering courage.

The shuffling sound came again as she crawled over a pile of fallen stones near the castle entrance. It seemed to originate behind the staircase, perhaps from a chamber more intact than the outer hall.

She glanced up at the devastated ceiling, noting with a shudder a number of jagged holes. Filmy whorls of fog seeped in like a miasma from the Middle Ages. The air was dank and chilly, the smell of decay too strong to ignore. If the strange noises hadn't persisted, she would have gladly abandoned her quest and returned to the cheerful confusion of the carnival.

Stiffening her spine, she managed a thready "Mr. Skelton, are you in here?"

The noises ceased abruptly, prompting her to call out again in a firmer voice. "Mr. Skelton, it's Lexie Hudson. I'd like to speak with you."

Her words echoed eerily inside the empty building, then gradually faded into nonexistence. If Skelly was indeed here, he evidently had no intention of showing himself, and Lexie had no intention of moving one step deeper into this death trap. Visions of Camelot gave way to images of wicked queens and black knights and the horrors of a dungeon she had no desire to explore. Enough was enough. She could corner Skelly in the fun house this afternoon. For now, all she wanted to do was get out of here.

Her Reeboks made a gritty sound on the pebbly floor. A tiny gust of wind whistled through the rafters, sending an icy draft of air tunneling down from the trees. She felt the first conscious flutters of fear in her stomach—irrational, yet real enough to bring goose bumps to her skin.

The fog appeared to be growing thicker. Maybe it was only her imagination, but suddenly even the wind seemed to be wailing a bleak warning.

Lexie fought to breathe normally. She was behaving like a frightened animal, reacting to a trick of nature, creating ghosts out of thin air.

Still edging backward across the dusty stones, she listened to the haunting gusts, to the tree limbs that scraped against the rough walls, to the sound of her heart thundering in her chest. But did she hear another sound, as well?

For a precious moment she stopped moving and strained to catch the mournful cry that underscored all those things.

She wasn't wrong. There was a voice being carried in the misty breeze. A lament. A silky thread of sound that contained a warning—or perhaps a threat.

"Death..." the soft whisper moaned again and again. "Death... Death... Death..."

Lexie's breath rushed from her lungs in a single panicky burst. A sense of overwhelming terror gripped her. She spun around on the floor, ignoring the few scraps of logic that somehow implanted themselves in her brain and ran straight for the castle entrance and the security of the open hilltop.

The sounds followed her, an amplified jumble of groans and scrapes. A horrible spray of pebbles showered down from the ragged ceiling, lightly at first, then more heavily as she drew closer to the archway.

She felt the abrasive particles on her cheeks, heard them clatter against the stonework beneath her and saw a flash of something in the gloom. Then, from out of nowhere, a pair of hands appeared to snatch her off the ground and drag her sideways.

Unbalanced, unable to maintain her footing, she stumbled, falling to the floor. A loud crash to her right sent shock waves echoing through her head and a fine cloud of dust billowing up in front of her eyes. And when at last the dust cleared, she could only stare in stunned disbelief at the slab of rock that lay in a broken heap not five feet from where she sat.

The erratic pounding of her pulse abated slowly, so slowly that it took several seconds for Lexie to become aware of the hands that were still clamped about her waist. Not Skelly's hands, she realized; someone else's. Someone on whose lap she'd conveniently managed to land. Too startled to scramble away, she twisted her head around—and found herself face-to-face with Rick Matheson.

An overwhelming feeling of relief swamped her. For a moment, she allowed herself to relax in his embrace, willing her breathing to resume its normal rate. His arm tightened briefly about her waist as Rick tugged her back against his chest and held her firmly in place on his lap.

Despite her shock Lexie recognized that a very large part of her didn't want to move. Absurd or not, she felt safe with him. Safe, secure—and just a bit too mindful of his warm body close to hers.

"You all right?" he murmured, his hand resting lightly on her rib cage.

Somehow she mustered the strength necessary to nod. With a reluctance she didn't dare analyze, she slid from his lap. "I'm fine. I—" Her eyes narrowed suddenly. "Wait a minute—what are you doing here?"

The smile that crept across his lips only served to heighten her uncertainty. "I followed you."

She blinked at him, positive she must have heard him wrong. "I beg your pardon?"

"I saw you slink out of the carnival after Skelly and I decided to follow you."

Lexie pushed herself to her knees, rubbing her palms on the legs of her jeans. It was stupid and she was probably a fool to take him at his word, but she believed him. After all, he might very well have saved her life. "I don't slink," she said calmly, not quite ready to offer her complete trust. "I simply wanted to talk to the man."

"In other words, you followed him."

"It's my job," she shot back. "I'm supposed to be looking for answers. At the risk of sounding ungrateful, I'm fairly certain that your duties at the carnival don't run along those same lines."

"That does sound a little ungrateful," Rick agreed, shaking the overlong hair from his face and looking up at the cracked roof. "But you should know this is a dangerous place, Lexie. Even Skelly wouldn't be brave enough to come inside."

A fearful tremor slid through Lexie's body. In the aftermath of her narrow escape, she'd almost forgotten the shuffling noises that had brought her into the castle.

She shifted her own gaze to the ceiling. "I heard something up there. Footsteps maybe, and a voice. That's why I came in. I thought it might be Skelly."

Shrugging, Rick held out his hand to her. "More likely it was the wind."

"The wind caused this particular stone slab to fall?" Lexie didn't buy that explanation for a minute, but Rick merely moved a dispassionate shoulder.

"I imagine time brought that about. Look around a bit. Other stones have fallen over the years. Undoubtedly they'll continue to fall for many more. And don't even think about it," he added as she tilted her head back to assess the upper landing.

"I'm not. I was just wondering."

"Whether someone might have gone up there and dislodged that rock?" He took her firmly by the hand. "Unless you want to wind up with a broken skull, you'd be well advised to keep right on wondering. One misstep and your job here will be finished. Permanently."

Gwendolyn's ill-disguised threat to that effect flashed through her head. Could it be the fortune-teller knew more about Wren Sherwood's death than she was willing to divulge? Could the same thing be true of Rick?

Lexie glanced down at the hand that held hers, resisting the urge to rip her fingers free. If she were honest with herself, she'd admit she really didn't want to, any more than she wanted to distrust him. Of course, she wasn't always as honest as she'd like to be.

"Come on, let's get out of here," Rick said as the wind began to rip through the rafters once more. "If you still want to talk to Skelly, he'll probably be back at the fun house by now."

Disconcerted, Lexie regarded her watch. Had she really left the carnival fifty-three minutes ago? "I guess so," she relented, letting him draw her forward.

The fog had grown patchy by the time they reached the safety of the gateway. It floated in vaporous layers about the tree trunks forming obscure patterns in the lower limbs. When Rick would have propelled her over to her car, she held back, angling for a clear view of the shrubbery where the green van had been parked.

"If you're searching for ghosts, you're going to be disappointed," he remarked in an amused tone. "The one that's supposed to haunt this place is said to inhabit the tower, not the bushes."

Sidetracked, Lexie stopped peering through the mist. "Let me guess. You're going to tell me that the weird sounds I heard inside were made by a ghost, right?"

Grinning slightly, Rick lounged against the rear fender of her Jaguar. "Actually, a lot of people claim to have heard this particular ghost. Lord Gerald Storm was reputed to be quite a boisterous man. It only stands to reason that his spirit would possess the same quality."

Lexie couldn't resist a small smile. "So what happened to this noisy lord? Why does he haunt the tower?"

"Because he died there, I guess." Pushing himself from the car, Rick planted his hands on her shoulders and turned her in the general direction of the town. He was so close that she could feel the heat of his body through her clothes, the warmth of his breath on her cheek.

"You can't see it through the fog," he told her, pointing down the hill, "but that old Roman fortress you noticed yesterday just beyond the carnival site was once connected by an underground tunnel to the tower of Wexford Castle. You have to know that or the story doesn't make a lot of sense."

Conscious of the clean, male scent of his skin and the hair that brushed lightly across her temple, Lexie managed to inquire, "What does an old Roman fortress have to do with Wexford Castle?"

Rick's lips tilted into a lazy smile. "Lord Storm prowls the castle tower while his alchemist, Algernon, haunts the fortress."

"Algernon's workshop," Lexie recalled, then she frowned. "I thought alchemists only existed in the Dark Ages."

"No, there were plenty of them around after that. In Lord Storm's case, he found Algernon in France, living in a small village near the Seine. The villagers were terrified of his pagan life-style and even more frightened of the potions he used to whip up in his marshy hovel. Algernon claimed to have discovered the secret to prolonging life, and of course Lord Storm, having reached the ripe old age of thirty-eight, was eager to learn that secret."

"So he took Algernon back to England with him?"

"In a manner of speaking. With the help of a local French count, Storm incited the villagers to riot. They drove the alchemist from his home and straight into Storm's waiting arms. When Algernon refused to share his secret, Storm had him imprisoned in the dungeon."

"Nice man," Lexie murmured, aware that Rick's thumb was idly grazing her collarbone. She knew she should move away, yet she was disinclined to budge. Maybe now would be a good time to insert her would-be fiancé's name into the conversation. She hesitated. Would-be? "Did Algernon ever share his secret?" she asked.

Rick shrugged. "The story gets a little blurry at that point. No one's really sure what kind of agreement the two of them reached, but within a year of his imprisonment, Algernon was apparently set free."

"And he went to live in the fortress?"

"No, he lived in the castle. He only worked in the fortress. Unfortunately, it wasn't the sort of work that endeared either Algernon or Storm to the people of Ashcroft."

Lexie could guess what was coming. "Did this 'work' of his involve murder?"

"Call it a series of mysterious disappearances," Rick drawled. "Whenever the fog rolled in from the north, someone from the village would vanish, never to be seen again."

How cheerful. "I take it Lord Storm and Algernon soon discovered that they weren't immortal."

"That depends on how you define immortal. Like any evil undertaking, this one had its downside. Immortality for both of them came with its own bitter price tag."

"You mean they didn't die?"

"Oh, they died, all right. Algernon in the fortress where he'd performed his most despicable rituals and Storm in the tower. From all outward appearances, the lord met his death by the alchemist's hand."

"And Algernon?"

"No one's really sure, but some say he made the mistake of drinking the potion that night. A poison brew Storm tricked him into concocting. Whatever the case, the two of them were doomed to an earthbound afterlife, separated by a cave-in in the tunnel, and unable to escape the stone walls at either end. Moreover, each night when the fog rolls down from the north, they're said to relive their own deaths, a fate they're destined to repeat for all eternity."

Lexie looked up at him. "You know, you really get around, considering you're a newcomer to the area. Tell me, where did you hear this story?"

Easing himself from the bumper of her car, Rick treated her to an enigmatic smile. "You'd be surprised at the things you can pick up," he began, then he frowned and swung his head around.

Behind her, Lexie heard a sudden roar, followed by an angry crunch of tires on gravel and something that sounded suspiciously like a gunshot.

"Son of a—" Rick bit the curse off, moving swiftly to his left, but Lexie was already one step ahead of him. She flung herself over the back of the car, knowing that he was right behind her.

A hastily drawn breath was knocked from her lungs as she tumbled into a prickly thatch of bushes. The hair that fell across her eyes prevented her from seeing much of anything, but she did manage to steal a quick look at the dark green van that barreled out of the mist.

Its headlights reminded her of a tiger's eyes. Cold and yellow and gleaming. Blinding. For one dreadful moment, she thought the vehicle was going to slam into her rear bumper. However, at the last second it veered away, leaving only a blast of dirt and stones in its wake.

From her sprawled position Lexie heard another loud bang ricochet through the murky air and she scrambled unsteadily to her knees, instinctively checking the ground for blood, half afraid one of them had been shot.

"Stay down," Rick ordered, grabbing her wrist and pulling her along to the front of the car.

She offered no protest but just let him drag her forward. It wasn't until she spied the gleaming black object Rick hauled from the belt of his jeans that her entire body went rigid.

A bolt of panic tore through her. A carny who carried a gun? Even given her limited exposure to carnivals, she knew that wasn't normal behavior.

Her breath constricted suffocatingly in her throat. With her free hand she began clawing at the fingers that held her wrist. "Let me go!" she gasped, looking around desperately for something to use as a brace. Far in the distance she detected another muffled blast. "Rick, let me go!"

To her amazement, the pressure of his fingers slackened. But her freedom was short-lived. Before she could react, he'd twisted her around in his arms, hauling her back against his chest and covering her mouth with his palm.

"Quiet," he instructed, his sharp eyes roaming the hilltop.

He handled the gun like a pro, Lexie noted as she continued her futile struggles. But a professional what?

Another blast, this one almost completely absorbed by the fog, reached her ears. It seemed to have come from the base of the hill, and for an instant her curiosity overrode her fear. Despite her fervent attempts to escape his hammerlock, Rick was paying surprisingly little attention to her. His gaze was focused intently on the road, and even in her muddled state of mind, Lexie couldn't miss the grim expression on his face.

"Must have been the van backfiring," he muttered, relaxing the muscles in his arm. To her astonishment, he flipped the safety back in place and slid the gun into his waistband.

Reaching up, Lexie snatched his hand from her mouth. Her breath came in short, uneven spurts, but it was anger now, not fright, that gave her the strength to lash out at him.

"Who are you?" she demanded belligerently. "And don't hand me that line about being a carnival roustabout. In the space of one short hour I've been threatened by an invisible specter, had a boulder come crashing down at my feet and almost been run over by a van. I've been grabbed, thrown to the ground and shot at, and now I find out that you're carrying a gun. A big gun that looks like it could rip a hole in the side of a barn. I want to know who you are, Rick Matheson, and what you're really doing here!''

Rick's features were infuriatingly unperturbed. "Are you finished?" he inquired, raising a negligent brow.

Lexie opened her mouth, then closed it again, unable to summon a suitably withering response. She jerked away from the hand he held out to her and continued to glare at him.

Shaking his head, Rick rose deftly to his feet. Before she could stop him, he'd circled her waist and lifted her from the ground, setting her unceremoniously in front of him and gripping her upper arms.

"First of all," he said, meeting her smoldering stare, "you weren't shot at. The van backfired, that's all."

"Oh, well, if that's all . . ." she began, then wisely let the sarcastic remark she'd been about to make die in her throat. She didn't trust the dangerous gleam that flashed in his eyes, and she trusted herself even less. "All right, tell me about the gun," she said. "What are you, a cop or something?"

His lips twitched, but there was no humor. "Or something," he murmured. He met her mistrustful stare. "Look, Lexie, it's a long story, and I'm not sure I'm in a position to tell it to you right now. One thing I will admit, though: there's something going on here, and I'm damned well going to find out what it is."

Lexie's antagonism faltered slightly as the memory of the two near accidents flashed before her eyes. A shudder ran through her. She could have been killed if it hadn't been for Rick. Suddenly, recklessly, she didn't care who he was or what he was doing at the carnival. All that mattered was that he was here with her right now.

Having reached that wholly irrational decision, she lifted her eyes to his, somewhat disconcerted to find him staring down at her.

"I think it's time we got out of here, don't you?" he asked. At her mute nod, he frowned a little and brushed his thumb lightly across her cheek, bringing a rush of heat to her skin. "You sure you're all right?"

Lexie's throat tightened. His touch, while doubtless intended to reassure, did nothing to sort out the growing confusion in her mind. Who was this man? Why couldn't she seem to think straight when she was with him? What was it about him that made her long to lean closer, to run her hands over his wonderfully broad shoulders, to turn her back on her relationship with Rodney... Rodney!

She stiffened abruptly. "I'm fine," she said curling her fingers around the cuffs of her sweater, determined not to let him see how he affected her.

Rick was less than helpful in that area. With his thumb and forefinger, he tipped her head back until she was looking straight into his eyes. "Make sure you stay that way," he said gently. "Trust me, Lexie. I don't want to see you get hurt. Do your digging at the carnival from now on. I don't know what happened here today, but I do know a few things about the people Wren Sherwood was connected to."

"For instance?" she managed.

He held her gaze and she thought she saw a flicker of something other than concern behind his steady stare. "Skelly," he said calmly, shattering her illusions. "He's an odd man at the best of times, very private and difficult to approach. But what you're probably not aware of is that he was once involved with Gwendolyn Sykes. And Gwendolyn dumped him a year ago for a three-month affair with Wren Sherwood."

RICK'S WORDS ECHOED sonorously in Lexie's head long after she left the castle. She spent the next few hours alternating between annoyance, confusion and grim speculation. This was supposed to be a carnival, not a den of liars, thieves and cutthroats. What on earth had she stumbled into down here? Gwendolyn wanted her out of the carnival. Skelly didn't want to talk to her. Gwendolyn had dumped Skelly for an affair with Wren. Maybe the motive here was passion rather than greed. Maybe it was a combination of the two.

"I'm sorry, Lexie, I really don't know what else I can tell you." Her client's weary voice dragged Lexie out of her disarranged thoughts. Diana was seated on the sofa in Gwendolyn's caravan, repairing a torn seam on her glittering Viking goddess costume. "I still don't remember seeing anything unusual the night Glen died."

Doggedly, Lexie perused the file she'd brought with her from London. "You're sure there was no sign of a struggie? Nothing out of place except the sofa cushion?"

"Just the gun." The teacup Diana had picked up began to rattle in its saucer. She blinked at it, then slowly raised her eyes. "And the cups," she added. "I forgot about them. But they were there on the counter, two of them."

A glimmer of hope prompted Lexie to flip hastily through the photographs. There were several different shots of Wren's compact kitchenette, yet none revealed any dishes on the counters. "Where were they?" she asked.

Diana put her costume aside and moved gingerly to the table. With her finger she stabbed at one of the pictures. "Right there, above the cutlery drawer. Two cups, no saucers. I remember now. Like the cushion, they were out of place."

They were also missing, Lexie noticed, her spirits lifting.

"Is this important?" Diana queried, her face pinched and drawn. "I mean, does it prove that I didn't, er, do it?"

"It's a start," Lexie told her. "And as luck would have it, it's also teatime. Victoria should have the key to Wren's caravan by now."

"You mean, you're going to...go in?" Diana seemed appalled by the idea, but Lexie was adamant.

"I have to. Those missing cups might be very significant."

"But how? Maybe the police put them back in the cupboard."

"They wouldn't do that," Lexie said, standing. She started for the door, then grimaced and retraced her steps. "I almost forgot. I need a description."

"Of the teacups?"

"Of all the dishes."

Diana twisted her hands together. "That won't be hard," she said with a nervous laugh. "The place settings are mine. My—my grandmother gave them to me. There should be four of everything, very old and faded, but all intact."

"What pattern?"

"Pattern..." Diana knitted her brow. "Oh, yes. They were floral. White bone china with pink flowers and a gold rim. Royal Albert."

"FOUR DINNER PLATES, four bread and butter plates, four saucers, four bowls, two teacups." Lexie muttered the list out loud. "Four of everything, except the cups."

Could they be the missing clue? she wondered, her excitement mounting. Had the neat and orderly Wren Sherwood received a visitor prior to his death? Had that person enjoyed a cup of tea at his table, then picked up the sofa cushion and the gun and shot him?

Maybe she should ask Rick, she reflected, giving the tinny cupboard door a disgruntled whack and gratefully exiting the kitchen. Whatever his game, he seemed to have a knack for picking up juicy little tidbits of information. Unfortunately, he also had a knack for throwing her completely off balance, for making her think and feel things she wanted no part of. Rodney was the man for her. Rick was nothing more than a passing attraction. A *dis*traction she refused to recognize.

She winced as she crossed the floor to the living area. Her entire body felt stiff and sore, as though she'd been hit by a cement mixer. One thing she would have to do was thank Rick properly for hauling her out from under that falling boulder at the castle that afternoon. Then she'd have to turn right around and do some in-depth prying into his background. If he wasn't going to tell her who he really was, she'd simply have to find out for herself. From a safe distance, of course.

The sofa springs groaned in protest when she sank down onto them. Raucous calliope music spilled in through the boarded-up window. Thank heaven for the sound of humanity and the good fortune that had smiled on her in the middle of an otherwise bleak day.

Lexie leaned back in her seat and absently checked her ribs for bruises. She'd been lucky indeed to intercept the Scotland Yard courier outside Victoria's caravan. Although she couldn't put her finger on it, there was something that bothered her about the carnival owner. No, *bothered* wasn't the right word. Victoria had done nothing to directly arouse her suspicions.

What was it, then? What had she said that struck a discordant note? She was certainly helpful enough. She'd given her statement quite openly to the police, and she was willing to testify as a character witness at Diana's trial. On the surface there seemed to be no cause whatsoever for doubt.

Sighing, Lexie rested her head on the trailer wall. Through her lashes she regarded the patched-up window. Beside it was the door and beside that another window. A grimy piece of glass with a smudged stick-figure drawing on it. Lines that resembled...

She snapped her head up so suddenly that she nearly gave herself whiplash. The blurred jumble came together with a jolt. Those lines weren't drawings on the glass. They were letters! And they spelled out the same word she'd heard at Wexford Castle.

Death!

She sprang to her feet, concurrently outraged and terrified. Fog swirled around the window, an eerie backdrop to the hideous symbols that hadn't been there ten minutes ago. She wouldn't have missed something as obvious as that. Whoever had written it knew she was in here. The threat was directed at her!

The air she breathed seemed to take on the properties of a poison gas. She began to tremble inside as the implications behind the warning sank in. Wren Sherwood had died at the carnival. If she continued her investigations, she just might wind up in the same condition.

"No!" she vowed angrily, clenching her fists. She wouldn't be frightened off by any perverse threat, no matter what it portended.

On shaking legs, she crept over to the window. Bracing her weight on the chair beneath it, she twisted the lock and inched the glass outward. Yet even with her senses alert, her body poised to spring away, the abrupt movement caught her completely off guard. She had no chance to scream, no time to close the window. An unaccustomed paralysis took over as something thudded soundly against the side of the caravan, a precursor to the grotesque face that rose with lightning speed to confront her.

She registered flattened lips, drooping eyes and a compressed nose, heard a vicious snarl emanate from deep inside a human throat. And then, suddenly, the growl ceased. The face vanished as unexpectedly as it had appeared. Only the fog remained, and in it the muffled sound of retreat, all but drowned out by the screams from the distant roller coaster.

The paralysis that gripped her made reaction impossible. She was like a granite statue, her muscles locked in place. It took a furious barb from her brain to shatter the outer edges of panic, to impel her away from the window and into the center of the caravan.

She didn't know what mysterious catalyst enabled her to bolt for the door. Maybe it was a lingering scrap of fury, or just a spontaneous burst of adrenaline. Whatever the case, in a matter of seconds she was yanking the door open and stumbling down the three steps to the grass.

The fog swallowed her up the moment she ventured into it, obscuring her vision. It was a perfect opportunity for the murderer to strike. There would be no one to witness the crime. Her screams would blend right in with the shrieks from the midway rides.

And yet, the person outside Wren's window had been wearing a stocking mask. That had to mean he or she didn't wish to risk exposure. Maybe she wasn't in as much danger as she thought.

She kept running toward the end of the site. More caravans rushed by. At long last, a break in the line signaled that she was approaching Victoria's living quarters. Again she felt that nagging in the back of her mind. However, the chance to analyze her doubts ground to a halt as the green trailer began to take shape ahead of her.

For an instant the fog parted, revealing the filmy outline of a man. Immediately Lexie dug her heels into the ground, but even as she did she knew the man had spotted her. He waved at the billowy whorls, squinted at her, then touched the brim of his bowler.

"I say, you seem to be in a bit of a rush," he stated in a typically clipped and proper English fashion. "Is there a fire somewhere?"

Only in her mind, Lexie thought, skidding to a stop. "Not that I'm aware of," she replied, keeping her distance. He looked to be a tourist, a businessman. And tourists had no business in the caravan row. "Can I help you with something?"

He smiled, showing long teeth, thin lips and a hawklike nose. One skinny hand went up to remove his hat, permitting a view of stringy brown hair that was slicked back from his shiny forehead. "Perhaps you might at that," he said, his limpid eyes running the length of her body. "I appear to have lost my bearings. Could you point me in the direction of the fortune-teller's tent?"

Lexie gestured to her right. This man didn't strike her as someone who'd want to have his palm read. He also struck her as strangely familiar. "Are you staying at the Pendragon Inn, Mr. ...?"

"Gideon," he inserted smoothly. "Charles Gideon. Webberly Bonbon Company, Exeter. And yes, I am staying at the inn. Don't tell me we've met. I'm certain I should never forget such a lovely face."

Lexie winced at the oily compliment. "No, we haven't met. I think I saw you, though, last night. You were getting out of the elevator. The lift."

His smile grew wolfish. "You don't work here, then."

"Not exactly."

"I see." An odd glimmer invaded his eyes. A flicker of recognition perhaps. Or was it something else? He replaced his hat, giving it a sharp tap. "Well, I'm sorry to have inconvenienced you, Miss ...?"

Now it was his turn to force the introduction. "Hudson," Lexie said, not elaborating. She had a feeling, however improbable, that he already knew her name.

He did nothing to confirm or disprove the unsettling notion. With a polite nod and a final sweeping surveillance of her tangled hair and closed features, he turned for the carnival, striding soundlessly into the fog from which he'd appeared.

Lexie let out a relieved breath as he vanished from sight. Charles Gideon posed no threat to her investigation, none at all. Her imagination was beginning to play nasty tricks on her. It was unfortunate, too, because as a rule she was a very trusting person.

Huddling deeper into her oversize sweater, she glanced at Victoria's trailer. And then it hit her. That niggling doubt she'd been unable to discard wasn't totally groundless after all. There was a sound basis for it. Alarming but justified.

By her own admission, Victoria had not been in her caravan when Diana found Wren's body. She'd said as much in her sworn statement. But what the police didn't know, what Lexie now remembered, was that it had been Victoria who'd told her about Skelly's habit of eating lunch at Wexford Castle, who had in fact made a point of calling out to him. It was also Victoria to whom Lexie had mentioned her desire to search Wren's caravan and Victoria who had quite likely seen her take possession of the key from the Scotland Yard courier.

The last was an assumption since the woman's trailer door had been open a crack when the courier arrived, but added together, the coincidences were enough to make Lexie's skin crawl. If she couldn't trust the owner of the carnival, then whom could she trust?

Suddenly, terrifyingly, the warnings of death seemed very, very real.

Chapter Four

"Coo, but you are a sight, mate," Fitz declared as Rick let himself into the ring-toss booth from the rear. "Alley cats have passed up more savory scraps than you."

Wincing, Rick dragged his battered body over to the counter. He wasn't prone to black moods, but he was dangerously close to one right now. It had been a lousy day, and the prospects for improvement weren't great. He was no closer to finding the damned Saxony jewels than he had been when he'd first come here, and now he had another problem to contend with. Three actually. Lexie's curiosity about him, her safety and a ridiculous fascination with her that he was powerless to combat.

At Fitz's grin, he bit out a rough "You're a real morale booster, mate. Try lugging twenty crates of frozen meat pies and thirty-five propane tanks from one end of the carnival to the other, and see how you feel." He worked a kink from the back of his neck. "Seen anything interesting during the past few hours?"

"Not since I closed down for tea," Fitz said with a chuckle. "Can't say as the lull's going to last, though. Could be there's some action about to start up in Gwendolyn's tent."

Rick frowned. "What are you talking about?"

"Have a listen and you'll see" was all Fitz would say. He rubbed his dextrous hands together. "Meantime, maybe you'd fancy a quick game of Scrabble. Perfect thing to remedy a foul mood. Got the board all set up, I have. We can pick up where me and Wren left off before he died."

"Forget the games," Rick countered irritably. "Stick to one subject for a minute. What's going on in Gwendolyn's tent?"

Before Fitz could open his mouth to reply, a furious succession of squawks erupted from across the midway, followed by a dull clang and another round of shouts.

"There's your answer, Inspector," the former pick-pocket revealed above the angry tirade. "Word to the wise, if I might. You'd best get over there before a certain copper in gent's clothing winds up with his shoulder holster wrapped around his neck. I don't think Gwendolyn's too fond of having her place of business violated by the likes of the man I saw creeping through the flap ten minutes ago. Right stuffy-looking sort he was, too. Tall, skinny, brown tweed suit, proper derby, scrawny mustache. Lower than you in rank, I expect, but I've no doubt he's from the Yard."

Charles Gideon! Rick swore between clenched teeth. Trust that idiot to get caught in the middle of an unauthorized search. Trust Fitz to be able to spot him.

He swung himself over the counter, forcing his protesting muscles to carry him across the nearly deserted midway. Thankfully, at four-thirty in the afternoon, there was very little action outside the food tents. With any luck at all, he'd be able to haul his bungling partner away before both their covers were completely destroyed.

Rick reviewed the few tidbits of information he'd been able to unearth about Wren Sherwood. The man had kept a decidedly low profile over the past two years. Apart from his affair with Gwendolyn, his relationship with Diana and his ongoing Scrabble games with Fitz, he'd maintained a polite distance from his co-workers.

There was one thing, though, one lead Rick recalled that he hadn't yet been able to follow up on. Sherwood had been responsible for collecting the daily take from the arcade booths. While the task seemed simple enough on the surface, it did raise a number of intriguing questions, not only about Wren Sherwood's reasons for accepting the job, but also about Victoria's reasons for giving it to him. As soon as the opportunity presented itself, he'd have to make a thorough search of the carnival owner's caravan, something he'd been unable to do yesterday with two other roustabouts helping him repair her leaking roof.

"I say, it was an honest enough mistake!" Charles's indignant exclamation rose above Gwendolyn's curses. "Nothing to get excited about, I assure you."

"In a pig's eye it was a mistake!" Gwendolyn spat. The side of her tent bulged as something weighty hit it. "You're a thief, that's what you are. A mangy no-good robber out to pinch my coin box. Give him the boot, Skelly, before I change my mind and send for Constable Chance."

Oh, God, no, not Constable Chance, Rick groaned to himself. The man was an insufferable stickler for propriety. He'd expose Charles in a second if he ever got wind of this little incident.

Rick had almost reached the fortune-teller's tent when he caught a glimpse of Lexie in his peripheral vision. She looked bedraggled but alert and completely irresistible in her faded jeans and baggy black sweater. If she hadn't been staring speculatively at the flap and undoubtedly contemplating the merits of venturing inside, he would have found the play of expressions on her face enchanting. Unfortunately, she was already making for the tent.

"Terrific," he muttered altering his course through the fog. This was just what he needed to set off an explosive situation.

The mist cleared slightly, and he saw her eyes flick to him, but only for a moment before she returned them to the tent. "What's going on in there?" she demanded in a tone that implied he should know. "Why is Gwendolyn so upset?"

Rick kept his features impassive, though he doubted there was much point. "Sounds to me like she caught an intruder. Probably nothing more than a misunderstanding."

The canvas bulged again. "Hold still, you." This time it was Skelly who grunted the order. "Won't help you any to hop about like a scared toad."

"See here," Charles blustered. "This is no way to treat a paying customer."

"A thief, you mean," Gwendolyn snapped. "The sign outside said Closed, and you know it."

"Sign?" Charles feigned surprise. "I assure you both, I noticed no sign."

Rick saw Lexie knit her brow. "I recognize that voice," she declared. "That's the bonbon salesman from Exeter who was wandering around by the caravans."

Wonderful, Rick thought with a sigh. Not only had Charles botched a search of Gwendolyn's tent, but he'd also come into contact with Diana's attorney. He couldn't have messed things up better if he'd planned it that way.

"Get out, and stay out," Gwendolyn snarled as Skelly, his hands clamped firmly around Charles's pale wrists, appeared at the entrance. "And don't let me catch you within ten meters of my coin box again."

Cheeks puffed, Charles stumbled on the slippery grass. "I really must protest," he caviled peevishly, then broke off as Skelly shoved him forward.

Despite the flurry of activity, Rick didn't miss the anticipatory gleam that lit Lexie's eyes. She'd cornered her elusive quarry at last. If there was any justice in the world, she'd tie him up long enough for Rick to drag Charles out of here.

But, no, that wouldn't be a good idea. The incident at Wexford Castle was all too fresh in Rick's mind. While Skelly didn't strike him as the type of man who'd try to run anyone down, that didn't prove he hadn't been driving the green van earlier today.

With a warning shake of his head that he hoped Charles would understand, he moved to stand behind Lexie. If she wanted to question Skelly, she was welcome to it, but whether she liked it or not he was going to back her up.

Gwendolyn and Skelly were both so busy glowering at Charles that neither seemed to realize they had company. Lexie didn't squander the opportunity. Taking a determined step forward, she said, "Mr. Skelton, I'm Lexie Hudson. If you have a minute, I'd like to speak with you."

Skelly's cadaverous features seemed more sunken than usual. He looked as if he wanted to glance at Gwendolyn, but he checked himself and settled for dipping his head. "I'm sorry, miss," he mumbled, "but I have to be getting back to the fun house. Can't tell you much, anyway."

"Can't and doesn't have to." Gwendolyn planted her hands defiantly on her hips. "You leave him be, Lexie. He had no cause to kill Wren Sherwood."

"I never said he did," Lexie replied. "I only want to ask a few simple questions."

"A perfectly reasonable request," Charles added, straightening his tie and hat. "I don't think—" He paused uncertainly. "Oh, yes, I forgot. I'm, er, supposed to be leaving, aren't I?"

Gwendolyn's eyes narrowed to slits. "Take the rubbish out, Skelly. And as for you—" she whirled on Lexie "—you can look for your answers someplace else. Go on, go back to Wren's caravan since you've obviously the stomach for such morbid surroundings. I said my piece this morning. You'll get nothing more from me."

Rick felt rather than saw Lexie stiffen. "But how—!" she began, then she halted and backed up until she bumped into his chest. "Never mind. I've seen enough for one day."

So had he, Rick decided as Skelly, his face averted, escorted Charles to the exit. "Come on," he said, wrapping his fingers firmly around Lexie's. "I'll drive you up to the inn."

She offered no more than a minor protest, and even that faded away when Gwendolyn stomped back inside her tent, ripping down the Closed sign as she went.

Rick paid no attention to the fortune-teller's poisonous display of temper. He had enough problems of his own. Like how he was going to keep Lexie from tracking Skelly to his fun house lair and possibly setting herself up for more trouble than she could handle.

She hung back as they approached the line of green vans. "I'd rather walk," she said, and he didn't pretend not to understand why. Instead he flipped up the collar of his red jacket and headed for the path to the village.

"Someone doesn't want me here," she stated flatly after they'd gone several meters in silence. "I don't suppose you'd know anything about that, would you?"

Rick averted his head. She looked more troubled than suspicious. "Has something else happened?" he asked carefully.

Her eyes glittered with anger and a measure of defiance. "Someone wrote the word 'Death' on the window of Wren Sherwood's caravan while I was inside. When I went to have a look, I saw a face with a stocking mask on it."

Years of training prevented Rick from reacting as he would have liked. "Did this person do anything else?" he grated evenly.

"No."

"Do you have any idea who it was?"

She sent him a faintly caustic look. "None. The only thing I'm certain of is that the message was a warning."

He hated to sound callous, but it was for her own good. "Then maybe you should heed it," he said softly, placing a hand in the small of her back and nudging her forward.

A spark of challenge entered her eyes. "What are you doing here, Rick? Or do you intend to keep up this roustabout charade of yours indefinitely?"

Shaking his head, he murmured dryly, "Not indefinitely. Just long enough to find the Saxony jewels."

She stopped walking to stare up at him. "That either makes you a cop or a crook. Which is it?"

Rick felt torn now between his desire to tell her the truth and a far more absurd desire to pull her into his arms and kiss her. Damn her, anyway. Why did she have to have such a tempting mouth?

He surveyed her with just a hint of a smile. "Tell me something. Do you make a habit of cross-examining everyone you meet, or do you save that treat for those few people who are willing to do more than grunt at you?"

She kept staring at him. "Why do you want the Saxony jewels?"

She was tenacious, he'd give her that. She was also gorgeous. It was all he could do to keep his hands to himself.

"I work for Scotland Yard," he revealed after a long pause. "Charles Gideon, the man you saw being escorted off the fairgrounds by Skelly, is my partner."

"And your assignment is to recover the Saxony jewels." She didn't sound entirely convinced. "I assume you have a badge."

For an answer, Rick dug a worn leather case from his inside jacket pocket and handed it to her.

"All right, so you're a cop," she agreed at length. "And you're looking for the jewels. Depending on who's in possession of them when they turn up, that could prove to be highly beneficial to Diana's case."

"It'd be more than beneficial, and you know it."

He impelled her forward once again, wishing he could rid himself of the notion that she was in danger, wishing he could view her situation with an impartial eye. To his relief, the Pendragon Inn took shape through the deepening mist. Like every other building in Ashcroft, it was old, probably dating back as far as the sixteenth century. In terms of security, it had little to offer, but at least it stood a fair distance from the carnival. Lexie would be as safe there as she would anywhere else in the village.

"Gwendolyn's thief," he heard Lexie murmur as he followed her into the lobby. A reluctant smile tugged at her lips. "I'd be willing to bet he wasn't your first choice for a partner."

Rick looked past her to the reception desk where a plump woman in a print housedress sat petting an orange tabby.

"Fresh linen, Mrs. Pendragon," Charles stated, rapping his knuckles on the scarred counter. "I really must insist on a change of bedding. Such shoddy housekeeping would not be tolerated in London for one tiny instant, I can promise you that."

"Exeter," Rick hissed under his breath.

Lexie glanced up at him. "Did you say something?"

He kicked the door closed with his foot. "Nothing important. Are you staying in tonight?"

She nodded. "I imagine so. I have some notes to go over and some phone calls to make."

"To Rodney?"

She didn't bat an eyelash, although he suspected she wasn't pleased with the question. "To Rodney," she agreed levelly.

"I say, Mrs. Pendragon, do I have your full attention here?" Charles demanded rather pompously, causing no less than five heads to turn in his direction.

He was going to strangle the man, Rick decided, keeping his expression bland and his mind fixed on his work. He was making a spectacle of himself, and all for the sake of some bedding.

"Rick?" Lexie's distracted voice drew him out of his dark reverie. "How much do you really know about the carnival?"

"What, you mean the operation?"

"That and its financial status."

He shrugged. "Not a lot. Why?"

"I was just wondering what the profits are like. I got the impression after looking around today that some of the equipment is awfully old, and yet the crowds seemed to be quite large. Have the numbers increased since Wren Sherwood was murdered?"

Rick leaned back against the door, jamming his hands into the pockets of his jacket. "You think Victoria might be involved in Sherwood's death?"

"I didn't say that."

"No," he agreed, "you didn't." He shifted his weight on the creaking floor. "Look, if you want me to, I'll see what I can find out about the financial situation. Don't get your hopes up, though. If the carnival's profits hadn't been relatively good, Victoria would likely have sold out when her nephew died. Even if she'd recognized Sherwood for what he was, I doubt she would have resorted to killing him, to say nothing of waiting two years to do it."

"Not unless she somehow got hold of the Saxony jewels," Lexie pointed out.

Rick nodded, but offered nothing more. There really wasn't a great deal he could add to that statement. For the moment he could only carry on with his investigation. And hope to hell that Lexie wasn't in as much danger as circumstances would have him believe.

PECULIAR.

It was the best word Lexie could think of to describe her day. Falling rocks, swerving vans, window messages—they ad to add up to something. However, for the sake of her client and her own scattered wits, she decided not to examine the total too closely.

"Will there be anything else, ma'am?" A bespectacled waiter stopped at the table in the quiet Golden Goose Restaurant.

"No, thanks," she replied, forcing a forkful of carrots into her mouth. "I'm fine."

"Very good, ma'am. I'll bring your pudding over shortly."

Lexie kept her expression pleasant, but in truth food was the farthest thing from her mind. She'd only come here so she could mull over the events of the day without fear of interruption.

Without calling Rodney, either, she acknowledged unhappily. A feeling of guilt engulfed her, but it wasn't enough to quell her burgeoning attraction to Rick. Why couldn't he have turned out to be a thief? Not a murderer, just a peripatetic opportunist, someone with the morals of a bilge rat. She could resist a man like that, even if he was the sexiest male on the planet.

Groaning, she propped her elbows up on the table and reached for her water glass. This wasn't helping her investigation at all. She had to concentrate on someone, anyone, other than Rick.

Victoria's name danced through her head, and Lexie grasped it with an urgency that bordered on desperation. No matter how hard she tried to rationalize the situation, it struck her as rather convenient that Victoria's nephew, Danny, should leave her the carnival at almost the same time as Wren Sherwood arrived on the scene looking for a place to hide out. But did it mean anything?

Her thoughts switched abruptly to Gwendolyn. "Go back to Wren's caravan!" she'd shouted—the operative word being "back," as though she'd known Lexie had been there only moments before.

And then there was the ever-evasive Leonard Skelton. Why wouldn't he talk to her? Why didn't Gwendolyn want him to talk? Was she afraid for him? For herself? For both of them?

The waiter returned to set a bowl of tapioca pudding on the gleaming table. Lexie waited until he'd gone, then let her gaze stray to the delicate teacup in front of her.

Two Royal Albert cups in Wren's caravan. There should have been four. What had become of the pair Diana had seen on the counter the night of the murder? Had someone sneaked in and removed them?

More muddled than ever, Lexie dipped into her unappetizing dessert. It tasted like chalk. With a shiver, she pushed it away. Forget food. What she needed was fresh air. The walk back to the inn would take at least ten minutes. Maybe it would also clear some of the cobwebs from her brain.

The fog hadn't dissipated in the slightest by 9:00 p.m. If anything it had grown thicker. The narrow streets were empty and dark, inadequately lit by the glow from the corner lampposts. The soles of her Reeboks made a squishy sound on the cobblestones. Ahead of her, she heard the jangle of a bicycle bell and saw the faint spot of yellow light that guided the rider along.

The sight offered little solace beyond reassuring her that she wasn't completely alone. For the most part, it only served as an unwelcome reminder of the van that had careered past her beautiful Jaguar up at Wexford Castle.

Immersed in thought, Lexie trudged past a row of blackened shops. Two more blocks, one flight of stairs and she'd be able to strip off her clothes and tumble into bed. Maybe in her dreams the confusion would clear itself up and provide her with the answers she sought.

A wall of stores topped with curtained flats made the night seem even gloomier. A BBC telecast brought a round of chuckles swirling down from above, but the laughter was distorted, emphasizing rather than diminishing the feeling of solitude that enveloped her.

She had to admire Diana for braving the moors alone at night. Picturesque though the setting was, Lexie much preferred the noisy streets of London to the isolation of the country. Fog slinking about the tower of Big Ben and the rooftops of Westminster Abbey and St. Paul's Cathedral had the power to enchant her. Here it felt downright spooky.

She plodded through the murky streets, focusing on the squelch of her sneakers and the plight of her client. The temperature had dipped to a chilly fifty degrees. An Austin Mini bumped past her, adding a cloud of exhaust to the already thick air. Her footsteps echoed on the wet cobbles, a steady tapping sound that she wouldn't have given a second thought if she hadn't happened to stumble on one of the slippery stones.

The tapping ceased as abruptly as the noises at Wexford Castle had done when she'd called out Skelly's name, sending a sharp stab of awareness to her nerve ends. It dawned on her with frightening suddenness. She was wearing sneakers—and rubber soles didn't make a tapping sound, not on any surface.

Catching her lower lip between her teeth, Lexie took an experimental step forward. Then another and another. It wasn't until the fifth that she heard the clicking footfall start up again. Hard-soled shoes on the slick cobbles, a stealthy advance that seemed to be coming from about twenty meters behind her.

The stride was off now, no longer matching hers. An apprehensive glance over her shoulder revealed nothing except a heavy blanket of darkness. Should she risk stopping again? Her instincts told her no, but what did she care about some obscure sixth sense? If someone was following her, she wanted to know about it.

Cautiously, she slipped up onto the narrow sidewalk. She groped for the damp, wooden facing of the clock shop beside her, halting in the locked doorway, listening to the eerie tap-tap that continued for only three more steps before giving way to an ominous silence.

The scrawl she'd seen on the window of Wren's caravan popped into her head, and her heart began to race. The fog was too dense, and death was entirely too final. Without a moment's hesitation, she pushed herself from the shop and bolted for the security of the Pendragon Inn.

No amount of logic could stave off the gory images that accompanied her as she ran. And all the praying in the world couldn't make the very real sounds of pursuit disappear.

The tapping grew louder, filling the street with sound, but Lexie refused to falter. Nor did she look back. Skidding ever-so-slightly on the worn stones, she shot past a sturdy lamppost. The inn was only a few short meters away now.

Morbid curiosity gave her the courage to twist her head around as the golden lights came into view. For a moment she saw nothing but blackness. Then, slowly, something began to take shape in the curling mist. At least, she thought it did. Before she could so much as blink, the fog closed in once more and the tapping broke off. When the lamppost became visible seconds later, all that remained in the dim amber glow was an empty street.

The person following her had vanished.

CHARLES WAS nowhere to be found. Rick checked the inn's sitting room, the dining room, the bar and the bathroom. On a hunch, he even hunted through the wine cellar. There was no sign of the man, just a small stack of fishing magazines on the nightstand in his room and an incomplete report beside his typewriter.

Irritated, Rick bounded down the stairs to the deserted lobby. He couldn't afford to be seen prowling around the inn, and tempting though the idea was, he didn't dare go near Lexie's room. She was too damned distracting, and he had too much on his mind to let it wander, even for a few minutes.

With a grunt of frustration, he stepped out into the gloomy night. He wasn't thinking straight, and that bothered him. It no longer seemed to matter that he and Lexie had very different jobs to do here. Until he figured out why someone was threatening her, he wasn't going to be able to devote his full attention to locating the jewels. Conversely, the less time he spent doing that, the greater the risk that they never would be recovered.... Especially if the charges against Diana were as unjust as he'd begun to think.

The air outside was cool, smelling of aged wood and wet leaves. Squeezing his eyes closed in an effort to block out the confusion in his mind, Rick took a deep breath. He promptly let it out again when he picked up on the sound of someone running toward him. Not jogging at a leisurely pace, but tearing along at a breakneck speed.

He squinted into the fog, moving away just in time to avoid a collision with the woman who flew past him. Or rather she would have flown past him if he hadn't reached out a hand to ensnare her wrist.

"Lexie, what are you doing?" he demanded, steadying both himself and her, barely resisting the urge to haul her into his arms.

She slid to a stop, her fingers clutching the sleeve of his jacket. "I'm not sure. I heard someone behind me."

With a frown, Rick looked over his shoulder. "Behind you, where? Where have you been?"

"At the Golden Goose, but I didn't hear the footsteps until I got to Market Street. Rick, someone was following me, chasing me." She leaned against his arm, and he gave up the struggle, hauling her close and pulling her head onto his shoulder.

"Did you see who it was?" he murmured against her hair.

"No, but I'm not imagining things."

"I know you're not. I saw the writing on the window of Sherwood's caravan."

Rick felt her shiver in the brisk night air. "Come on," he said, drawing her gently through the door. "I'll walk you to your room and get you something hot to drink. Then I'm going to take a stroll down Market Street and see what I can find."

She went rigid in his arms. "No, you can't—I mean, you shouldn't." She lowered her eyes, adding a quiet, "You might get hurt."

A hint of a smile touched the corners of his mouth. He tipped her head back with the side of his hand, forcing her to look at him. "I appreciate the thought, Lexie, but I do this sort of thing every day, remember?"

"I remember."

He heard the sigh in her voice and immediately gave himself an exasperated mental kick. Doubtless his unfortunate phrasing had caused her to remember a few other things, as well. One of them being a "friend" by the name of Rodney Boggs who couldn't possibly be good enough for her.

A wave and a loud harumph from a sleepy-looking Myles Pendragon effectively put an end to Rick's uncharitable thoughts. Dropping his hands reluctantly to his sides, he ushered Lexie over to the front desk.

"Message in your slot, Miss Hudson." The man held out her key and a plain white envelope with her name stenciled on the outside. "Wasn't there last I checked afore dinner. Must be someone stuck it in while me and the missus were enjoying our cuppa round the kitchen table."

Rick positioned himself behind Lexie's shoulder, standing close as she ripped open the flap and removed a single piece of white paper. Something was wrong; he could feel it in his bones before she even unfolded the sheet. Before he saw the five fateful words typed in bold black letters upon it.

LEAVE THE CARNIVAL, OR ELSE...

SHADOWS AS BLACK as chimney soot hung in the lane beside the Pendragon Inn. Busy shadows, the murderer thought, taking care not to make any jerky moves.

Pleased eyes locked on the figure who squatted beneath Lexie Hudson's darkened second-story window. Splendid. Highly transparent in some ways, but considerate nevertheless. The writer of this afternoon's death threat had struck again, issuing yet another stark warning.

Leave the carnival, or else...

Such a melodramatic phrase, the murderer reflected, recalling the note that had been carefully slipped into the pigeonhole that held Lexie's room key. Of course, it wouldn't work, but that was hardly important. All that mattered was that she would read it and wonder about its origins. Who knew—maybe she'd even trace it back to the person who'd painstakingly composed it. Straight back to the person who was presently crouched in the shadows beneath her window.

Suppressing a laugh of pure pleasure, the murderer crept from the lane. Surely the truth would never come out now.

Chapter Five

"I'm not going back to London," Lexie maintained stubbornly. She kept her voice low but her tone resolute as she and Rick crossed the carnival grounds early Wednesday morning. "Last night's note proves that someone here had something to hide. I won't leave until I find out who wrote it and why."

Rick cast her a level sideways glance. "Your legal firm could send a private detective down to look for those answers, Lexie."

"There isn't enough time for that. Besides, I'm not a quitter."

"If yesterday was any indication, you might not have much to say in that regard."

He was trying to frighten her into leaving, but Lexie wouldn't be dissuaded. Nothing was going to happen to her. The note was a hollow threat. She'd spent almost an entire sleepless night convincing herself of that. She wasn't prepared to let Rick wipe out such a hard-won conviction, even though she could believe he really did have her best interests at heart.

He strode easily over a large patch of mud, his eyes scouring the sparsely populated meadow. It was a lucky thing she'd worn her hiking boots. She practically had to run to keep up with him.

At 7:30 a.m., the sun was already beginning to break through the haze. The forecast called for an uncommonly warm and muggy day. That should put everyone at the carnival in a fine mood, Lexie thought with a regretful sigh. Between the heat and the crowds, tempers would likely be at a precariously low ebb. Even Rick was exhibiting signs of impatience, although in his case, maybe she could understand it. He'd made no secret of the fact that he was concerned for her safety. He'd even gone so far as to spend the night in his partner's room. And, in all fairness, he still had his own assignment to think about.

They arrived at the main food tent—a huge canopy stretched over long rows of wooden tables and benches—in tandem with a wave of early-morning carnival workers. The canvas walls had been rolled up on three sides, permitting a warm breeze to blow through the eating area. At the far end of the tent, two flushed cooks dished up boiled eggs, toast, ham, blood sausage and something that looked suspiciously like gruel to the hungry mob.

"Tea?" Rick asked as he ushered Lexie under the canopy.

"Coffee," she corrected, looking around.

For the first time that morning, a grin crossed his mobile mouth. "Find us a seat," he said with a trace of humor in his beautiful blue eyes. "I'll be right back."

Lexie nodded, then promptly stifled a cry of pain as a heavyset ticket seller elbowed her into the corner of a table.

"Blimey, but you're in a bit of a snit, Gertie." Fitz appeared out of nowhere to shove a stubby hand under Lexie's elbow and whisk her deftly away from the crush of hungry diners. "You have to make a few allowances for this lot, miss," he confided with an impudent grin. "Queer ducks, most of them, not fit to call themselves human until they've partaken of their morning tea—or pint, as the case may be. Engage them before that and you'll be in for a right good ticking off." To emphasize his point, he gestured humorously at Gwendolyn, who was glowering at one of the burly maintenance men.

"Listen up, you twit," she snapped. "Are you daft or something? I said turn the cup three times, not thump it on the blooming table until the tea leaves drop to the bottom."

Muttering an unintelligible response, the man across from her pushed his cup aside, got slowly to his feet and ambled out of the tent.

"Dolt," Gwendolyn grumbled under her breath. She lifted her turban-wrapped head, treating both Lexie and Fitz to an acerbic stare. "Is there something I can do for you?"

Fitz dug a badly bent cigar from the pocket of his baggy jacket. "You could give us a smile," he suggested cheerfully.

"I could, but if I were you, I wouldn't hold my breath waiting for one." She slid her gaze to Lexie. "So you're still here, are you? I don't suppose you dropped in to say goodbye."

Lexie's hackles rose along with her suspicions. Gwendolyn was entirely too anxious to be rid of her. "I told you I don't plan on going anywhere until I've finished my investigation," she said in her most reasonable tone.

Snatching up the English muffin she'd heaped with strawberry jam, Gwendolyn stood. "Yeah, well don't say I didn't warn you," she snarled.

Lexie didn't flinch. "Which warning was that?"

A glimmer of something she couldn't comprehend rippled through the woman's dark eyes. It seemed to Lexie that she sneaked a quick look in Fitz's direction; however, he gave no indication that he noticed. His attention appeared to be fastened on Victoria, who was issuing her daily load of instructions to the grounds' crew outside the tent.

More and more curious, Lexie reflected as Gwendolyn hitched up the hem of her skirt and stalked away from the table. She felt as though everyone around her had a deep, dark secret to keep. Everyone with the possible exception of

Rick, she recalled, allowing herself a brief smug smile. She'd already exposed his secret. She could only hope and pray he never exposed hers.

Fitz's countenance could only be described as cheeky when he regarded her from beneath the brim of his battered derby. He didn't say anything, just watched her with that ever-present twinkle in his eyes. Maybe now would be a good time to learn what she could from him.

Leaning forward on her elbows, she ventured a deliberately nonchalant question: "I hear you and Wren Sherwood were neighbors in the arcade."

The twinkle in Fitz's eyes deepened. "You heard right, miss," he agreed, his prudent reply undermined by his lopsided smile.

Lexie studied his narrow features. He reminded her of a fox, cunning and devious, masterful in his ability to endear himself to whomever he chose—and undoubtedly tricky to a fault if she was any judge of character.

"Did anything unusual happen the night Wren was killed?" she asked, watching for the slightest indication of guilt.

Fitz bit down on his cigar. "Could be it did. But me, well, I find it suits me purposes best not to take notice of a neighbor's, er, deviations."

Lexie narrowed her eyes. "Are you saying that Wren was acting strangely before he died?"

"Can't say as I knew him well enough to answer that one, miss."

"Lexie."

"Right you are, Miss Lexie. You see, me and Wren, we didn't get too cozy on private matters. Just played our Scrabble games and pretended like both our slates were squeaky clean."

"You pretended," she echoed. "Did you recognize him, Fitz?"

A cagey little smile appeared on his lips. "Coo, such a round of queries. Fairly makes me head spin. Next, I suppose you'll be wanting to know where I was the night Wren cashed it in."

"Okay, where were you?"

A spark of mischief gleamed in his squinty eyes. "Locking up me booth, of course."

"Alone?"

"Only takes one pair of hands to pull down a flap and snap a bolt in place," he told her.

"So you don't have an alibi."

He shrugged, but appeared unruffled. "Didn't know as I'd be needing one." A shrewd brow was raised in her direction. "Given that, though, alongside me questionable credentials, I reckon I can see how I'd look like a top possible to someone such as yourself."

Lexie stared at him. "A what?"

"A prime suspect," Rick supplied, coming up behind her. At her trenchant expression, he smiled and shook his head. "Come on, let's go find someplace quiet to sit. Fitz has work to do, don't you, mate?"

"If you say so." Fitz made a polite show of tipping his derby. "Right nice chatting with you Miss Lexie. Come by me booth later if you fancy a distraction. Never can tell when me memory might be due for a good jog."

While Lexie pondered that curious remark, Rick handed her a steaming cup of coffee and propelled her out of the tent. She couldn't decide whether Fitz was purposely misleading her or whether he really did know something about Wren Sherwood's death. One thing was certain, the man was an inveterate flimflammer. He'd very neatly avoided telling her if he had indeed recognized his carnival cohort for the thief and murderer he was.

Another thought suddenly occurred to her, and she glanced sharply at Rick. "You knew about Fitz's record before you joined the carnival, didn't you?"

He grinned. "I should. I've arrested him three times over he years."

"And now you're using him to spy for you."

"In a manner of speaking."

"Do you trust him?"

"To a point."

"Do you think he might have the jewels?"

"Maybe, but he wouldn't be my first choice of suspects." Rick swallowed a mouthful of coffee as they strolled hrough a motley collection of storage tents on the outer dge of the carnival. "Fitz is clever enough to know exactly how far he can go in terms of breaking the law. Wallets and watches are fair game to him, the Saxony jewels would be a bit out of his league."

Although it was virtually impossible not to like the little man, Lexie didn't entirely buy that theory. "If Fitz is so clever, couldn't he be using your opinion of his limitations to his own advantage?"

Rick waited until they'd cleared the tents before answering. "The thought crossed my mind," he admitted finally, squinting at the sun that shone brightly through the fast-dissipating haze.

They'd drawn abreast of Algernon's workshop, and while Rick vaulted over the remains of an old stone wall, Lexie took a moment to observe him. It was an indiscreet undertaking, but she couldn't seem to stop herself. There was no denying that he was a frighteningly sexy man. He moved with a catlike grace that she found completely captivating—so much so that she failed to register his subsequent actions. Not giving her a chance to object, he clamped his hands securely around her waist and swept her with remarkably smooth dispatch over the eroded barrier.

He set her down in front of him, his eyes on hers, his beautiful body only a few inches away. For one rash moment Lexie longed to forget all about her life in London and a low-risk relationship that suddenly seemed to be lacking in many areas. It would have been easy to do with Rick standing there in front of her, looking so tall and lean, so wonderfully male in his faded jeans and white T-shirt that hinted at the strength of muscle beneath.

He said nothing, but his hands slid with practiced slowness to her ribs, lingering there for a fraction of a second longer than necessary. His breath on her temple was warm, the scent of him clean and masculine and enticing. When she could drag her eyes upward, Lexie was surprised to see a glimmer of something closely akin to regret in his expression—although what he could possibly have to regret was hard to imagine.

If only she hadn't felt so guilty, so confused about everything, she would have been sorely tempted to sway a little closer to Rick's broad chest, to let her hands explore the sleek contours of his back and shoulders...

She caught herself in the nick of time, stepping backward and giving herself a firm mental slap as his arms dropped reluctantly to his sides. It was madness to want him, to even think about wanting him—and thoroughly frustrating not to be able to interpret the expression in his shielded eyes.

A smile worked its way across his mouth, as though he could tell what she was thinking. Good for him, she reflected crossly, because she couldn't begin to sort out the turmoil in her mind.

She chose not to try. Instead, she took idle stock of the ancient fortress, visible just past his shoulder.

Situated on a rise near the perimeter of the carnival, Algernon's workshop was in a far more advanced state of decay then Wexford Castle. Its one-time battlements had caved in to the point where they were little more than jagged pillars of stone. Three rocky steps covered with dirt and weeds led to the only wall that remained erect. From there darkness took over completely.

"That's the entrance to Algernon's lab," Rick explained, his voice neutral.

She peered into the inky blackness. "Can we go down there?"

He hoisted himself onto the rampart and picked up his coffee cup. "It isn't against the law," he said, "but not many people would be willing to risk an encounter with Algernon's ghost."

Maybe in her case, a foray into the alchemist's underworld laboratory would be worth the risk. If Algernon's ghost was typically nocturnal, he might have seen who'd killed Wren Sherwood. However, barring that unlikely circumstance she could think of only one way to expose the murderer. Unfortunately, no matter how logical her arguments, she had a hunch her plan was going to meet with more than a few objections.

"You know, Rick," she began with feigned nonchalance, "I've been doing a little thinking. Actually, a lot of thinking. We agree that whoever shot Wren almost certainly had to be after the Saxony jewels, right?"

His eyes on hers were steady. "That's the general consensus."

"Well, if that person wanted to throw Scotland Yard off the trail, wouldn't it make sense to frame someone else for the murder?"

"Someone like Diana?"

"She did live with Wren," Lexie pointed out. "Anyone who works at the carnival would have known or could have found out about her habit of taking a walk every night after her last show."

"In other words, she was frameable," Rick clarified, his eyes never leaving her face. "Added to the fact that someone's been threatening you, I'll admit the likelihood of a setup does seem quite strong, but it's nothing that hasn't been considered before. What are you really driving at?"

He was too damned perceptive, Lexie thought, checking a sigh. "I want to help you search for the Saxony jewels," she said with commendable serenity. "You admitted that there's a good chance the murderer has them. Therefore, it would be advantageous to both our causes if we worked together on this."

His eyes darkened, but she noticed he didn't trash the idea outright. "It would be dangerous," he told her after a lengthy pause.

In more ways then one, a small voice in her head mourned. "I've had my fair share of danger already," she murmured obscurely, standing still as Rick hopped lithely from the wall. "I'm getting used to it."

"Are you?"

He advanced with a predatory swiftness that both alarmed and excited her. She should have moved out of range. She told herself she wanted to. But the lie was apparent even in her muddled state.

Did Rick know, she wondered desperately. Could he see it in her eyes, the desire she couldn't seem to erase? Lexie promptly lowered her gaze—and immediately wished she hadn't as her eyes found the front of his faded jeans.

The response she'd been about to make stuck in her throat. Her skin felt hot, her mouth dry. Somehow she managed to lift her head, facing him with the merest hint of a blush staining her cheeks. But he was too close, and suddenly she couldn't remember what she'd been about to say.

His features were, as always, inscrutable. "I must be crazy," he muttered more to himself than to her. His fingers curled warmly around the back of her neck, coaxing her head up farther until she was staring directly into his eyes. "If I had an ounce of common sense I'd talk you into getting in your car and driving straight back to London."

"You'd try," Lexie retorted, struggling to remain unaffected by his touch, knowing it was a hopeless undertaking. "Is it a deal?"

A mocking smile crept across his lips. His fingers tight-ened their grip and he drew her forward, slowly inclining his head toward her.

Lexie didn't move a muscle. She almost didn't breathe as his mouth covered hers in a kiss that effectively forestalled any protest her conscience might have made. Logic de-serted her, and she found herself savoring the taste of him, the heat and the scent and the texture of him for those few brief seconds of contact. Contact she would have deepened if a million alarm bells hadn't started clanging in her brain.

Regret and an unmistakable glimmer of desire darkened Rick's blue eyes when he lifted his head. The alarm bells stopped as abruptly as they'd started. However, the name, the face, the feelings that should have had her shoving him away simply refused to materialize. Sweet, kind, unde-manding Rodney was nothing more than a blur in Lexie's memory. If she hadn't wanted so badly for Rick to kiss her again, she would have been furious with him for flinging her into this completely unwarranted emotional turmoil.

A wry smile pulled at his lips, but he continued to stare down at her. "If I said I wouldn't work with you, would you go back to London?" he queried, distracting her now with his eyes.

She set her jaw. "No."

"In that case," he said, dropping a quick, gentle kiss on her still-bemused mouth. "It's a deal."

SHUDDERING DELICATELY, Diana recited the words typed on the paper Lexie held in her hands.

"GET RID OF YOUR ATTORNEY, OR ELSE..."

"I found it last night when I came back to the caravan. It was—" she shivered at the memory "—stuck under my pil-low." Too agitated to stand still, she wandered about the tent that doubled as storage space for a multitude of carni-val props and costumes and a wardrobe cum makeup area for the dancers.

Lexie perched on the corner of an overflowing vanity. This wasn't good news at all. So why, she wondered, irritated with both herself and the man she'd just left, was it so hard for her to get her mind back on track? Why did she feel as if she'd betrayed Rodney by kissing Rick? No, by *letting* Rick kiss her, she answered hastily. Fair was fair. He'd made the first move, even if she hadn't lifted a finger to fight him off.

She squirmed a little inside and forced her mind back to her client. The chaos of her personal life would have to wait its turn. She had a job to do, and that job certainly wasn't getting any easier as time went by.

"You should have called me the moment you found the note," she said, trying to sound prosaic rather than panicky. Diana was nervous enough. If her lawyer fell apart, she'd likely follow suit.

Diana's drawn face appeared above a rack of brilliantly colored boas. "I couldn't call you, Lexie. For one thing, Gwendolyn's cordless phone doesn't work, and for another, I was too scared to leave my room. You don't know how easy it is to break into our caravans. A trained chimpanzee could do it blindfolded."

A trained chimp or a cold-blooded killer, Lexie thought, alternating now between fear and wrath. She considered telling Diana about the similar warning she'd received, then thought better of it. It was going to be tricky enough confronting Rick with this latest development. She couldn't be expected to thwart his attempts to send her packing, deal with her own emotional traumas and Diana's problems and watch out for a murderer all at the same time.

She shoved the note into the pocket of her khaki shorts. "Do you still take your walks after the show?" she asked.

Diana ducked under a laden clothesline, carrying her horned Viking's helmet. "No." Her eyes clouded. "I did want to mention something, though. I don't know if it's important, but I saw someone coming down the slope from the village late last night.''

Lexie shrugged. ''Don't some of the people who work here occasionally go to the pub after the carnival closes?''

''Oh, yes, but they usually head up in a group, have a quick pint and come back the same way. Ever since Burt Drury's dog took a nip at Gwendolyn's ankle two weeks ago, she makes sure she's surrounded whenever she goes near the Rose and Crown.''

''Brave dog,'' Lexie murmured.

''Actually,'' Diana said with a faint smile, ''Gwendolyn tried to have Constable Chance arrest both owner and dog. However, when that didn't happen, she decided to trade fortunes for protection. But that's beside the point. It wasn't a bunch of workers I saw. It was just one person.''

Lexie eased herself from the vanity. ''Do you know who it was?''

''No.'' Diana sounded deflated now. ''It was past midnight and I couldn't sleep, so I got up to get a book. When I looked through the window, I noticed that the fog had started to lift and the moon had come out. That's when I saw someone creeping down the hill into the caravan row. Nothing really happened. I just have this funny feeling that whoever it was stopped for several seconds outside Glen's caravan.''

''And then?''

''Nothing.'' Diana stepped around a pile of fuzzy pink elephants. ''Maybe I'm going crazy. A cloud floated over the moon and the person disappeared. With my luck it was probably Algernon's ghost I saw. Algernon's the local phantom, you know.''

''So I've heard.'' Lexie glanced at her watch; 8:20. Only forty minutes to see how many of her client's churlish associates she could coax into a conversation.

While Diana's story piqued her curiosity, she couldn't see the advantage of belaboring it. Disappearing people had become aggravatingly commonplace around here, but until one of them could be caught she'd be better off pursuing more substantial leads.

After a few false words of reassurance, she left Diana in the tent and stepped out into the humid morning air. It felt like a sauna. She shook her head in disbelief. How could it be so cool and misty one day and like a tropical jungle the next?

Lifting her hair from her neck, she turned for the midway, but she'd scarcely taken a few steps when she caught sight of someone emerging from between two droopy equipment tents.

Skelly!

The instant his flint-hard eyes landed on her, he halted, dipping his head and searching for a means of escape. She opened her mouth to call his name, then promptly snapped it shut when he executed an abrupt about-face and strode back the way he'd come. Heartily tired of his evasion tactics, Lexie followed, scrambling over the tent's outer rigging, determined not to lose him again.

With an agility belied by his lanky frame, Skelly threaded his way through the carnival. He was heading for the fun house, Lexie realized as she slipped around the side of the tilt-a-whirl. Damn the slippery man! If he made it inside that exhibit, she'd never catch him.

The sun had broken through the haze now. Wisps of steam rose from the wet grass. Concentrated blasts of noise and heat poured from the roller coaster's engine, but she ignored them both and darted beneath the maze of steel girders that supported the tracks.

It was difficult to keep her eyes trained on Skelly's rigid back without tripping over a metal peg and breaking her ankle. More than once, she banged her shins on the crisscrossed poles and had to bite her lip to stop from swearing out loud. While he didn't slow down, she noticed with relief that he did change direction away from the fun house, and silently, she thanked the trio of barkers lounging by the ticket booth. Now, if she could only catch up to him before he lost her in the snarl of midway stalls.

Forty yards ahead of her, Skelly swung himself over a chain-link fence and began striding for a wood and canvas building that Lexie couldn't identify. She climbed over the remaining girders, somehow managing to clear the fence without getting tangled up in the wire. Neverless, by the time she dropped to the ground on the other side, he'd already reached the building's rear entrance.

Taking a deep breath, she covered the distance to the unmarked door. A tentative twist of the knob proved that it was unlocked; a determined inward shove caused it to creak back slowly, opening on a thick ebony curtain that looked as though it would have been right at home in Gwendolyn's tent.

Although she had no idea where she was, Lexie suspected it wouldn't be wise to venture too deeply into this place. Unlike her, Skelly knew the carnival inside out. Maybe he'd led her here for the express purpose of losing her in the shadows.

"Well, think again, mate," she muttered under her breath as she groped for an opening in the curtain. A bump on the far side indicated the presence of another person, but Lexie had no intention of calling out and announcing herself. Instead, she tugged the heavy drapery until she'd pulled it apart just wide enough so she could slip through.

An eternity passed before her eyes grew accustomed to the darkness. It took even longer for her to become aware of the shimmering black walls that surrounded her as she fumbled her way down a network of narrow corridors.

As a rule she didn't suffer from claustrophobia, but the farther she walked the more she could have sworn that these particular walls were beginning to close in on her. A glistening radiance brushed the gloomy passageways, a trace of silver lay over a coal-black framework. The effect was magical, haunting—and intimidating. Lexie felt the smooth texture of glass beneath her fingers, saw a stray filament of light bounce weakly off the panels beside her head and knew with a sudden shiver of recognition that she'd made a horrible mistake.

She'd followed Skelly right into the house of mirrors!

Chapter Six

"Here you go, Inspector. One wrought-up sergeant delivered safe and sound, as promised."

Beaming, Fitz squired a crotchety-looking Charles across the stage in the Viking dance tent. Limp strands of hair fell across the sergeant's shiny forehead; his hat sat at a lopsided angle on his head and the collar of his overstarched shirt was turned up on one side. He appeared flustered, untidy and suitably offended.

If Rick hadn't been in such an irritable mood, he might have found Charles's condition amusing. But his mind was on Lexie now, as it had been for most of an uncomfortable night and every damnable minute in between. The whole thing was ridiculous, this compulsion he'd developed for a woman who probably put her career above any relationship. If he'd thought it would get her out of his system, he would have refused to work with her. If he had a brain left in his head he'd concentrate on finishing the job he'd been sent to do and keep his personal feelings completely out of it.

It annoyed him that he couldn't seem to concentrate properly on his investigation. He'd just spent the better part of an hour searching for the Saxony jewels. In the process he'd been forced to tear apart, then carefully reconstruct, the fleet of Viking sailing ships that dotted the stage. He was hot and sweaty and in no fit mood to deal with his partner's pompous affectations.

A knowing little smile lit Fitz's face. "Did me best to avoid traffic, mate," he confided, "but I can't say as someone might not have taken notice of the fuss this one kicked up when I stuffed him under the canvas out back."

The mental picture evoked by the thought of Charles being "stuffed" anywhere was enough to cut through Rick's annoyance. While Fitz strolled to the front of the tent and assumed a lookout position on a crate near the entrance, he swung himself under a large Viking figurehead and watched as Charles plucked pettishly at the cuffs of his shirt sleeves.

"I say, Rick," he admonished, "it was downright unsporting of you to send a blackguard to the inn to fetch me. You could have rung me up instead."

Rick didn't feel like playing games. "I would have if I'd thought you'd be there. I spent the night in your room, mate. You still hadn't shown up by the time I left at seven-twenty."

An odd blend of expressions crossed Charles's face, ending with a lordly indignation that didn't quite ring true. He drew himself up to his full height, nostrils flaring, lips set in a thin line. "Need I remind you, Inspector, that my time off is none of your concern?"

"Need I remind you, Sergeant, that we have an assignment to carry out?"

"An assignment, not a banishment to bloody Botany Bay or Sing Sing or wherever it is you originally called home."

Rick's eyes narrowed dangerously. The urge to ram his fist—along with several of Charles's teeth—down the man's throat was almost too strong to resist. However, he forced himself to hold back and leaned against one of the huge firebrands, regarding his partner with a bland smile. "I'll see what I can arrange. In the meantime, suppose you tell me where you were at nine o'clock last night."

"I . . ." Charles sucked in his cheeks, then gave his vest a tug and assumed a huffy posture. "I was out," he said, but his attempt at insolence fell short, diminished by the gruffness in his voice. "A private matter."

"Visiting a sick friend?" Rick suggested softly, aware of the perspiration breaking out on Charles's forehead.

"Business." Charles flapped an impatient hand. "Entirely personal. Now, if you don't mind, I should like to end this unwarranted interrogation. As the Saxony jewels aren't likely to surrender themselves to us, we certainly shan't find them by standing around all day, bickering."

Rick had to give him marks: he'd managed not to answer a single question. He'd also made a valid point. The jewels weren't magically going to jump up and announce their hiding place to the world. They weren't even going to be found if Rick didn't make a concerted effort to keep his mind on his work—and off Lexie Hudson.

He pushed himself from the firebrand, knowing that he should squeeze the truth from Charles's scrawny hide, yet reluctant to force the issue at this juncture. The man had only missed one job-related rendezvous and an indeterminate one at that. It was hardly cause for the jumble of vague suspicions that had been drifting through his head for much of the previous night. Suspicions he couldn't quite shed.

Someone had followed Lexie from the Golden Goose restaurant, and Charles hadn't been around the inn at the time. Someone had slipped a threatening note into Lexie's key slot, and Charles just happened to be residing in the same building. And on a more ambiguous note, Sergeant Charles Gideon, a mediocre detective by any standards, had conveniently been vacationing in Dartmeet at the time of Wren Sherwood's murder. However remote the chances, it was possible that he'd spotted Sherwood at the carnival—and then what? Killed him and stolen the jewels? Decided to risk a prison sentence in an attempt to pad his meager retirement fund?

Rick gave himself a sound mental shake. He couldn't justify his doubts. And at this point he had no real cause to try.

"Begging your pardon, gents." Fitz caught Rick's attention by stabbing his cigar at the entranceway. "We appear to be in for a visit." He hopped from his perch. "Perhaps me and the good sergeant should take our leave through the rear exit."

Charles stopped fiddling with his clothes. "I beg your pardon? Did you say this place has a rear exit?" He looked affronted. "I hardly think that's cricket, old chap. Crawling under the tenting, indeed. I say, you might have seen fit to bring me in through this exit of yours."

Fitz grinned. "I did, mate." At a nod from Rick, he clamped a wiry hand around Charles's arm and towed him, spluttering and indignant, across the stage.

Rick heard the grunts of protest his partner emitted as he was propelled under the canvas, but it was doubtful Diana could. She wandered into the tent, clutching her glittering costume and helmet and offering him a wilted smile that bore testimony to the oppressive heat and humidity.

He hopped from the stage in one agile bound, unobtrusively watching her as she approached. She didn't look like a murderer, which didn't mean a damned thing, as he'd learned a long time ago. While the nature of Lexie's investigation tended to lead her away from her client, Rick wasn't prepared to overlook any possibility. He'd been obliged to search the dance tent this morning, even if wisdom had dictated that he do it behind Lexie's back.

He halted by a stack of chairs, aware of Diana's rather wistful gaze sliding down his body, but ignoring it. He kept his expression blank when he asked, "Didn't I see you with your lawyer earlier?"

"Lexie?" Diana nodded, lifting her eyes to his and expelling a tiny sigh. "You probably did. We were talking over in the wardrobe tent. I— Well, I've seen you with her a few times myself." Another sigh, punctuated by a contrite smile, escaped her. "I hope for her sake that you're not a jewel thief in disguise as Glen—I mean Wren—was."

Rick's smile was dispassionate. "I'm not. Do you know where she is?"

"Not really. The last I saw of her, she was following Skelly through the storage tent area. That would be fifteen or twenty minutes ago, I guess."

Following Skelly? Rick refrained from groaning out loud. feigning a lack of concern, he tugged his work gloves off with his teeth and tossed them onto the stage. "If you see Victoria, tell her I'll finish reinforcing that loose pole after lunch," he said over his shoulder as she made for the entrance.

Diana nodded. "I will. And Rick?" He glanced back at her troubled face. "When you find Lexie, tell her to be careful. I don't think that note I received was an idle threat."

Rick's eyes darkened. "What note?"

"The one I got last night." She ran a restless hand along her arm. "Somebody around here wants me to be convicted of murder, and I'm afraid to think just how far he or she might go to make sure that happens."

A CHILL CRAWLED DOWN Lexie's spine. The house of mirrors had become a house of horrors. An endless tunnel with only a few spindly cobwebs of light to shatter the gloom.

She halted her uncertain advance, telling herself there was nothing to fear, no cause for alarm. In the darkness, she was as much an invisible specter as Skelly.

Not moving she looked up at the ceiling, then across at the shimmering black walls that formed an illusory cage around her. A light film of sweat broke out on her skin as an unaccustomed feeling of vertigo assaulted her. She knew it wasn't possible, but the walls seemed to be swaying, spinning in large, lazy circles that threatened to affect her balance as well as her stomach.

She leaned on the glass for a minute, closing her eyes and pressing her forehead against the cool, silver-black surface, struggling to regain what little self-control she could muster. The sounds that filtered in from the carnival had a surreal tinge to them, making the shadows more oppressive and far more terrifying than they would normally have been.

A surge of indignation momentarily expunged her fears. Skelly had lured her here on purpose. He'd wanted her to trail him into this nebulous realm, and she'd obliged him. For all she knew, he might be long gone, back to his own world of cackling puppets and the cleverly hidden springs that made them leap out of the woodwork when people least expected it.

Anger gave Lexie sufficient strength to push herself away from the wall. It didn't quite give her the courage to move forward. She'd settle for backing out of this eerie maze while she still retained a fragment of her self-possession and worry about a confrontation with Skelly later.

She couldn't prevent the uneasy tremors that rippled through her. The sounds of machinery and human laughter were little more than a fractured buzz in her head. She had trouble distinguishing between mirror and glass, and no matter which direction she chose, it always seemed to be the wrong one. Her feet were moving, but was she really getting anywhere?

Frustration joined the chaotic medley of emotions swamping her. Her skin was damp with perspiration, her breathing labored, her mouth dry. The background noises had subsided to a mere thread of sound, and it was all she could do to keep from screaming for help.

In a distant part of her brain she recalled looking at her watch when she'd left the storage tent. It had to be almost nine by now. Surely anyone visiting a carnival would want to explore the house of mirrors. She was bound to have company in a few minutes.

Expelling a shaky breath, she turned to brave the tinseled darkness behind her. With her hand she felt for the nearest corner, then pulled up short as a burst of moist air suddenly skated along her bare arms.

She considered shouting to whoever might hear her, but discarded the idea. Skelly might still be in the vicinity. He'd probably like nothing better than to know he had reduced her to a bundle of quaking nerves. Follow the direction of the breeze, she ordered herself instead, and somehow, miraculously, her cramped muscles obeyed.

The shades of darkness altered subtly with every step she took. Elfin patches of light streaked through the steamy air, reflecting off the mirrors, gilding the corridors with a strange, luminous glow. Lexie's spirits lifted a fraction as the breeze wafting over her grew more pronounced. Thank God, she must be going in the right direction at last.

A feeling of relief gripped her. But it had scarcely begun to settle in when the air stopped circulating. Stopped, only to be filled with an eerie rumble from somewhere so close to her that she couldn't help flinching.

"What d'you want from me?" a man's voice—Skelly's, she presumed—demanded in an amplified monotone.

Lexie plastered herself to the nearest wall, endeavoring to breathe normally as a sense of desperation washed over her and a thousand frantic thoughts crowded into her head.

"I—I don't want anything from you," she managed to croak.

"You been following me, hunting after me like I was a prize buck," Skelly accused. His words echoed along the corridors, ghoulishly augmented by a built-in electronics system. "I told you yesterday, I got nothing to say about Wren Sherwood."

A small measure of Lexie's terror faded. Through parched lips, she forced herself to respond. "I only wanted to ask a few simple—"

The sentence broke off, ending with a strangled gasp she couldn't suppress. Directly in front of her, a grotesque figure began to take shape. The body was distorted, the arms and legs hideously long and thin, the fingers curled like the talons of a hawk. The facial features, too, were deformed, elongated, as though they'd been constructed of wax that was slowly being melted.

"Leave me be," Skelly's voice warned, the waxen mouth mimicking in caricature every word he spoke. A bony finger was raised until it pointed straight at Lexie's slamming heart. "Go away from here, now. Nothing can change what is. Diana shot Wren dead. That's all I know, and all I got to say."

The face assumed a scowl so repellent that Lexie didn't dare put up an argument. She doubted if she could have found her voice in any event. She felt as if an unseen hand had wrapped itself around her throat. It was a struggle just to fill her lungs with air.

The breeze she'd noticed earlier swept across her trembling body. She tore her gaze from Skelly's forbidding countenance long enough to ensure that he hadn't crept up beside her, then returned it to the mirror.

Her fingers curled into fists and the sudden intake of breath that reached her ears had to be her own. Damn the man! The misshapen image was starting to dissolve. No, strike that, she amended. It was mutating, taking on a new and terrifying shape that had the power to hold her in place for several interminable seconds.

The eyes, cold and malevolent, slowly became hollow cavities. The mouth dropped open in a mocking travesty of a smile. Stretched limbs metamorphosed into strips of bones.... She was looking at a skeleton!

Lexie blinked at the apparition, unbelieving, then swallowed hard as the mirror resolved itself into a wall of darkness once more.

The silence, almost tangible before, seemed deafening now. Abandoning the last vestiges of her self-restraint, she catapulted away from the glass. Overhead, a profusion of blue lights flickered and gradually settled down to a cool, aquamarine glare that allowed her to see where she was running. Polished metal, plate glass, reflections both real and imagined, she raced past all of them, intent on escaping the deceptive realm and everything it contained.

She wished she could also escape from the memory of what she'd just seen, from the word that kept shooting through her head. She wished she could find a way out of here!

Tendrils of fear pulled at her as she ran. She felt lost, disoriented, like a puppet caught in a supernatural limbo, the horrible fairy-tale world that was supposed to exist on the other side of the mirror. A hideous place, ravaged and tangled and lonely...

No, not lonely, she realized, stumbling to a halt as a shadow fell across the floor in front of her. She wasn't alone. There was someone in here with her.

Afraid to breathe, Lexie crouched, wrapping her fingers around the edge of a clear glass panel and watching for any sign of movement. It had to be Skelly, her terrified brain informed her, and he was standing between her and the door. From where she was huddled she could see the reflections of striped awnings, blue sky and green grass. God help her, freedom was only a few short meters and one long shadow away.

With a cautiousness born of unmitigated panic, she crept forward. To her relief, the mirrors remained empty. No sign of the person casting the shadow, and thankfully no obstacles in her path.

She held her breath as a blast of hot, sticky air spilled over her cheeks, then almost choked when a dark, completely menacing shape suddenly filled the silvery glass on her left.

Instinctively, she flattened herself against the nearest wall, biting down hard on her lip, trying not to make a sound. Her chances of reaching the door were slim at best, but what choice did she have if she wanted to get out of here?

The reflection turned—away from her, Lexie prayed—and somehow, she found the courage to bolt down the final corridor.

She kept visualizing the figure she'd seen earlier, A skeleton. The ultimate personification of death. Gwendolyn's crystal-ball prophecy come true.

She raced past the last mirror in her path and made a dash for the threshold. But it wasn't the sweltering morning air she slammed into, it was a human barrier. Very tall, very solid and very much in her way.

She reacted swiftly, without thinking, bringing her knee up and shoving hard with her palms. A grunt of pain told her she hadn't missed her target. A muttered curse and the sound of her name gave her pause to snap her head up and view her attacker.

"Rick!" His name tumbled from her lips in a cracked whisper. She stared at him in patent disbelief. How on earth had he found her?

With a reminiscent shiver, she let herself be pulled firmly against him, let his arms close about her shaking body. She felt the warmth, and the reassuring strength of him as he urged her head onto his shoulder and knew for the first time since she'd plunged into this horrible mirrored world that she was safe.

He held her close for several long seconds, until she no longer cared about the glimmering walls that surrounded her, or the images she'd seen, or even the fact that Skelly had undoubtedly lured her in here. All that mattered was the feel of Rick's fingers stroking her back, his warm breath stirring her hair, the smooth delineation of muscle and bone pressing into her heated skin. She could hear the beating of his heart beneath her ear, slightly accelerated but soothing and steady, a balm to her battered senses.

One by one, her fears began to subside, wiped away by a vastly different set of emotions that still had the power to confuse her. Something that had to do with the touch of Rick's body and the heady male scent of him. A strange jumble of feelings that made her long to forget all about propriety and duty and plain common sense.

A thread of rationality worked its way into her mind as Rick's voice penetrated her hazy thoughts. He made no move to put her away from him, just slid his hand to the nape of her neck and tipped her head back until she was staring into his eyes.

"What happened?" he demanded in a controlled tone that Lexie realized might have been brought about partly by pain.

A faint blush rose in her cheeks at the memory of her defensive action, but she didn't lower her gaze. "Skelly," she managed. "He told me to leave him alone, to go away."

"That's why you were running?"

Lexie sincerely wished they could drop the whole distasteful subject. Skelly's words still hovered uneasily in the back of her mind. The last thing she wanted to do was rehash them. Besides, being this close to Rick no matter what the circumstances wasn't exactly conducive to conversation.

Suppressing a sigh, she eased herself from the security of his embrace. Now was no time to be indulging in errant sexual fantasies. "He tried to scare me, and it worked," she said, aware of Rick's hands still resting lightly on her hips. She shivered despite the cloying heat. "I think he wanted me to come in here."

"Did he threaten you?"

"Not exactly." She explained briefly about the distorted image she'd seen and how it had changed into a skeleton. "He must have planned the whole thing. It's obvious he wants me to—"

"Leave the carnival," Rick concluded flatly, placing a firm hand in the small of her back and propelling her out of the building. His jaw was set in an unrelenting line. "Diana told me that someone slipped her a note last night."

Lexie had neither the desire nor the mental energy for the confrontation she knew was coming. If she was casual enough, maybe she could put him off. She glanced over at him. "It was nothing. How did you ever find me in there?"

"I followed your trail from the supply tent. A couple of barkers saw you go into the house of mirrors after Skelly." Rick wrapped his fingers around her arm, pulling her to a halt on the grass. "What did Diana's note say, Lexie?"

So much for putting him off. Wordlessly, she dug the folded paper from the pocket of her shorts and gave it to him. "Whoever did this must be afraid that if I stay here long enough, I'm going to learn the truth about Wren's murder."

"That *we're* going to learn the truth," Rick said, surprising her. She'd been expecting him to use this latest development to try to persuade her to return to London. Instead, he handed her the note, then shifted his attention to a point well beyond her right shoulder. "We have an audience."

She twisted her head around. From the shady reaches of a dark gray canopy outside the fun house, a man's figure stirred. And Lexie didn't have to see him clearly to know that Leonard Skelton's vitriolic glare was aimed directly at her.

SHE WAS BECOMING PARANOID, Lexie decided. Either that or everyone at the carnival was watching her. In her less fretful moments that day she suspected a lopsided combination of the two. The carnies were keeping their collective eye on her, all right, but whether those stares contained any real malevolence was hard to say. It might have been the remnants of Skelly's surveillance that had her looking over her shoulder every five minutes.

By the time two o'clock rolled around, she was tired and hungry and ready to collapse on the first patch of unoccupied ground she could find. At least the sun was no longer beating down on her head. A mass of gray-white clouds had blown inland from the channel just after eleven that morning, sending the mercury down to a reasonable seventy-five degrees and bringing a few of the shorter tempers back in line.

"Lexie?"

The unexpected sound of her name hit her like a physical blow. Her spine stiffened as she automatically turned to regard the speaker.

"I'm sorry—did I startle you?" Victoria approached from the direction of the temporarily out-of-service Ferris wheel.

The ingratiating expression on her face was highly questionable in Lexie's mind. Nevertheless, she forced a congenial smile. "Not really. I was just thinking about—" she paused for a moment "—uh, Wren Sherwood's relationships," she finished for lack of a more original idea.

"You mean other than the one he had with Diana?" Victoria rubbed a work-roughened hand on the leg of her black pants. "I'd venture to say there were very few. Not a particularly sociable man was our Glen."

"Wasn't he involved with Gwendolyn once?"

"Ah, so you've heard the scuttlebutt. The prognosticator and the superstitious felon. Quite an intriguing combination, I must say." Victoria indicated a grouchy-looking mechanic who was revving up the Ferris wheel's noisy motor. "I have to take a test turn on the wheel. If you're not afraid of heights, perhaps you'd like to join me."

Lexie stole a furtive look at the belching motor. She'd heard more promising grumbles from the Sea Tiger submarine in "Operation Petticoat." "I'd love to," she replied, lying through her teeth. She waited until they were settled in their seats with the safety bar solidly locked in place before venturing a casual, "Tell me, how did Wren get along with Mr. Skelton?"

Victoria's lips compressed ever so slightly. "As well as one might expect, given the awkward circumstances. Skelly is completely devoted to Gwendolyn. Has been ever since he signed on."

"One and a half years ago." Lexie wanted to be certain of the time. "Six months after Wren showed up."

"And seven months after my nephew, Danny, died." Victoria's voice was rather clipped, her knuckles white around the crossbar. "I remember it all very well. The carnival was in a dreadful state when I was called upon to take over. Danny was no bookkeeping wizard, but then neither am I, unfortunately," she muttered in an embittered undertone that Lexie would have addressed if the Ferris wheel hadn't shuddered into sudden, spasmodic motion.

Lexie loved airplanes and ski lifts and skyscrapers with open balconies. But she didn't like any feeling akin to a free fall, and she neither liked nor trusted the drunken lurches of this particular carnival ride. Holding her breath, she closed her eyes and clung to the crossbar, while Victoria offered a few more succinct remarks about her nephew and his decided lack of business acumen.

The motor, now a hundred feet below, coughed and sputtered and blew out clouds of noxious black smoke before emitting a final desperate wheeze that brought the wheel stuttering to a halt mere seconds before it could begin its horrible downward plunge.

Lexie didn't know if she should feel relieved or not. She opened her eyes to find Victoria leaning out of the car as far as she possibly could. "Is it the bearings?" she shouted.

An unintelligible response drifted up along with a cloud of smoke that smelled like burned rubber.

"All right, bring us down when you can." Victoria dropped into her seat, looking defeated. "He warned me this would happen. I'd hoped he was exaggerating. Now I'll have to replace the entire engine. A word to the wise, Lexie. If you ever inherit a carnival, find a buyer. You'll save yourself a great deal of heartache in the end."

Lexie relaxed her stranglehold on the crossbar and assessed the mass confusion in the meadow. "You've got a very good crowd today," she said, gesturing at the jam-packed midway. "Surely you'll have turned a decent profit by the time you pull up stakes."

"One can only hope," Victoria murmured.

Her tone was just obscure enough to revive Lexie's doubts. However, before she could sort through them, her eyes lighted on the caravan row, the one area of the carnival that was virtually devoid of activity in the midday crush.

She squinted at the solitary person who stood on the top step of the red trailer. It could have been a man or a woman; there was no way for her to tell from such a vast height and distance. But one thing was sure: no person of either gender had any business being on the stoop of Wren Sherwood's former home.

She flashed a quick look at Victoria who gave no indication that she noticed the would-be intruder. Not that her unrevealing countenance proved a single thing, Lexie thought.

It seemed like hours before the Ferris wheel's motor chugged to life again, long enough that she was able to see the person outside Wren Sherwood's caravan give the door a final abortive shove, then edge reluctantly down the stairs, holding a shapeless bundle under one arm. A sack, she guessed, or maybe a hat.

She leaned forward in her seat, unable to get a clear view of anything except the smoke that billowed up in a sooty black wave. Even the breeze made no effort to cooperate. It blew the suffocating fumes into her face throughout the wheel's descent, although after the first convulsive tremor shook the cars, her only salient thought was that she be delivered safely from the clutches of the ailing mechanical beast.

She shuddered inwardly, certain her lungs would burst if the downward motion didn't end soon. Thankfully, with one last hiccup from the engine, the ride was over. Sending a prayer of gratitude to God and the Fates, Lexie pushed the crossbar aside and jumped shakily to the ground. She took a deep breath, exchanged a few banal words with Victoria, then set her sights on the caravan row.

As always when she was in a hurry, the entire flow of carnival traffic seemed to be against her. After being bumped and jostled and nearly bowled over by a man carrying a huge Pink Panther, she fell into step behind a hefty carny who zigzagged between booths and rides and people with no trouble whatsoever.

She was weaving a path of her own through the concession stands when she happened to spot Rick. He was sprawled on the grass behind one of the snack bars, munching on a hamburger and unobtrusively watching the action in the arcade. Wearily, Lexie joined him, dropping to her knees on the spongy ground and trying not to fall on his food.

Her thespian talents must have been in low supply. The moment he looked at her, a grin spread across his lips and he handed her his half-eaten lunch.

It was manna from heaven, complete with onions, tomatoes and a big leaf of lettuce. She savored every bite, ignoring Rick's amused expression and her former sense of urgency. The person outside Wren's caravan would be long gone by now. She didn't have to die of starvation to come to that logical conclusion.

"Coke?" Rick asked, passing her the can.

The British didn't believe in ice, and sometimes Lexie doubted they had much interest in refrigeration of any type. She washed down a mouthful of hamburger with the tepid soda. "I went up on the Ferris wheel with Victoria a few minutes ago," she revealed, ignoring the fact that his head was mere inches from her breasts.

"That was brave of you." Reaching out, Rick wiped a smudge of ketchup from her chin with his thumb. "Last time I went up, I had to climb down."

"Well, we did sort of get stuck," she admitted between bites. "But only for a couple of minutes. It gave me a chance to look around."

"See anything exciting?"

"I think someone might have been trying to break into Wren Sherwood's trailer."

All traces of lazy amusement faded from Rick's eyes. He drew himself to a cross-legged position, facing her. "Who was it?"

"I couldn't tell."

"What about clothes?"

"Pants and a long-sleeved shirt, maybe a jacket. Black or possibly some other dark color."

"Sex?"

Lexie managed not to choke on her food. "I was too far away to see," she responded with admirable self-possession. "Whoever it was also had some kind of bundle under one arm."

She stopped speaking as Gwendolyn, decked out in a pair of skin-tight jeans and a brown leather jacket, stepped from her tent. She'd clipped her frizzy blond hair into a loose bun and topped it with a man's black bowler. She had a knapsack in one hand and a square of cardboard in the other. With a whack she slapped the closed sign on the tent flap, slung the knapsack over her shoulder and marched into the midway throng.

Lexie stared after the fortune-teller, dumbfounded, her hunger forgotten, the last scrap of burger poised in midair halfway to her mouth. "Where's she going?"

Calmly, Rick polished off the final bite, licking her fingers and rising to his feet with his own inimitable grace. "Luckily, away from the caravans." He tugged her, Coke can, sticky hands and all, from the ground. "Come on, let's see if we can figure out what your sexless visitor was doing outside Sherwood's place."

Lexie would have preferred trailing along behind Gwendolyn, but since that idea was rooted more in curiosity than any tangible suspicion, she clamped her mouth shut and accompanied Rick to the caravan row.

The area was deserted and unnaturally hushed despite the intrusive sounds of humanity only a short distance away. Irrational or not, Lexie kept expecting a face to pop up at the now-clean window of the red trailer. When none did, she fixed her attention on the silver lock that Rick was inspecting.

"Anything?" she asked, trying to see over his shoulder without lying on top of him.

He nodded, then moved aside, taking her by the wrist and pulling her down beside him. Even with her inexperienced eye Lexie would have been hard pressed to overlook the tiny scratch marks next to the keyhole. For whatever reason, someone had indeed tried to break into Wren Sherwood's caravan.

IDIOT!

The murderer punctuated the charge with a creative round of obscenities that would have done Wren Sherwood's felonious associates proud. Unfortunately, swearing wouldn't solve this newest problem. At issue was ineptitude. At stake was a setup that had to be completed as soon as possible.

Blundering fool! How hard could it be to pick a bloody lock? You'd have thought the nitwit was trying to have a go at the gates of Dartmoor instead of a two-bit carnival caravan. At this rate, the damaging evidence would never turn up—and that was a situation that could neither be accepted nor allowed.

The matter must be dealt with straightaway. No more sitting back and waiting. No more counting on blind luck, Irish or otherwise. It was time to take decisive action.

First, the necessary clues would have to be planted, the groundwork for suspicion laid. Then as a precaution the jewels would have to be moved.

And, of course, the murderer asserted with a vengeful mental thrust, anyone with the misfortune to get in the way would have to be killed.

Chapter Seven

"You had to see it, mate," Fitz declared. He sat on his cot with his back propped against the side of the tent where a number of the carnival workers bunked, waving his cigar around the darkened interior. "Flailed about like a stuck pig, he did. And the words that came from his mouth... Blimey, such ribaldry I'll wager you've never heard. How is it you got yourself partnered with a gent of that ilk?"

Rick's answering grunt was swallowed up in his pillow. His entire body hurt, even his skin. It was ten-thirty, the carnival was closed and he still had twenty minutes left before he'd have to rouse himself from the lumpy cot. He didn't intend to move a muscle until it was absolutely necessary. And talking about Charles Gideon was definitely not necessary.

In the back of his mind, Rick thought he detected a strange hissing sound. He blocked it out and concentrated on his plans for the evening, instead. Knowing that those plans would involve Lexie sent a pleasurable surge of heat to his extremities. Knowing what their course of action would ultimately be brought a groan of pain to his lips.

He was too tired, too sore and too mentally drained to undertake a moonlight treasure hunt. As the newest roustabout, he'd been the one elected to climb up and repair a worn strip of track on the roller coaster. He'd also been dealt the backbreaking chore of hauling a mammoth stock-pile of trash to the village dump. A hot shower hadn't re-vived him, and the prospect of prowling around the carnival in the dark, searching for the Saxony jewels, only made his desire to crawl into bed that much stronger.

Of course, he didn't necessarily want to be alone, he re-flected with a dry grin. He might be exhausted, but he wasn't dead. And neither was Lexie, even if she'd been trying very hard today to remember her supposed involve-ment with Rodney Boggs.

"Sssst..."

The hissing sound broke into his thoughts once again, and this time Rick lifted his face from the pillow to look at Fitz, who was puffing away on his cigar. "What is that?"

Fitz cocked his head. "Can't rightly tell. Off the top of me head, I'd say it's either a snake on its last legs, a popped steam pipe, or—" his eyes twinkled "—a certain copper with the smarts of a shriveled gooseberry and the word stock of an old Cornish salt."

Charles.

Rick held back the growl that burned deep in his throat. Murmurs from a group of workers engrossed in a poker game at the other end of the tent probably covered his part-ner's sibilant bids for attention, but that didn't make him any less of a jackass for pulling such an idiotic stunt.

Fitz blew a fat smoke ring. His eyes were half closed, the look on his foxlike features indolent but shrewd. "If it isn't out of line, mate, you'd be as well to give that bloke the heave. He's not the craftiest beggar I've ever hobnobbed with, but mark me, he's the kind who'd peddle his mother in a trice and never think the worse of himself for doing it. He's a humbug, that one, keen on serving his own interests before those of any other."

"Tell me something I don't know." Rick tossed a sneaker at the taut canvas wall to shut Charles up, then dragged himself from the cot and pulled on his work boots. He had the authority to dismiss a subordinate officer if he so chose, and he was damned close to exercising that authority right now. The only thing stopping him was the point Fitz had made about Charles's unqualified self-absorption. There was more than a grain of truth to that statement. The man had his own best interests at heart. He always had, and undoubtedly he always would, which raised some highly compelling questions in Rick's mind.

Just how far might Charles's misplaced egotism take him? Where did his loyalties really lie—with Scotland Yard or with himself? Cut loose from this investigation, what would he do? Could he be trusted?

Ruthlessly, Rick shoved the unsupported thoughts aside, grabbed his jacket and slipped out of the tent. He'd spent enough time on the force to keep his footsteps silent as he approached Charles from behind.

"What are you doing here?" he demanded coldly, watching with grim satisfaction as the shocked sergeant flung himself against the trunk of a nearby beech tree.

Despite being caught off guard, Charles adopted his usual affronted air. "Steady on, old chap," he rebuked, but Rick cut off his feeble protestations, taking him roughly by the arm and hauling him into the sparse stand of trees that dotted the meadow beyond Algernon's workshop.

"What are you doing here?" he repeated, his teeth clenched, his fingers itching to wrap themselves around Charles's throat. "And no more evasions, mate. This isn't the first time you've jeopardized my cover, but it's sure as hell going to be the last. Now tell me what's so urgent that it couldn't wait till tomorrow."

Too arrogant to be easily intimidated, Charles mustered a scowl, but Rick noticed he was quick enough to reply. With an awkward tug he adjusted the lapels of his dark gray suit. "I saw the blond woman, the fortune-teller," he disclosed stiffly. "She came to the village this afternoon just as

I was preparing to leave for the carnival. Most inelegantly attired, I must say.''

"Get to the point," Rick snarled.

Charles bristled, but complied. "The point, my dear chappy, is this. I not only saw her, I took the time to follow her. Discreetly, of course, as is my wont. I thought it might interest you to know just how your waspish soothsayer chooses to spend the coins I was so rudely accused of conspiring to pinch.''

Rick shoved his hands into his jacket pockets. Mere orders didn't work with Charles. It was doubtful that anything short of a good right to the jaw ever would. Weariness joined impatience in his voice. "All right, what did she buy?''

"A box.''

The announcement was made so smugly that Rick felt certain he'd missed something. His eyes narrowed. "You came down here after hours, dragged me out of my tent, risked my cover and your own just to tell me that Gwendolyn bought a box?''

Charles raised a haughty brow. "A strongbox, Rick, with a very stout lock. Made of a rustproof metal alloy. Suitable for storage in damp surroundings. Am I making myself clear?''

"You think she's planning to store this box somewhere wet?" Rick's amusement got the better of him.

"The Saxony jewels will have to be hidden well," Charles elaborated in his most profound tone. "Hence, the need for a proper containment vessel.''

Rick's lips twitched. "Does this mean you now believe that she killed Sherwood and stole his cache?''

One thin hand batted at the air. "What I do or do not believe with regard to Wren Sherwood's death is entirely beside the point. I'm sure I needn't remind you that our goal is to locate the missing jewels. To that end, I feel your time would be best spent keeping one Gwendolyn Sykes under close scrutiny."

"*My* time?"

Charles flushed a little. "Yes, well, you are in rather a more favorable position than me, aren't you? Besides," he added, bridling, "if you'll recall, the one and only time I had the misfortune of meeting the woman, she instructed that loutish henchman of hers to chuck me out on my ear."

A move that could hardly be held against her. Rick's irritation began to mount again, but he knew he couldn't let his personal feelings blind him to the very real possibility that Gwendolyn might have the jewels. "I'll watch her. And, Charles." His unimpassioned gaze didn't mask the silky note of warning in his voice. "If you endanger my part in this assignment one more time, you'll be deskbound for the rest of your days with the Yard."

Although his mustache twitched, Charles offered no rebuttal. Treating Rick to a tart look, he rearranged the angle of his bowler, squared his narrow shoulders and strode off into the copse.

Rick watched him go until he was swallowed up by the night. There was no hint of guilt in his thoughtful stare. As a partner Charles was useless, more of a hindrance than a help. It was patently obvious that he didn't want to be here, and yet he'd allowed himself to be pressed into service. He'd had an easy out. Why hadn't he simply refused the assignment and finished his vacation? Because he was still bucking for the promotion to subinspector that he felt had been unjustly denied him? Or was there another reason?

Rick tossed the questions around for several seconds, then gave his head a brooding shake and glanced at his watch. He'd told Lexie he would meet her in the pub at eleven o'clock, and it was already ten minutes past. He knew she wouldn't be particularly pleased by his tardiness, but he'd rather find her at the Rose and Crown, cursing his late arrival than wandering around the carnival by herself, getting into God only knew what kind of trouble.

He fought the shudder that slid along his spine when he recalled one of the barkers telling him that she'd followed Skelly into the house of mirrors. Evidently, the erstwhile undertaker had no intention of talking to her.

As he drew closer to the village, Rick let his mind drift back over the other events of the day. He still couldn't figure out why anyone would want to break into Wren Sherwood's caravan. If that person had half a brain, he or she couldn't have been planning to search for the Saxony jewels. The place had been torn apart the day after the murder by a team of professionals. In total, they'd turned up six shillings, two dusty rhinestones and a sliver of broken blue glass, likely from Diana's dance costume. There'd been no sign of any valuables and no map to pinpoint the location of Sherwood's illicitly obtained fortune.

Though the blistering heat of the morning had long since abated, the night air still felt damp and heavy. Rick took a deep breath, savoring the coolness, letting his mind wander well beyond the limits of his investigation. Once again his thoughts stopped short on a stunning and entirely too-stubborn lawyer who'd probably slug him if he kept her waiting another ten minutes—assuming she'd even waited the first ten.

Ignoring the painful protest from his muscles, Rick lengthened his stride on the village path. The night was too dark, the carnival too big and empty for anyone to be prowling around it alone. Especially when that person had her sights set on exposing a murderer.

'BIT OF A BARNEY, that's all it was. Me and the missus, we've had bigger rows over what to watch on the box than those two did that night.'' The pub owner set a dry cider on the polished table and gave Lexie a conspiratorial wink.

"Only person from the carnival who ever raised a ruckus hereabouts would be that fortune-teller."

"Gwendolyn?" Lexie's spirits lifted considerably. Rick was already ten minutes late and she'd spent every one of those minutes fidgeting in her seat, trying to work up enough courage to walk down to the carnival and find him. She'd been chiding herself for her cowardice when the bartender had strolled over and struck up a friendly conversation about Diana and her impending trial.

At the mention of Gwendolyn's name, a crusty old man with long, pointed whiskers and a shock of white hair let out a derisive snort. He didn't turn from the dart board he was aiming at, just shook his head and gave his wrist an experimental flick.

"She's a nasty creature, that one," he commented sourly. "Tried to have me locked up and my dog put down a couple weeks back. Stepped on Gordon's sore paw, she did, then started crowing like the furies when he took a wee nip at her ankle." The man whom Lexie assumed must be Burt Drury, made a coarse sound in the back of his throat and flipped the dart at the much-used board. "Cost me a day's wages to get his paw bound up again. She deserved to feel his teeth, that one did. Anyway, I don't see as she could have been up to much good loitering about like she was in a dark lane."

Lexie looked at the ruddy-cheeked pub owner. "Did the dog actually bite her?"

"What, Burt's old hound?" His laughter rang out in the smoky room. "Why old Gordon wouldn't so much as scratch at a flea. Ain't but one person I've ever set eyes on he didn't take a fancy to straightaway. Lick you to death, he will, but put his teeth in your leg?" The bartender wiped his thick fingers on a white dish towel. "He'd be as like to bite himself first."

He ambled over to the bar, still smiling, leaving Lexie to her own devices. She leaned back in her sturdy chair, sipped her drink and studied the small pub with only a moderate amount of interest.

It was an old building, much like the Pendragon Inn. Walls of dark wood gleamed under the flickering light cast by a fire burning low in the grate. The panels were covered with remnants of an era gone by. There was a rusted scythe, a cracked bell and a wheel that might have belonged on a seventeenth-century carriage. The latter, minus two spokes, reclined against a stack of wooden barrels beneath a shelf crowded with an intriguing assortment of dusty green bottles and hand-turned pots. In the far corner of the room sat an old cider press and beside that stood a collection of stained jars and firkins once used to contain the fermented apple beverage.

Over the rim of her glass, Lexie surveyed the pub's patrons, villagers for the most part as well as a small group from the carnival. In light of Burt Drury's remarks about Gwendolyn, it was probably just as well the fortune-teller hadn't stopped in for a nightcap. But if she wasn't here, that almost certainly meant she was down at the carnival, and after seeing her that afternoon, Lexie could only speculate on what she might be doing right now.

Impatiently, she shoved back her chair, paid her bill and marched over to the front door. Rick was late, and she was tired of waiting. She'd have to take a chance on finding him at the carnival.

She shivered a little as the cool night air washed across her face. While it wasn't really foggy, she did notice a light mist swirling about the tops of the lampposts. The gauzy veil seemed to be sweeping down the hill from the direction of Wexford Castle, and for a moment Lexie allowed herself to recollect the tale Rick had told her yesterday. Whenever the fog rolled in from the north, one of the local villagers would mysteriously disappear....

An involuntary shiver shot through her. Spooky or not, it was only a story. Algernon wasn't going to materialize and whisk her off to his fortress laboratory.

The grass beneath her feet had been trampled flat by the crowds, but it still served to absorb the sound of her hiking boots. With the lights of the village behind her, she could see the outlines of motionless rides, deserted tents and poles topped with silent loud speakers. Somewhere off in the distance, likely from the caravan row, the reassuring lyrics of "Penny Lane" reached her ears.

She lifted her head to regard the trailers. Most of them were bathed in darkness. Only the odd lamp burned, one of them in Victoria's living quarters. Since her gaze happened to be fastened on the caravans, she took no notice of the shadow that approached her on the winding path. She might not have seen it at all if a twig lying on the grass hadn't snapped loudly under the foot of the advancing figure.

Lexie swiveled her head, eyes widening in sudden alarm. A scream rose automatically to her throat, one that would have alerted the entire constabulary of Ashcroft had she released it.

"It's just me, Lexie."

Rick's low voice drifted out of the darkness, bringing a feeling of relief that was so overwhelming that Lexie could scarcely keep her knees from buckling. Sheer force of will gave her the strength to continue walking.

"You're late," she accused without umbrage. Her voice came out a bit shaky, but at least she didn't sound as unmanned as she felt. Or as disturbed, her brain added when the clouds parted to let the moon beam down on Rick's head. He looked rumpled and sore and impossibly sexy in his work boots, jeans and jacket, and Lexie couldn't prevent the spark of excitement that flared up inside her at the prospect of working with him. "I thought maybe you'd decided to renege on our deal."

His slow smile brought a sigh of regret to her lips. "I probably should," he returned, reaching for her hand. "But then I've never been the most sensible person in the world."

"Or the most punctual," she murmured. She devoutly wished she could ignore the warm pressure of his fingers on hers and the stream of moonlight that dusted his hair with silvery highlights and changed his eyes from sky blue to a deep shade of cobalt.

He turned those beautiful eyes to her as they walked toward the carnival. "You can blame Charles for the delay, Lexie. He showed up insisting he had some important information about Gwendolyn."

Lexie raised a hopeful brow. "Did he?"

"I'm not sure. I doubt it. He says he followed her into the village this afternoon and that she purchased a strongbox from one of the local merchants. It's his theory that she's got the Saxony jewels and that she's going to stash them in the box and bury it somewhere until the carnival pulls up stakes at the end of the week."

The idea sounded reasonable enough to Lexie. A little conspicuous perhaps, but, like any lead, worth exploring. "Don't you think it's possible for Gwendolyn to have murdered Wren and taken the jewels?"

"Lots of things are possible," he said, but she noticed the contemplative look he slanted in the general direction of the Pendragon Inn.

It didn't require a great deal of brainpower to interpret that look. "You don't trust your partner, do you?"

He shrugged. "I question his motives for accepting this particular assignment. I also have a doubt or two about the coincidence of his being on holidays in Dartmeet at the time of Sherwood's death."

The last was news to Lexie. Mentally, she added Charles Gideon's name to her ever-expanding suspect list. Piece by tiny piece, Diana's chances for an acquittal were beginning to improve.

Indistinct silhouettes evolved into more familiar objects as they drew closer to the gates. Canvas awnings flapped in the breeze. Bald metal couplings creaked monotonously, at odds with the thumps and bangs of loose sidings that emanated from the arcade.

Lexie concealed an apprehensive shiver. Even in Rick's company, the closed carnival struck her as a desolate place, rife with shadows and murky hollows and blackened spaces that she wouldn't have had the nerve to probe alone.

She trained her eyes on an area just past the arcade. They had to start somewhere, she reasoned, pulling insistently on the hand that was wrapped around hers. "Maybe we should search Gwendolyn's tent first," she suggested.

A grin touched the corners of his mouth. "Should or want to?"

"Want to," she confessed, still tugging. "Look, I don't know how reliable your partner is—"

"He isn't."

"All right, then we should search his room at the inn, too. That's not the point I'm trying to make. Whether you trust him or not, you have to admit he isn't the only one who's been acting strangely."

"Neither is Gwendolyn," Rick remarked, letting her drag him forward.

They crossed the midway to the fortune-teller's tent. Eyes alert for any unusual movement, he lifted the flap and allowed Lexie to precede him inside.

She paused on the threshold, unable to see anything except a wall of blackness. "I don't suppose you brought a flashlight?" she asked as he came up close behind her.

He chuckled. "Do I really seem that inept to you?" She felt the slight movement of his body just before he placed something hard and cylindrical in the palm of her hand. "Make sure you keep the beam down," he cautioned, switching on the second torch. "Gwendolyn's caravan isn't very far away."

Mutely, Lexie nodded. Part of her wanted to put some distance between them; another part was tempted to step back and press herself against the strong, solid length of him. With an effort, she cast the impulse aside and ventured deeper into the tent.

While Rick wandered over to inspect the trunk Gwendolyn kept there, Lexie shook the pillows, examined the toadstool ottoman and the crystal ball, peered behind the shrouds and a picture of Nostradamus, checked under the table and finally focused her attention on a black lacquered cabinet she discovered behind the folding screen. It wasn't locked. Unfortunately it wasn't brimming with jewels, either. Except for two sets of gaudy plastic earrings, a flattened turban, three black cups, a copper kettle and a box of Earl Grey tea, the cupboard was bare.

She was sifting idly through the tea leaves when she detected a sharp snap from the other side of the screen. Hastily she stuffed everything back into the cabinet and peered around the screen only to find Rick crouched down, calmly rifling the contents of the formerly padlocked trunk.

Flipping off her flashlight, she crossed the straw-covered ground and dropped to her knees next to him. "How did you do that?" she demanded doubtfully.

"Trick of the trade," he replied with a grin.

"Your trade?"

"Fitz's." He handed her a shoe box tied up with a frayed, yellow ribbon.

"So Mr. Fitzwilly picks locks as well as pockets, does he?" Lexie untied the ribbon. "I guess that means he wasn't the one I saw trying to break in to Wren's caravan this afternoon."

"Not unless he's lost his touch."

"Maybe that's what he wants you to think," she said, poking through the magazine clippings in the box. "There's nothing but recipes in here, Rick." She looked up at him, disconcerted to find his hooded eyes on her. "Have you searched Fitz's booth?"

He smiled, moving closer. "Not yet."

"Are you going to?"

"If we finish up in this tent before the carnival opens for business tomorrow, I might consider it."

Lexie refrained from sticking her tongue out at him. "As far as I'm concerned, we're already finished."

A speculative light she'd begun to recognize shimmered in his eyes. "No, we're not," he told her. "Not by a long shot."

With the same graceful economy of movement that characterized all his actions, he shifted position on the hard ground, impelling her backward with the lightest of touches until she felt the barrier of smooth, satin-covered cushions against her spine. One determined hand grazed the side of her jaw, then slid to the nape of her neck, holding her steady while the other brushed several long strands of hair from her cheek.

She began to tremble inside. "Yes, we are," she lied while she still could. "I don't want to be involved with a man right now."

He continued to stroke her cheek. "Not even Rodney?" he queried humorously.

"Rodney's different," she defended. "He's . . ."

"A friend?"

"A close friend," she snapped, knocking his hand away. "We're almost engaged."

"Almost?"

"We don't want to rush into anything. Now will you please let me up before Gwendolyn storms in here and has us both arrested?"

Rick grinned but didn't move. "You sound like my Italian grandmother. She believes in polite courtships, four-year engagements and fiftieth wedding anniversaries."

"Your grandmother sounds like a very wise woman."

"She's a saint. Why don't you want to rush into anything?"

Lexie caught his errant fingers before they could slide beneath her sweater. "My ancestors were Puritans. Maybe some of their beliefs rubbed off on me."

"Or maybe you don't love this almost-fiancé of yours."

Maybe she didn't, but Lexie wasn't about to admit that to anyone, least of all to Rick. "Let me up," she repeated through clenched teeth.

Smiling, he raised her hand to his lips and began kissing her fingers. "I'm not holding you, Lexie," he murmured, and with a start she realized he was right. He was hardly even touching her at this point. She could have scrambled away from him any time she chose...so why hadn't she?

"You know, you won't be happy marrying a man you don't love."

As he spoke, Rick pushed back the sleeve of her sweater, giving his mouth access to the soft skin of her inner arm. A hot shiver swept through her. "You keep saying that," she said, her voice not quite steady. "How can you be so sure I don't love him?"

He ran his tongue lightly over the inside of her elbow. "Do you really want me to answer that?"

Was there any point? Lexie knew she cared for Rodney, but she'd never deluded herself into believing she loved him. For that matter, neither had Rodney. "No," she said, then swallowed a tiny gasp as Rick's mouth left her arm to find the pulse at the base of her throat.

Shifting his weight slightly he rubbed his thumb over her lower lip. His mouth slid along the side of her neck, stopping halfway to hers, and for a split second Lexie thought he was going to say something more. When he didn't, she held her breath, waiting, not fighting the giddy little waves of desire that assailed her. In the dim light, she saw the hunger he made no attempt to hide and with a tremor of anticipation felt his lips brush across hers, gently at first, then with a much greater insistence.

She ran her hands over his chest to his shoulders, eager to touch this man who could make her feel things she hadn't felt in years, if ever. Her fingers twined in the layers of his long hair and she pulled him forward, reveling in the hardness of his warm body, arching herself closer in response. His mouth traveled teasingly over her lips, his tongue parting them while his hands began a provocative exploration of their own.

She couldn't hold a rational thought, didn't want to. To think was to acknowledge the pangs of guilt that had been gnawing at her for the past few days, and guilt was the last thing she cared to feel. Not with Rick's fingers sliding deftly over her waist, his lips roaming over the flushed skin of her face.

Lexie wasn't sure how the lonely little fragment of reason managed to sneak into her brain. She wished it would go away. But then Rick raised his head for a moment, and the fragment became a half-formed thought, one she resented, yet couldn't disregard when she caught the overpowering scent of honeysuckle incense she'd somehow missed before. A groan built in her throat. This was absurd, to say nothing of dangerous. They were in Gwendolyn's tent!

"Rick, this isn't a good idea," she began, then stopped and almost pushed the thought away when his lips found the corner of her mouth. "What if Gwendolyn shows up?"

"In the middle of the night?" He kissed her eyelids. "Why would she want to come here so late?"

"We're here," Lexie reminded him in a soft voice. "I wouldn't put it past her to have her tent bugged."

To her relief, Rick rolled away, sitting up and pulling her with him. "That's a paranoid thought," he murmured in her ear.

IT'S FUN! IT'S FREE!
AND IT COULD MAKE YOU A

MILLIONAIRE

If you've ever played scratch-off lottery tickets, you should be familiar with how our games work. On each of the first four tickets (numbered 1 to 4 in the upper right)—there are PINK METALLIC STRIPS to scratch off.

Using a coin, do just that—carefully scratch the PINK STRIPS to reveal how much each ticket could be worth if it is a winning ticket. Tickets could be worth from $5.00 to $1,000,000.00 in lifetime money.

Note, also, that each of your 4 tickets has a unique sweepstakes Lucky Number...and that's 4 chances for a **BIG WIN!**

FREE BOOKS!

At the same time you play your tickets for big cash prizes, you are invited to play ticket #5 for the chance to get one or more free book(s) from Harlequin. We give away free book(s) to introduce readers to the benefits of the *Harlequin Reader Service*®.

Accepting the free book(s) places you under no obligation to buy anything! You may keep your free book(s) and return the accompanying statement marked "cancel". But if we don't hear from you, then every other month we'll deliver 4 of the newest Harlequin Intrigue® novels right to your door. You'll pay the low members-only discount price of just $2.24 * each—a savings of 26¢ apiece off the cover price. And there's no charge for shipping and handling!

Of course, you may play "THE BIG WIN" without requesting any free book(s) by scratching tickets #1 through #4 only. But remember, the first shipment of one or more books is FREE!

PLUS A FREE GIFT!

One more thing, when you accept the free book(s) on ticket #5 you are also entitled to play ticket #6 which is GOOD FOR A VALUABLE GIFT! Like the book(s) this gift is totally free and yours to keep as thanks for giving our Reader Service a try!

So scratch off the PINK STRIPS on all your BIG WIN tickets and send for everything today! You've got nothing to lose and everything to gain!

Here are your BIG WIN Game Tickets, worth from $5.00 to $1,000,000.00 each. Scratch off the PINK METALLIC STRIP on each of your sweepstakes tickets to see what you could win and mail your entry right away. (See official rules in back of book for details!)

This could be your lucky day - GOOD LUCK!

TICKET 1
Scratch PINK METALLIC STRIP to reveal potential value of this ticket if it is a winning ticket. Return all game tickets intact.

LUCKY NUMBER

1D 235222

TICKET 2
Scratch PINK METALLIC STRIP to reveal potential value of this ticket if it is a winning ticket. Return all game tickets intact.

LUCKY NUMBER

3W 236258

TICKET 3
Scratch PINK METALLIC STRIP to reveal potential value of this ticket if it is a winning ticket. Return all game tickets intact.

LUCKY NUMBER

51 235978

TICKET 4
Scratch PINK METALLIC STRIP to reveal potential value of this ticket if it is a winning ticket. Return all game tickets intact.

LUCKY NUMBER

5D 235304

TICKET 5
We're giving away brand new books to selected individuals. Scratch PINK METALLIC STRIP for number of free books you will receive.

FREE BOOKS

AUTHORIZATION CODE

130107-742

TICKET 6
We have an outstanding added gift for you if you are accepting our free books. Scratch PINK METALLIC STRIP to reveal gift.

FREE GIFT

AUTHORIZATION CODE

130107-742

YES! Enter my Lucky Numbers in THE BIG WIN
Sweepstakes and tell me if I've won any cash prize. If PINK METALLIC STRIP is scratched off on ticket #5, I will also receive one or more FREE Harlequin Intrigue® novels along with the FREE GIFT on ticket #6, as explained on the opposite page.

(U-H-I 05/90) 180 CIH RDC6

NAME _____

ADDRESS _____ APT. _____

CITY _____ STATE _____ ZIP _____

Offer limited to one per household and not valid to current Harlequin Intrigue® subscribers.

© 1990 HARLEQUIN ENTERPRISES LIMITED

PRINTED IN U.S.A.

Carefully
detach card
along dotted
lines and
mail today!
Play your
all your
BIG WIN
tickets
and get
everything
you're
entitled to—
including
FREE BOOKS
and a
FREE GIFT!

Lexie tugged at the hem of her sweater. "Lawyers are notoriously paranoid people, especially when their lives have been threatened."

Wrong thing to say, she realized, biting her tongue as Rick's eyes narrowed. She opened her mouth to downplay the remark, then closed it again when he held up a warning hand.

He appeared to be listening to something, and Lexie's first thought was that Gwendolyn was about to come bursting through the flap in a full-blown fury. A giggle beyond the canvas walls shot that idea down, but it still wasn't a welcome sound. Neither was the low chuckle that accompanied it.

Before Rick could stop her, Lexie was crawling over pillows and straw to the heavy flap. Inching it back, she peered out into the gloom—and promptly jumped back again after almost banging her head on a pair of stumpy legs.

"What are we going to do?" she whispered to Rick whose arms resided calmly around her ribs.

He grinned, brushing his lips across her temple. "Use the rear entrance, what else?"

"There is no rear entrance."

"This sounds like a conversation I've heard before," he murmured obscurely. "Come on."

"Where? Through the wall?"

"Under it."

"Why did I ask?"

It took the better part of a minute for Lexie to wriggle out from under the taut back wall. She emerged in a fog bank that was much thicker at ground level than it would have been a foot higher. Just as well, she thought, waiting for Rick to join her. Gwendolyn's caravan stood a mere twenty feet away, and Lexie didn't doubt for a minute that the fortune-teller had the eyes of a hungry eagle.

"Let's go."

Rick's voice in her ear surprised her. "How did you get out so fast?" she demanded, tempted to laugh. "And don't tell me Fitz taught you that, too."

"Your faith in my talents is staggering," he noted with a mocking smile. Keeping his hand pressed firmly to the base of her spine, he moved her away from the tent, not letting her straighten up until they were well out of range of the caravans.

He kept his fingers linked with hers as they headed toward the line of shuttered arcade booths. Relaxed, her composure slowly reasserting itself, Lexie forced her mind back to the task at hand, "Have you searched the shooting gallery yet?"

His ever-watchful eyes combed the area. "Not as carefully as I would have liked."

She watched him extract a slender file from the back pocket of his jeans and couldn't resist a smile. "My God, you're a walking hardware store. It's lucky for Victoria that you're not a crook."

"She's safe enough," he said in wry amusement. From a different pocket, he dug out what looked like a skeleton key. "Keep an eye on the caravans and watch for those carnies we saw earlier," he instructed her, squatting at the far end of the arcade. "This isn't one of the better keys."

Arms wrapped around her waist in an effort to combat the evening chill, Lexie turned to regard the row of trailers. Her mind was a ball of confusion. The imprint of Rick's kisses lingered on her lips, an infinitely more enticing thought than the prospect of hunting for a bunch of jewels. Enticing—and disturbing in the sense that it set off a chain reaction of related thoughts about Rodney and the kind of life that, until a few days ago, she'd convinced herself she wanted.

Restlessly, she ran her gaze down the caravan row. Almost all the lights had been extinguished. Victoria's desk lamp might have continued to burn, but it was difficult to see that far through the thickening mist. Actually, it was increasingly difficult to see beyond the end of Wren's former home.

She glanced at the boarded-up window. A wispy layer of fog blurred the edges, giving the entire trailer a ghostly appearance. She started to look away, then paused and fixed her gaze on the door. Something about it wasn't right. The shades of darkness didn't quite match, as though . . .

"Rick!" Lexie hissed his name through gritted teeth, stepping hastily into the shadows and nearly tripping over him in the process. Eyes riveted on the partly open trailer door, she grabbed a handful of his jacket. "Look at Wren's caravan. There's someone inside."

Rick's response was automatic. Pivoting on his heel, he brought her down next to him. His hand was poised by his waistband, but she noticed he didn't pull his gun. He must have seen the tiny yellow beam moving past the unlatched door, though, because he motioned for her to keep absolutely still.

The mist formed a delicate white pattern against the side of the caravan, and for a second Lexie lost the pinpoint of light. Beside her, she felt Rick's coiled muscles, the tension radiating from his body. He was going to do something. She only hoped it wasn't something rash.

"Stay right here," he began, but he got no farther than that as a resounding crash inside the caravan suddenly rent the calm night air. The explosive blast seemed to galvanize the intruder. Another noise, this one more of a dull clank, was followed by an abrupt surge of motion as a black-clothed figure burst across the threshold at a dead run.

Before Lexie could fully comprehend what was happening, Rick was on his feet and moving, the soles of his boots making no sound on the hard-packed earth. Yet as fast as he was, she knew the intruder had a very definite advantage. To the left stood the other caravans, thirty or more strong, each one a refuge of dark walls and looming shadows, unbroken by even the most fragile ray of starlight. Once there, the number of hiding places would be virtually endless.

Not stopping to consider the consequences of her actions, Lexie scrambled from her knees and started running toward the next caravan in the line. Rick was heading straight for the intruder. If his human target eluded him, she might at least be able to tell him which direction to take.

The figure hesitated for only a fraction of a second outside the door. Then, with one nimble bound, a pair of black-sneakered feet landed on the grass beneath the boarded-up window. A gloved hand immediately went up to catch the jutting ledge, using it first for balance then for leverage to push off in the direction of the neighboring trailers.

The scene unfolded with lightning speed so swiftly that Lexie had trouble absorbing it all. However, the few thoughts that managed to separate themselves from the clutter in her brain were reasonably encouraging. For one thing, the intruder showed no sign of having a weapon. For another, both she and Rick appeared to be gaining ground.

The corner of Wren's trailer loomed before her. She saw the figure race around the side, saw Rick a scant thirty yards behind and realized with a surprised jolt that neither of them were turning down the caravan row. For some unknown reason the intruder had chosen to plunge into the sparse stand of trees that stretched out in a thin line along the upper edge of the meadow.

Lexie kept her eyes trained on the blackened silhouette. It seemed the mist intensified the deeper they ventured into the meager woodland, but that didn't prevent her from seeing the intruder dodge a narrow briar patch, pause, then dart jerkily between two scrawny birch trees.

Rick was only a few steps ahead of her now. When he pulled up, so did she. Vaporous tendrils of white wove an oblique design between the two slender trunks. The silence was unnerving, as was the sudden cessation of movement among the trees.

Lexie's fingernails dug into Rick's forearm. The intruder had squatted down on the rough ground, the human form taking on the properties of the inanimate object. A shapeless black boulder or...

Her breath caught tightly in her throat as Rick drew her around the larger of the two birches. Mist danced tauntingly across the top of the malformed object before them— an object that possessed not a single trace of humanity. Where a figure clad in black had once crouched, there now stood a decaying tree stump.

The intruder had disappeared.

Chapter Eight

"I don't care what happened in Algernon's time," Lexie muttered. "People in this century don't just vanish into thin air."

Thick air, Rick wanted to correct, but he held his tongue and resumed his examination of the lock on Wren Sherwood's caravan. Not surprisingly, he found no sign of a forced entry. The scratch marks from that afternoon remained, but there were no additional scorings, nothing to indicate that tonight's prowler had done anything more drastic than use a key to get in.

He dragged himself to his feet, wincing at the stiffness in his shoulders that was increasing as the evening wore on. Kicking the door closed behind him, he picked up a flashlight that sat amid the large chunks of a broken glass ashtray. The beam end had been taped so that only a small shaft of light could escape. It was an old trick, not especially clever, but an effective enough tool for an amateur burglar.

"Did you find anything?" Lexie asked from the kitchen.

He tipped the flashlight over, studying the chipped orange paint on the old-style casing. Both the tape and the torch were carnival issue. "Not much," he said, staring down at the shattered ashtray, the source of the crash they'd heard earlier. "After you left here yesterday, what did you do with the key?"

Her head emerged from the cupboard she'd been ransacking. "I gave it back to Victoria. Why?"

"Because whoever we were chasing didn't have to jimmy the lock to get in."

"Which means that whoever we were chasing probably wasn't the same person I saw trying to break in here this afternoon."

"Not unless that person took a crash course in breaking and entering, or somehow managed to get hold of Victoria's key." Rick nudged the broken glass with the toe of his boot. There really wasn't any delicate way to present the other alternative, so he simply said it straight out. "Do you know what Diana did with her key?"

A completely confident smile curved Lexie's tempting lips. "As a matter of fact, Diana turned both her key and the two spares that Wren had cut a month ago in Rotterdam over to Scotland Yard."

Rick worked a cramp from the back of his neck, checking a weary grin. "You don't have to look quite so smug about it."

"Yes, I do. It's all I've got to be smug about." The smile faded, and she reached into the cupboard, producing four floral-patterned teacups. After setting them down in a line she leaned her elbows on the counter, staring at each one as though it were part of a confounding rebus. "These weren't here yesterday," she said, chewing on her lower lip.

Rick sent her a narrow-eyed look. "What do you mean?"

"The cups. Two of them, anyway. They shouldn't be here." Quickly, she filled in the gaps for him, ending with a puzzled "Someone went to a lot of trouble to make sure the police didn't find these the night Wren was killed and an equal amount of trouble to put them back. Why?"

"Probably because they prove something." He returned the cups to their proper shelf and closed the flimsy tin door. Before she could object, he wrapped his fingers around hers and gave her a gentle but firm tug away from the counter.

"Whatever it is, we're not going to figure it out by standing around and guessing for what little is left of the night."

"No, but . . ." She hesitated, frowning as she scrubbed at a smudge of dirt on her cheek. "I guess you're right. I just wish we'd found the cups before rather than after whoever took them had a chance to break in here and put them back."

Rick's lips quirked with amusement. Even covered with bits of bark and peat she fascinated him. Hell, who was he kidding? He couldn't remember wanting any woman as much as he wanted Lexie. He plucked a twig from her hair. "Is that statement supposed to make sense?"

She shrugged, but her eyes were on him and vaguely wary. "Maybe I'm too tired to make sense. What time is it?"

"After two. We spent a good hour trying to find our disappearing phantom."

She held up a scraped and grimy fist. "It was a hideous hour, and phantoms don't go around putting cups back where they belong."

"No," he agreed, bringing her clenched fist to his lips and kissing her knuckles. "They don't."

He resisted the urge to haul her into his arms and let his mouth explore the faint smudge on her cheek. Actually it wasn't so much mental resistance as physical exhaustion that held him back. When he made love to Lexie—and there was no doubt in his mind that they would—he intended to be wide awake and much more alert than he was right now.

Keeping his hand around hers, he ushered her onto the stoop. Out of the corner of his eye he saw her squint through the fog and along the line of caravans to the yellow one where Gwendolyn lived. He didn't have to ask or even look at the expression on her face to understand the thoughts that were spinning around in her head.

Reduced to their simplest form, the facts were telling. Wren Sherwood had been a superstitious man, and Gwendolyn Sykes was a fortune-teller, whose talents included the reading of tarot cards, palms—and tea leaves.

Rick followed Lexie's gaze to the yellow trailer, acknowledging the questions he couldn't seem to shake off. Was it possible that Gwendolyn had been here the night Wren Sherwood died? Had she seen his future in the bottom of his teacup? Or had she instead decided that he would have no future at all?

A BLUE-WHITE streak of lightning snaked through the stormy predawn sky, outlining the edges of Lexie's dreams with an electric glow. She flipped onto her stomach in the four-poster bed but couldn't banish the nightmare. Gwendolyn's raw laughter filled her ears as Lexie clawed at the side of the huge teacup she was trapped in.

"Two people will never leave this carnival," the fortune-teller promised, sitting inside a disengaged Ferris wheel car, feet propped up on the safety bar, wearing Fitz's barker's derby and smoking his bent cigar. "We don't like outsiders, do we, Skelly?"

The fun house operator appeared beside her in the car. Only he wasn't a man, Lexie realized frantically; he was a skeleton, and he kept flashing a mirror in her eyes, blinding her. His jaw gaped open in a mocking travesty of a smile as one bony finger reached out to push a button—one long, white finger that slowly changed size and shape and was suddenly attached to Victoria's capable hand. Grinning, the carnival owner waved at her, then held up the key to Wren's caravan.

Lexie fought to escape the vibrating teacup that was now part of the tilt-a-whirl, pounding on the bone china sides with her fists, until she heard the deadly rumble that shook the ride, causing the cup to shatter into enormous, razor sharp pieces around her.

She was going to die. Darkness and danger pressed in. But suddenly, she was no longer alone. Rick was with her. She couldn't see his face, but she recognized the feel of his body as he reached for her, hauling her away from the shooting fragments, pulling her into his arms, keeping her safe from Death's cruel grip. . . .

A furious crack of thunder tore through the heavens, shaking the foundations of the old inn. Lexie awoke to find herself sitting straight up in bed, her mind an uncertain tangle of nightmares, disoriented reality and an infinitely more erotic feeling that had to do with the memory of Rick's touch. Rick's, not Rodney's. She wondered distantly how she could be so certain of that when she hadn't seen a face, but certain she was.

With an effort, she shook the dream away. It took her a long moment to understand what had intruded so rudely on her fitful sleep, but then the thunder came again, the bedframe rattled and the answer was clear.

Pushing back her hair, she wrapped her arms around her upraised knees and turned her eyes to the window. Runnels of rain streamed across the glass. She could hear the heavy drops pelting the roof, splashing on the cobbles below. The fog was gone, washed away by the storm that had hurtled inland from the south coast about the time Rick had walked her back to the inn. While the temperature remained moderate, the humidity had risen considerably making everything, even the sheets, feel damp and sticky.

Lexie glanced at her travel alarm on the ancient mahogany nightstand: 4:20 a.m. She hadn't even slept for two hours. At this rate, she wouldn't be able to able to keep her mind on her work, to say nothing of keeping her eyes open.

Groaning, she dropped back on the soft mattress and willed the drumming rain to lull her into a restful slumber. She didn't want to dream about any of her suspects. Not Gwendolyn or Skelly or Fitz or Victoria or anyone else at the carnival. On the other hand, she wanted to dream about Rick very much. But how could she do that and not feel like a complete rat? She already felt as though she'd committed some unpardonable sin, and yet she wasn't exactly sure what she'd done that was so wrong. Well, maybe she did, but it wasn't as if she'd actually agreed to marry Rodney or even given the matter much more than a passing consideration.

"Oh, hell," she half-grumbled, half-wailed. Why did she have to meet Rick? Why did life have to be so complicated? Why didn't she just admit she loved the man and deal with all the problems that little bombshell caused from there?

Another deafening clap of thunder rocked the building, and Lexie knew she wouldn't be getting any sleep until the storm passed, if then. Expelling a frustrated sigh, she sat up, pulled the rough wool blanket from the foot of her bed, gathered it around her shoulders and crossed to the chair by the door. She was trying to figure out a gentle but noble way to tell Rodney that she couldn't marry him when a familiar creaking noise overrode the deluge outside, capturing her attention.

Now that was odd, she thought, turning her head. Who would be using the lift at four-thirty in the morning? Not the Pendragons or their negligible night staff. Only one young boy had faith in the antiquated cables and clacking runners, and he finished work at ten o'clock every evening.

A spark of curiosity she couldn't douse had her switching off the lamp and stepping toward the door. Cautiously, she twisted the rickety knob and peeked into the hall.

Somber night shadows lurked in every corner of the unfurnished corridor. At the top of the stairs, a single bulb burned inside a dusty glass orb throwing a dull pool of light onto the carpet and a host of sinister shapes onto the paneled walls.

The lift stopped creaking on the heels of a violent thunderbolt that rattled the rain-lashed windowpanes and flooded Lexie's room with an eerie blue radiance. Tugging the blanket closer, she strained for an unimpeded view of the lift doors, all the while lecturing herself on the evils of snooping.

The lecture halted midway when the floorboards moaned feebly beneath someone's weight. Seconds later the figure of a man began to take shape in the dusky light. He crept along the hall, hugging the panels, tiptoeing with an exaggerated care reminiscent of an old Laurel and Hardy movie.

As the man approached, Lexie caught back an astounded gasp. She recognized him instantly, but only because of his thin mustache and beady brown eyes. Aside from that, she saw nothing of the stuffy Scotland Yard sergeant she'd met yesterday.

Charles Gideon was currently creeping down the hall in stocking feet that looked to have a coating of mud on them. His suit pants were wet and badly creased; his hat was gone, and his hair was hanging in long, thin strings over his forehead. He wore a jacket as wrinkled as his pants, but no shirt or vest, nothing to cover the hairless white skin of his chest.

Lexie studied him closely as he drew nearer, noting the large bundle he cradled under his right arm. It looked soft, like a parcel of wadded laundry. But there were no Laundromats open at this hour. In fact, there was nothing open in Ashcroft at four-thirty in the morning.

Although her fingers itched to rip apart the nondescript bundle, she forced herself to step back into her room and close the door before Charles could see her. Rick's words echoed in her head, grimly augmented by the fury of the summer storm. He didn't trust his partner's motives or the coincidence of his presence in Devon at the time of Wren's death.

Moving around the chair, Lexie went to stand by the window. The weather lately seemed to be in constant flux, changing from hour to hour like her thoughts and suspicions. She closed her eyes, breathing in the wet smell of rain on the cobbles and the perfumed scent of lilacs from a bush down the lane, trying to reject the feeling of discouragement that enveloped her.

For a brief time, Gwendolyn had looked so guilty, but two teacups didn't make her a murderer. Millions of British people drank tea, Scotland Yard sergeants included. One of those people had killed Wren Sherwood. And Lexie knew that person would do whatever was necessary to avoid being caught—even if it meant killing again.

THE OPPORTUNITY TO SEARCH the shooting gallery didn't arise until late the next afternoon. Rain continued to pour from the swollen, black sky throughout the day, although it was hardly the deterrent Lexie had hoped it would be. Fortunately, a return of the previous night's thunder and lightning soon sent the carnival crowd scurrying for shelter, leaving the midway all but deserted and only Fitz to watch both the arcade and her as she climbed over the counter and hopped down onto the floor.

Throwing off the bright yellow slicker Diana had loaned her, she shoved back the sleeves of her peach cotton blouse and took her first real look around Wren's old booth. It was about what she'd expected, utilitarian and drab. A line of little white ducks, complete with dents and rust spots, sat motionless on a stretch of frayed conveyor belt. Dime-store prizes had been stuffed into every available space on the shelved walls; a limp, brown curtain tacked to the counter hid another group of shelves used for the storage of gallery guns and pellet boxes, while a second strip of cloth curtain near the front had been drawn back to reveal a portion of Fitz's cramped ring-toss booth.

The wily ex-pickpocket lounged blithely against the partition separating the stalls, eyes sparkling as he puffed on the stub of his cigar. "If you've a mind to be looking for any pretty pebbles this fine afternoon, you best be warned; the bloke who tends this place now has already given it a right good sniffing out. Likewise for the lads from the Yard."

Lexie was only interested in one "lad" from the Yard. Although they hadn't specifically planned to meet in the arcade, she knew he'd show up. Somehow he always seemed to find her. Giving her damp hair a toss, she asked, "Has Rick been here today?"

Fitz's darting eyes came to rest on her face. "Here now, Miss Lexie. He's a roustabout, our Rick is. That lot seldom get the time to visit a game booth."

"She knows, Fitz," a dry voice inserted, and Lexie turned to find Rick vaulting smoothly over the counter. "You've got customers," he added, arching an lazy brow at a group of waterlogged teenage girls with trendy haircuts, platform shoes and white lipstick who were huddled under his awning, eyeing the rows of prizes.

Obligingly, Fitz moved away from the partition, giving Lexie a chance to grab Rick's arm and drag him to the back of the booth. Since it was the first time she'd spoken to him all day, she hadn't yet had a chance to tell him about Charles. Of course, the telling would have been a great deal easier if he hadn't been shrugging out of his sodden rain gear, down to a pair of damp jeans and a white T-shirt that clung to every sleekly muscled contour of his body.

Biting back a groan, she lifted her eyes and related the scene she'd witnessed earlier that morning, finishing with a shake of her head and a cranky "I should have gone out in the hall and bumped into him. Maybe I could have knocked that bundle he was carrying loose."

"And maybe you would have wound up staring down the barrel of a gun." Rick offered the gentle reminder of his partner's profession. With one long finger, he traced the delicate line of her collarbone, sending a shiver across her skin. "If it turns out that Charles did have something to do with Sherwood's murder, he might prove to be a dangerous adversary. Crooked cops make first-class felons."

Lexie's answering nod was purely mechanical. He was doing it to her again. One look, one touch, one minute in his company and her mental balance was shot. It was a peculiar sensation to be so completely caught up in her emotions. She wasn't sure if she liked it or not. She *was* sure, however, that she liked the little tremors of excitement that shot through her as he slid his fingers to the side of her neck.

A day's work in the rain had brought an earthy scent to Rick's skin that stirred every one of her senses. She couldn't move, though she knew she should. Of course moving closer wouldn't be a problem; it was stepping away that she couldn't seem to manage.

God, this was all so confusing. Weren't Australian men supposed to be arrogant and sexist and a whole lot of other contentious things? No, wait, maybe she was thinking of English men. Or French men. Then again, maybe she was simply losing her mind. She'd never met a stereotypical person of any nationality. And from what little he'd told her about himself, Rick's ancestry could only be described as hodgepodge. He was a little bit of everything and a lot more than her abused senses could presently handle.

She looked up into his blue, blue eyes. "You know you're making me crazy, don't you?" she demanded in a voice that sounded treacherously husky.

He didn't really smile, but a spark of laughter glittered deep in his eyes. "Then I guess that makes us even," he said, and before she could utter another word, he covered her mouth with his.

A surge of heat raced through her body, wiping out her confusion and any weak protest her brain might have launched. When he kissed her she stopped thinking. Completely. Nothing mattered except the touch of his hands on her back, the feel of his lips on her mouth, her face, the side of her neck.

Thankfully, Rick's self-control was in slightly greater supply than hers. But only very slightly, Lexie realized on an abstracted note of pleasure as he reluctantly raised his head.

"I'm sure this isn't why I came in here," he said in a voice too low for Fitz in the ring-tossing booth to hear.

His breath was warm on her lips and she shivered, aware that her body was still responding to him quite strongly. At least she wasn't alone in that regard, she thought, glancing down, more than a little tempted to press herself against him once again. "I'm sure it isn't," she agreed instead. "We should get back to work."

"Uh-huh." Rick ran his hands along the curve of her rib cage, letting his thumbs pause teasingly on the hardened nipples of her breasts and leaving Lexie with only two options.

In broad daylight, in the middle of the carnival arcade with an erstwhile pickpocket who could probably hear a proverbial pin drop lurking in the next booth, what else could she do? Stiffening her spine, she slapped at Rick's wandering hands. "We're supposed to be conducting a search, remember?"

He grinned, unrepentant. "I am."

"Of the booth, not me."

Again she swatted his arm and this forced her feet to carry her back a pace. His grin broadened, but he made no attempt to stop her. She could likely thank the trio of bedraggled boys passing the counter for his forbearance. Thank or blame—at this point she couldn't decide which.

Fitz's voice drifted over the partition, capturing Rick's attention. Brushing her wanton thoughts aside as far as she could—which wasn't far at all—Lexie applied herself to the task of clearing the shelf under the counter and examining everything she pulled out. What she found was a tidily stacked but unexciting collection of damaged guns, a paperback copy of *Rebecca* with the name Glen Barrie printed neatly on the inside cover, a calculator, a lined scribbler with several pages torn out and two ballpoint pens. Not exactly the bonanza she'd been hoping for.

Ten minutes later, after every square inch of the cramped booth had been covered, she tossed the last stuffed fox back onto a high shelf, lifting her head just as Fitz reappeared at the partition.

"You might want to step up the pace of your search, mate," he said to Rick who'd come up behind Lexie's shoulder and was toying with the ends of her hair. "I shouldn't think the bloke who works the gallery will be absent much longer. He's a real apple polisher, that one. Keen on worming his way into Victoria's affections and taking over Wren's old job of totting up the daily take. Got a fair taste of it, he did, that last night. Gathered up the spoils just as cheeky as you please and trotted them out to the green caravan. Chirping like a cricket, he was, too, over his snap."

Lexie understood most of Fitz's speech, but the meaning of the last remark eluded her. She appealed to Rick for a translation.

"The kid was pleased with his alacrity in getting the money to Victoria," he clarified in wry amusement.

Reaching down, he scooped their dripping rain gear from the floor, then spread his warm fingers across her lower back and steered her over to the partition that was actually a gate in disguise. Fitz immediately rubbed his clever hands together, emptying the two cluttered stools his booth had to offer while Rick swung the chipboard barrier closed behind them and drew the curtain.

Perching herself on the high, three-legged seat, Lexie regarded the spry little informant curiously. "You said 'that last night,' Fitz. Do you mean the night Wren died?"

"The very same." He squatted next to where Rick was standing and started rooting through the clutter under the counter. "Got me a bottle of good Irish whiskey somewhere in here. Should be some glasses too, mate, if you've a notion to give me a hand."

His expression thoughtful, Rick crouched and joined the hunt. Lexie watched distractedly, as racing forms, scratch pads and crumpled cigar boxes piled up on the floor.

In a distant corner of her mind she recalled one of the official reports she'd read in London. Wren Sherwood had left the arcade early the night he'd been killed, somewhere around nine. A premature departure would account for the fact that the man who'd filled in for him that evening had also assumed responsibility for collecting the arcade profits, but it didn't explain where Wren had gone or why he'd left early in the first place.

When she posed the question to Fitz, he merely shrugged his narrow shoulders and blew a layer of dust off the two-thirds full bottle of whiskey he'd pulled from the shelf. "Can't rightly speak his reasons for him, Miss Lexie. All I can tell you is he left me sitting on a high-point Scrabble word." His eyes twinkled. "Could have used all me letters, too, and what does the silly beggar do but give me a queer look and scuttle on out the door like Beelzebub himself was nipping at his heels."

Rick extracted a cracked glass from beneath the counter. "You sure you don't know what made him leave in such a hurry, mate?"

"Sorry, Inspector." Fitz sounded sheepish. "Two hundred and ninety-three points I had, sitting there in front of me waiting to be scored. A Scrabble player's dream come true. No, mate, that was one night me mind was fixed on matters other than those that sent Wren dashing into the darkness." With a waggish grin, he slid his hand back under the counter and withdrew the Scrabble board. "Couldn't bring meself to pack in such a plum word. Been waiting, I have, for someone to come along and help me finish the game."

Lexie hopped from the stool and went to have a look at the board. *"Quatorz?"* Doubtfully she read the word spelled out on the letter stand.

"It needs an *e* on the end," Fitz explained. "I'd have used this spot right here and scored me a passel of points."

"Quatorze? What does it mean?"

"It comes from another game," Rick informed her, idly flipping Wren's letter stand around. "Piquet."

"That doesn't help," she muttered, then gave a little start as a very different word came into focus in front of her. Rick must have seen it at the same time because his fingers curled firmly around her wrist, squeezing gently to gain her attention as he gave his head an imperceptible shake to silence her reaction.

"Right you are," Fitz announced cheerfully. "Three glasses with a wee dram of Irish whiskey in each."

Lexie felt something smooth being pressed into her free hand. Bemused, she lifted the glass to her lips and swallowed a mouthful of the potent drink . . . and promptly proceeded to gulp a lungful of air as the alcohol burned a fiery trail down her throat.

Whiskey was good for one thing, she realized. Like a giant hammer, it smashed right through her disorientation, leaving in its wake a legion of questions she couldn't begin to answer. Her eyes flicked to Fitz who was calmly pouring himself another drink, then to Rick who was scrutinizing his informant's every move over the rim of his glass and finally to the word spelled out on Wren Sherwood's letter stand.

Actually, it wasn't a word at all. It was a name. The first name of the man who had helped Wren steal the Saxony jewels.

AIDAN . . .

COULD AIDAN O'BRIEN be alive?

The question pounded through Rick's head until his temples began to throb. Lexie didn't even have to ask it. The unspoken words hung in the air between them as they trudged along the path to the village.

The rain had subsided to a steady drizzle, and the smell of flowers and wet vegetation was strong in the afternoon air. Already, the midway was filling up. Fitz had returned the Scrabble board to its proper shelf, capped the whiskey bottle and shifted his attention to a fresh round of customers, seemingly oblivious of the discovery they'd made in his booth. But was he really as guileless as he pretended, or was he merely putting up a good front?

Rick felt Lexie staring at him, and he slanted her a discerning sideways look. A subtle twist of humor curved his lips at the tacit challenge she issued with those incredibly expressive eyes of hers. "Yes, I'm going to call and check on O'Brien's death," he said patiently. "No, I don't completely trust Fitz, and no, I don't think we can afford to dismiss any other possibilities just because we happened to find the name Aidan spelled out on a letter stand that Sherwood was using the night he died."

"Supposedly using," Lexie corrected, still staring up at him from beneath the hood of Diana's oversize slicker. "Fitz, or for that matter someone else, might be purposely trying to mislead us...me." Her smooth brow wrinkled. "Uh, Rick, do you think...?"

"That the murderer knows I'm working undercover?" He shrugged, unconcerned. "Probably. Both Charles and Fitz have known from the start, and even if neither of them is guilty, chances are still good that whoever broke into Sherwood's caravan last night realizes I'm not a carny."

She lifted exasperated eyes to his even features. "Doesn't that worry you?"

"There's nothing I can do about it, Lexie. So far the truth hasn't come out. I'm not going to get panicky over something that hasn't happened yet."

"That kind of logic is really irritating," she muttered, pushing the drenched hood away from her face and giving him a cross look that lightened his mood considerably. She was gorgeous when she was angry and damned near irresistible when she was soaking wet on top of it. "Are you going to call Scotland Yard from the inn?" she asked, and he had to squash the provocative image of his hands stripping away not only her slicker, but the rest of her clothes, as well.

Nodding, he ventured a bland "It'll probably take some time to get the details about the fire. Since I can't trust Charles, and since any message left for you could easily be intercepted, I'll have the reply put through to my answering machine in London and retrieve it from there."

"Do you have any idea how long it'll take to find out if it really was Aidan who died two years ago?"

The note of forbearance in her voice revealed a deep understanding of the red tape that couldn't be avoided in any legal undertaking. "I don't know," he admitted. "By tomorrow night if we're lucky."

"And if we're not?"

A lazy smile crossed his lips. "Are you always this pessimistic?" he queried, arching a mocking brow. "Or is the rain starting to get to you?"

They'd reached the edge of the village now, and she picked her way carefully around a large puddle in the road. "I'll have you know I'm a very optimistic person in any kind of weather," she flung over her shoulder. "What you're forgetting is that my assignment and yours are two entirely different things. You want to find the Saxony jewels. I want to find proof that Diana isn't a murderer. So far all I've managed to turn up are questions, and as intriguing as they are, they won't be of much use to her in court."

"In that case, we'll just have to look harder for the answers," Rick returned softly. He pulled open the door of the inn. "Charles is still at the carnival. As soon as I finish calling the Yard, I'll go through his room and see if he's hiding anything."

"If he is, it won't be in his room," Lexie informed him. "Mrs. Pendragon is extremely thorough when it comes to straightening up personal belongings. I'm positive she dusted the inside of my suitcase yesterday."

Amusement tugged at the corners of Rick's mouth as he trailed her up the stairs. "Charles has been here longer than you," he reminded her, watching with undisguised interest as she shed the yellow slicker. "I doubt if Mrs. Pendragon has much curiosity left about his personal effects."

She seemed skeptical, but offered no resistance to his plan. Instead, she dug her room key from the pocket of her jeans, handed it to him, then reversed direction on the stairs. "I'd better keep an eye on the proprietress while you make your phone call. I don't care what you say, people who dust suitcases are bound to have a penchant for eavesdropping." She grinned. "After all we've been through together, I'd hate to see your cover blown by a cantankerous busybody who hasn't sunk her teeth into a really juicy bit of gossip since Wren Sherwood was killed." A delicate shudder swept through her. "I guess I'm lucky Mrs. Pendragon didn't have a chance to read the note that was left in my mail slot."

Rick closed his fingers around the key. His lusty thoughts vanished swiftly, wiped away by a more disturbing set that had to do with the question of Lexie's safety and his ability to ensure it.

Working undercover for Scotland Yard meant taking risks. He'd learned that simple lesson a long, long time ago. He'd accepted it, and if it became necessary, he knew he could protect himself as well as or better than many of his cohorts.

But what about Lexie? he wondered darkly. Could he be sure of protecting her, too?

The answers were cloaked in an uncertainty he flatly refused to acknowledge, leaving only one choice open to him. He had to help her expose Wren Sherwood's murderer. Fast.

"AFTERNOON, MA'AM."

The stately-looking gentleman who passed Lexie in the corridor gave her a courteous nod before continuing on to is room. Once there, he paused, summoned an uncertain mile, then shook his head and stepped inside.

Expelling a relieved breath, Lexie let her own forced smile lip. So far in her new role as sentry, she'd encountered four guests in four minutes. This end of the hall must be a heavy raffic area, she decided, pivoting away from the staircase. She rarely ran into anyone outside her room.

Ears alert for the first hint of a creaking floorboard, she udged open the door to Charles's chamber a bit wider. 'It's like the underground at rush hour out here, Rick," she aid impatiently. "The least you could do is hurry."

Rick didn't dignify the fractious remarks with a response, but she glimpsed the flicker of amusement that danced through his eyes before he directed his attention to Charles's nightstand.

She bit her tongue and whirled back to face the hall, leaving the door open a crack and leaning on the rough rame. Shoulders hunched, she tried to sort out a few of the myriad facts she'd compiled in the three ridiculously long days she'd been here.

One by one names and faces flashed before her eyes: Charles, the starchy Scotland Yard sergeant with his mysterious bundle; Gwendolyn who used teacups to tell fortunes; Skelly who appeared willing to do her bidding and whom she had dumped for an affair with Wren; Fitz, the scrabble playing ex-pickpocket in whose booth they'd found lettered squares that spelled out the name Aidan and Victoria, current owner of the carnival, in possession of the only key to Wren Sherwood's caravan.

Lexie rested her head against the wooden jamb, flirting with yet another half-formed theory. "Are you finished et?" she asked Rick without turning.

Somewhere along the line, she'd come to accept the fact hat nothing about this case was going to be simple. It herefore didn't surprise her when Rick came out of his partner's room and negated the look of inquiry in her eyes.

"No bundles and no jewels," he said, tugging on h
jacket. "Just a pile of muddy clothes on the dresser, a bro
ken *R* key on his typewriter and part of an orange feathe
stuck in the zipper of his shaving kit."

Despite her disappointment, Lexie smiled. "Mrs. Per
dragon strikes again." They started down the corrido
"Rick, I was thinking while you were in there."

"About Charles?"

"No, about Aidan—and Victoria."

He frowned. "What, you think they're connected?"

"I'm not sure." She stopped at the corner near the stai
well. "Maybe I'm grasping at straws, but isn't it true tha
Wren Sherwood was supposed to have killed his partner
little over two years ago?"

"As far as we know it is. What's your point?"

Lexie met his striking blue eyes. "Victoria's nephew
Danny, also died just over two years ago. One month be
fore Wren joined the carnival."

For a long, silent moment, he stared at her, as if weigh
ing all the possibilities. Finally, a tiny smile touched his lips
"I'll make another phone call," he agreed.

"And after that?"

His smile widened. One hand slid around the back of he
neck while the fingers of the other trapped her chin, tip
ping her head up so that she was again looking into h
beautiful eyes. She felt the warmth of his breath on her lips
then his mouth came down, opening over hers in a brief bu
searing kiss that left her momentarily speechless.

"After that," he said, not releasing her, "we go for di
ner. You can tell me all about your Puritan ancestors and I'
tell you all about my great-great-great-great grandmothe
Leska Foscani. She was a Romanian Gypsy. So were two c
her husbands."

Lexie stared at him. "You're a Gypsy?"

"I have a colorful family history," he reminded her, stroking the smooth skin of her jaw with his thumb. "If you'd rather, I could fill you in on my Alaskan forebears. I'm told some of them lived in caves."

Lexie couldn't help laughing. Only she would fall in love with a man who could claim to be descended from Gypsies and cave dwellers.

For a moment she thought about Rodney, about the face-to-face explanation she owed him—the one she vowed to give him the moment she returned to London. Was that enough? Was it fair? She considered the questions for several long seconds, then relegated the entire jumbled mess to a place well beyond the confines of her consciousness. Right or wrong, her decision was made. Tonight she'd have dinner with Rick. Everything else could wait until tomorrow.

CURSE THEM. Both of them. They were getting close. So very close. They knew more than they should. They'd seen far too much. They'd become a serious threat. A danger that would have to be dealt with.

Against swirled gray clouds, the vibrant colors of the carnival danced in a wild profusion before the murderer's eyes. The memory of a face took shape, floating misshapenly between the tents. Not smiling, not frowning. Just staring. Coldly. Spitefully. He'd tried to hide himself in the shadows that night, but it hadn't worked. His face had told a tale of discovery—and so much more.

Wren Sherwood deserved to die!

The vengeful thought burst forth in a furious rush, effectively shattering the hazy image. The murderer's eyes snapped away from the midway crowd, rising to the edge of the village, to the danger that lurked there like a time bomb, ticking away, waiting to explode.

They had the knowledge . . .

The teacups were back where they belonged. The jewels had been moved to a safer place. All the little things had been taken care of. Only one question remained.

How much longer could Lexie and Rick be permitted to live?

Chapter Nine

"This is not a good idea," Lexie hissed from her low crouch in the shadows of Victoria's caravan. "What if she gets halfway to the village, decides she's tired and comes back before we can get out?"

"Then we'll have some explaining to do," Rick said so unconcernedly that she wanted to kick him.

Their perfectly wonderful dinner last night had given way to a perfectly wretched day, filled with dead-end conversations and thwarted searches. They'd received no firm answers from Scotland Yard regarding either Aidan O'Brien or Victoria's nephew, found no new clues about the murder or the stolen jewels and had no opportunity to get inside the carnival owner's trailer. Until now, at 10:30 p.m., a full half-hour after the gates closed.

Lexie glanced apprehensively at the trees behind them, then back at the green caravan. Ghostly tentacles of fog stretched out across the moors, but the meadow remained clear beneath a sweep of silver stars and a partial moon that seemed to be casting its pearly beams in all the wrong places. She felt as if she was on public display. Even if Victoria didn't notice her when she walked through the door, surely everyone else in the area would.

"Here she comes," Rick said, his voice close to Lexie's ear.

The woman's boot heels hit the metal steps, then the hard-packed earth. With Rick positioned in front of her, Lexie couldn't see a thing, but she did hear a murmur of female voices followed closely by a squawk of laughter as four other sets of boot heels joined Victoria's.

"And there she goes." Rick kept his eyes on the receding figures. "Fitz said the five of them go up to the pub every Thursday night without fail. Looks like he was right."

"It looks that way." Lexie knew a moment of raw tension when Victoria paused and seemed to glance back at them. But then she turned and continued walking, and Lexie released her tightly held breath. Burglary even for a good cause was hard as hell on the nerves. She lifted her eyes to the caravan's outer walls. "Why do I feel like a sneak thief?"

"Probably because you aren't one." Rick pulled her around the corner into a whole new batch of shadows. Firmly, he pushed her down low while his eyes made a quick sweep of the area. "Stay here until I get the door unlocked."

A silent nod was Lexie's only reply. She needed to toughen up. Part of her was still balking at the prospect of involving herself in such an intimate search. Asking questions and hunting through booths and tents was fine; digging through someone's underwear drawer struck her as despicable and low, not to mention unpalatable.

Perspiration broke out on her palms. She tipped her head up to look at Rick. "How long does she usually stay at the pub? Did Fitz say?"

"No later than midnight, but she seldom gets back before eleven-thirty." A tiny click signaled that the lock had been breached. Rick stood and made another surveillance of the area. Satisfied that there was no one in sight, he reached for her hand. An understanding smile flitted across his lips once they were inside, and he indicated the compact living room. "You start in here. I'll take the bedroom."

Lexie nudged a large laundry bag with the toe of her Reebok. "You've done a lot of this, haven't you?" she asked.

"Enough," he admitted, checking to make sure all the shades were drawn. "If it makes you feel any better, this isn't my favorite job. It's just something that has to be done."

No guilt there, she thought. It must go with the territory. She eyed the time-worn furniture distastefully as Rick headed toward the bedroom at the end of a short hall. "Have you searched Skelly's caravan yet?"

"I haven't had a chance. He bunks with two of the midway barkers. It's hard to find a time when the place is empty."

And harder still to find the fun house operator himself, Lexie reflected sourly. So far, she hadn't been able to dredge up the courage to beard him in his puppet-filled den, but she'd have to eventually. Unless, of course, the jewels or some other piece of highly incriminating evidence could be unearthed here.

Careful not to leave a mess in her wake, she prowled about the room, checking chairs and tables, lamps, bookends and even wastepaper baskets.

"Nothing," she murmured as she scooped up the trash she'd dumped on the carpet by the desk. "Rick, are we looking for jewels that are in or out of their settings?"

"Two years after the fact?" His voice seemed to come from the bathroom. "Probably out."

"So they wouldn't be very bulky, would they?"

"Not particularly." He sounded closer now, and she looked up from the floor to find him lounging near the living room entrance, one shoulder propped indolently against the wall and an unfathomable smile quirking his lips as he added, "Forget it, Lexie. It'd be too risky for whoever has them to be carrying them around."

Setting the garbage can aside, she got to her feet. "No riskier than hiding them in his or her caravan. Either way the evidence would be damning."

"True, but don't forget, as far as a lot of people are concerned, the fact that Diana's been charged with Sherwood's murder automatically makes her a prime suspect in terms of the Saxony jewels. The person who's got them likely feels confident that the thrust of any further police investigation will be aimed at her."

Lexie flipped open a large accounting book that sat amid a pile of calculator tapes and invoices on the desk. "While we're on the subject, how many times have you searched Diana's trailer?"

She had to give him credit; he didn't bat an eyelash, just left the wall and came to perch on the corner of the desk. "Hers and Gwendolyn's," he pointed out. "And the answer is, twice."

"Well, at least you're honest..." The sentence trailed off as her eyes landed on a row of figures in the right margin of the ledger book. Sums that had been circled several times in red ink.

"Did you find something?" Rick slid from the desk and moved up behind her.

"I'm not sure. Maybe." She ran her finger from the top of the page to the bottom. Victoria's handwriting was terrible, more like chicken scratches than letters and numbers. There were ink blots marring several of the entries, illegible notes around the border with arrows that ran to various numbers, asterisks that didn't seem to mean anything and all sorts of smudged erasure marks. "I think these figures circled in red might be the monthly totals from the arcade booths. R.T. would be ring toss; S.G., shooting gallery; B.B., basketball and so on."

Reaching around her arm, Rick indicated the date at the top of the page. "Twenty-one months ago. According to

Fitz, that's when Sherwood was given both the shooting gallery and the responsibility of collecting the daily take."

Lexie frowned. "Well, if I'm reading this right, while the earnings fluctuate for the different booths, the overall profits appear to be decreasing."

"And in such a way that Victoria might not have noticed it."

"Maybe." Lexie examined the most recent entries. "The profits are way up now. But so are the attendance figures," she recalled.

"The attendance figures weren't up when Sherwood died," Rick reminded her. "He didn't collect the money the last night, and look at the difference between that total and the previous ones."

"Do you think he was skimming?"

"It's a good bet."

Lexie chewed her lip in consternation. "If he was and Victoria found out about it, she might have confronted him. That could explain why she happened to be so close by when Diana found Wren's body. Still, that doesn't tell us whether or not she killed him or if she knew the details of his sordid past. Unless there really is a connection between her nephew and Aidan O'Brien." She knitted her brow. "Rick, could they—"

A brittle snap beyond the caravan walls caused the question to lodge in her throat. It might have been a twig or maybe one of the branches on the hemlock bush underneath the front window, she thought uneasily, but neither she nor Rick stopped to try and identify the source. He had the lights extinguished before she could slam the ledger book closed and bury it beneath the loose coils of adding machine tape.

The room was instantly transformed into a coal-black pit. The only particle of light Lexie could detect came from a tiny crack at the base of the window to her right. She didn't call out to Rick, even though she knew he'd lifted the shade a fraction to see who or what had made the noise. Instead, she uttered a silent prayer that she wouldn't slam into any of the furniture as she groped her way to the far wall. After what seemed an eternity, her fumbling fingers found his back, and she crouched next to him, her mouth dry, her heart thundering in her chest.

"Someone's out there." His voice was so low that she could barely hear it. She felt his fingers circle her wrist. "Stay behind me, and keep down."

Mannequins were more graceful then she was, Lexie thought in frustration. Grinding her teeth, she ordered the tension in her limbs to abate. Luckily, her eyes had adjusted enough that she could distinguish furnishings from shadows, making her vision that much more acute when they reached the front stoop.

At first there seemed to be no movement at all. Not a leaf stirred on the hemlock bush, and the only artificial light came from inside one of the caravans a good fifty meters in the distance. Fog still wreathed the moors, the membranous shroud creeping ever closer to the fringe of the meadow, twining in stealthy, white fingers about the outer stalls.

Rick sheltered her body with his as his gaze roamed the open spaces around Victoria's caravan. Lexie found herself following the direction of his eyes, certain he had a better idea of what they were looking for than she did. Hopefully nothing more than a stray dog.

Blood continued to pound in her ears, though she wasn't really sure why. As the seconds ticked away in a steady succession, the only things that moved were the awnings. As far as she could see there was no one here.

She'd almost convinced herself that they were both starting to imagine things when a blurred flash of motion suddenly disrupted the darkness in the caravan row. For a second, a running figure was outlined by moonlight, then it settled down to a vague shadow. A shadow that bolted rather clumsily across the grass toward the heart of the carnival.

Lexie's reflexes took over, keeping her close on Rick's heels as they raced around the wardrobe tent and through the tricky tangle of rigging between two of the smaller storage tents. She bit down hard on her lip when her foot got caught up in one of the taut lines but swallowed the cry of pain, blanking her mind to everything except the shapeless black figure that had cleared the ropes and was now climbing the fence that girdled the octopus ride.

"Wait." Rick slowed his approach, eyes locked on the runner's indecisive actions. Reaching behind him he stopped Lexie's flight, holding her back when she would have moved up beside him.

"Wait for what? What's he doing?"

"Baiting us."

Sure enough, the figure edged around the huge spider-like arms as if daring them to follow. "Bad bait," Lexie said. "What do we do now?"

"Nothing."

"Rick, I could have come up with that idea."

He shrugged. "Would you like me to shoot him?"

"That's sick."

"I'm open to suggestions."

"You could bluff. Warn him that you're armed. Tell him you'll fire if he doesn't surrender."

"I thought you didn't want me to shoot."

She swore under her breath. "I said bluff, not blow him away."

Not that it mattered anymore. Either sensing failure or simply too impatient to wait around while they made a decision, the figure spun on its heel and charged the far side of the fence. Metal clattered as hands and feet clawed at the links. A single vigorous pull and the blackened form hoisted its body over the top to land with a leaden thud on the broken ground.

Lexie groaned to herself as the chase began again with the runner weaving an erratic path between shuttered food stalls and ticket booths. It darted around the perimeter of the carousel, then jumped up on the platform, dodging the painted horses until it reached the other side.

Despite the haphazard route, Lexie sensed they were being led somewhere very specific, just as she had when she'd trailed Skelly into the house of mirrors. The memory of that aborted pursuit sent a nervous tremor skating along her spine, but she forced her legs to keep moving.

The figure seemed to be laboring slightly. Thank God. Lexie's own lungs felt seared and tightened from the flat-out run. A half stride ahead of her, Rick didn't appear to be suffering the same fate. Rather than question his stamina, she used it to drive herself on.

Already the edge of the carnival loomed before them. Wisps of fog curled teasingly about her ankles. She peered through the layers of darkness at the last set of obstructions between meadow and moor and realized with a start of recognition that the house of mirrors was directly in front of her.

But only for a moment. Before she could check her stride, the figure, struggling visibly now, veered sharply to the left and lurched into the ebony-hued confines of the fun house awning.

Without being told, Lexie tucked herself in behind Rick who'd rearranged the position of his gun in his waistband for easier access. She fought to breathe quietly, though her depleted lungs definitely didn't appreciate further privation. Together, they slipped under the jutting canvas and approached the entrance.

The figure was nowhere in sight, but doubtless that was to be expected, as was the fact that the door had been left unlocked. It swung back with a single twist of the handle, opening into a narrow corridor that had a pitchy quality even more malignant than the silvery darkness that had enveloped her in the house of mirrors. She should have told Rick to shoot, she decided spitefully, her pacifist attitude strained where this particular murderer was concerned. If indeed it was the murderer they'd been chasing....

A picture of Skelly's gaunt features flew through her head. He'd lured her into one exhibit. Might he be doing the same thing again? And if so, what nasty surprises would he have in store this time?

She didn't have to wait long for an answer. Less than two meters inside the door, her entire body went rigid as a blue light flashed on and a huge malformed blob dropped from the ceiling. Only it wasn't a blob, it was a bat. A gruesome-looking vampire, hanging upside down, its blood-red eyes opening slowly to stare at her, its malleable black wings unfurling until they spanned the width of the hall. She saw white fangs protruding from the vicious little mouth and had absolutely no idea how she managed to suppress the scream that jumped into her throat.

"It's okay, Lexie. It's only one of Skelly's puppets." Rick's quiet words helped. So did the feel of his fingers curling warmly around hers. But even his calm reassurances couldn't override the sight of the cold scarlet eyes that seemed to be boring right into hers, or the long fangs that looked needle sharp in the arctic blue light. Who'd ever thought to call this a fun house?

She let herself be drawn beneath the dangling creature, noting with a grimace that the light was instantly doused. The corridor was once more swathed in darkness, and heaven only knew what lay ahead.

To her relief, Rick stopped before they had a chance to find out. She couldn't see him, but she did feel his breath on her temple, the solid, lean length of his body pressed against hers, the coiled tension that radiated from him. "Did you hear that?"

From farther down the hall, she caught a tiny rasp that could have been a shifting foot. "Our phantom?" she assumed. "Aren't there any lights in this place?"

"Look at it this way, Lexie, we're all at an equal disadvantage."

"Why don't I believe that?"

Rick squeezed her hand in response, and they started forward again, moving cautiously along the darkened passageway, trying to pick up on any other noises the figure might make.

Beside Lexie's face, an orange light flared. Her head shot up automatically, and she steeled herself to encounter a tarantula or some other disgusting arachnid.

Nothing happened. No spiders dropped from the ceiling. No cobwebs brushed her cheeks. Maybe the mechanism was broken, she thought, breathing a fervent prayer to that effect.

The orange light continued to glow even after they'd passed beneath it. From somewhere nearby, a door squeaked. At the same time, Lexie felt the floor begin to tremble...and then she lost track of everything as an unearthly screech suddenly filled the vibrating corridor.

"Come on." Rick strengthened his grip on her fingers. At least she thought he did. No sooner had she raised a hand to the wall for balance when she felt herself toppling sideways into yet another dark place where the wild shrieks instantly resolved into a series of ghoulish moans that caused the hair on the back of her neck to stand on end.

Her fingers were torn from Rick's as she stumbled backward. A small terrified part of her brain registered the sound of slamming doors, but she had no chance to think about that. The subtle tilt of the floor made it impossible for her to regain her balance. She staggered for several steps and finally smashed into something hard and lumpy that simultaneously broke her fall and knocked the breath from her sore lungs.

Above her, a feeble ghost light drizzled down from an unseen source. Shaking the hair out of her eyes, she slowly levered herself away from the furry obstacle she'd banged into. A tuft of something touched her neck. It felt dry, almost mossy, smelled faintly of mothballs. She automatically batted it aside with her fist and lifted her head.

A scream of revulsion bubbled to her lips, escaping before she could stop it. She leaped away from the collection of bony limbs, shed clothing and clotted hair, away from the loose joints and lax jaws that clacked and rattled like marionettes being forced to dance at the end of a string. Hollow eye sockets gaped at her as she spun around and began hunting desperately for the door.

Skeletons, her shocked mind informed her. Graveyard ghouls. Three of them this time, all bemoaning their fates. Not real, but not mere reflections, either.

The clattering persisted behind her, and Lexie had to clench her teeth to keep from screaming out loud again. By clinging to the crudely fashioned wall, she was finally able to locate a corner. She sensed it wasn't the same place she'd entered, but at least she was in a corridor of some sort. Sooner or later it would have to lead her out of here.

Shoving back her terror, she fumbled her way through something that felt like an open door. She longed to call Rick's name, but couldn't bring herself to do it. He could be anywhere—and so could the black-clad figure who almost certainly had to be Wren's murderer. No, she wasn't going to do anything stupid. She'd keep walking, keep the worst of her fears under control and find the nearest exit from this unwholesome exhibit.

Beneath her shifting palms, the walls changed from plywood to chipboard. Almost immediately a weird green light flared overhead. Lexie ducked underneath it, ready to spring aside at the first sign of a falling creature.

Relief, tempered by the experience she'd had only moments before, swept through her when she passed the light unscathed. Then she lowered her eyes, her fingers encountered a slick gelatinous substance, and she knew her relief had been premature. More green lights flickered on and a raw cackle split the shadowy air, the sound seeming to spill from the mouth of the witch who swooped down from the rafters on her raggedy broomstick.

She was a frightful crone complete with sallow green skin, a hooked nose, warts and clawed, scabrous hands. The toes of her long shoes were curled at the ends, her hair resembled black straw and her eyes looked like a pair of burning coals.

Lexie managed to absorb all the lurid details as she edged along the rubber-coated wall. The witch scudded past in a raucous frenzy, hanging much too low on her wire. If she hadn't jumped clear, Lexie's throat would have been speared by the tip of the broomstick.

Around her, the cackles grew deeper, more jarring. She heard a barely perceptible clunk and watched dry mouthed as the swinging witch dropped lower and lower until her feet began to scrape across the floor.

That did it. The black eyes continued to burn, even after the glow from the green lights faded out. Choking back a craven desire to run, Lexie launched herself from the wall, forcing her strained muscles to respond to the directive of her brain. She hadn't panicked in the house of mirrors and she'd gotten out. She would get out of here, too, just as long as she remained calm.

That bolstering thought lasted for maybe five seconds. Then her fingers found the end of the rubbery slime, something slammed hard into her back and she was shoved without ceremony across a murky threshold.

RICK FELT as though he'd been hit with a giant sledgehammer. He hadn't, but the result was the same. The pounding in his temples was eclipsed by only one other thought. He'd lost Lexie. Somewhere in this god-awful exhibit that should have been shut down more than an hour ago, they'd become separated.

Kicking aside the wooden troll that had tripped him up and sent him sprawling through one of Skelly's secret panels into a storage closet, he retraced his steps to the main corridor. He didn't know enough about this exhibit to have any idea where Lexie might be, and while he wanted to, he realized he couldn't risk calling out to her. For all he knew Sherwood's killer could be looking for her. If he shouted her name and she responded, the murderer would be on her in a minute.

A number of thoughts, none of them pleasant, ran through his head. The person they'd been chasing had entered the fun house only a few seconds before he and Lexie had. The control panel for the puppets, the light switches and all the other machinery were housed in one of the chambers in the rear of the building. That meant the exhibit had been live before any of them had gotten here. And that in turn meant the killer planned to lead them here all along.

Why?

He chose not to explore the many possible answers to that question. First he'd find Lexie, then he'd concentrate on motives.

If his memory was correct, the main passageway snaked back and forth several times before emptying into a place the other carnies called checkerboard square—a black-and-white room with tilted floors and sloped walls, disproportionate in design and illusive in every conceivable sense of the word. The roller, a huge, rotating tube, led to the control room and ultimately to the exit, but getting to either place wasn't going to be easy. Whether on purpose or by chance, the phantom guide lights that normally burned at a superlow wattage had been left off. The hallway was pitchblack, illuminated only when a beam was tripped, activating one of Skelly's puppets.

Swearing softly, Rick dodged a multieyed tarantula that skittered out of a hidden niche near his shoulder then disappeared into the darkness overhead. Skelly had been given free rein in terms of the fun house. He'd constructed most of the figures himself and those that broke down he fixed in his workshop, wherever that was. Probably sequestered in some black hole just beyond the walls of this soot-dark labyrinth, Rick reflected, shouldering his way past a bellowing green-eyed cyclops that materialized directly in front of him.

The bellows ceased as soon as the accompanying light was doused. Though he listened for any hint of movement that might lead him to Lexie, he heard nothing except the sound of his own footsteps. Had she gotten out? He wanted to believe that, but he couldn't be sure. He'd have to reach the control panel. Once the machinery was off and the lights were up, he'd stand a better chance of locating her.

Ignoring the motley assortment of creatures that leaped out at him, Rick felt his way to the door at the end of the passage. Checkerboard square. Good. All he had to do now was get across it to the roller and he'd be able to flip the light switch.

The checkered chamber turned out to be as dark as the rest of the place, although by rights it should have been brightly illuminated. Rick didn't bother trying to analyze the murderer's strategy. His goal was to find Lexie. Anything else could wait.

Less than a meter over the threshold, he heard the witch start to cackle. The sound was deadened by layers of black cloth and chipboard, but it was there. Someone had tripped the beam.

Instinctively, he tugged the gun free of his waistband, positioning himself just inside the door, waiting for whatever telltale noises might follow.

For a long time, all he heard were grinding gears and a bizarre gabble that had to be the issue of a damaged tape.

When those things faded away, an unnatural silence seemed to take over. Rick remained by the door, not moving, his patience worn but intact.

The frenetic eruption of sound and motion came with little warning. He caught a discreet footfall, followed almost immediately by a rapid pounding that might have been sneakers on the wooden floor. His reaction was automatic. Gun poised, he hurled himself from the wall—and would have made for the corridor if someone hadn't lunged straight at his chest.

The unexpected impact robbed him of breath, but little else. With one agile twist he clamped the fingers of his left hand around a flailing wrist, spun the figure around and locked his right arm across its neck. *Her* neck, his brain corrected, and he frowned, able to feel but not see the woman who was clawing at the sleeve of his jacket.

"Lexie?" The clawing stopped as he slackened the pressure on her windpipe.

"Rick?" Her voice came out in a raw whisper, and he didn't waste a second, turning her around and folding her into his arms. "What happened?" he demanded, pulling her closer, welcoming the surge of relief that tore through him.

"It's a very long story," she began. Then she stiffened and he heard the note of sudden alarm in her tone. "Rick, someone shoved me in here. There's—"

She halted sharply when the overhead lights snapped on, flooding the chamber with a blue-white glare so intense that it was momentarily blinding.

Rick's relief vanished. Swiveling his head, he squinted through the dazzling glow, drawing Lexie with him as he took an experimental backward step. The floor appeared level enough; however, he knew that could change at any time. They had to get out of here now, while they had the chance.

The chamber was designed to mislead, and it succeeded in doing exactly that. Large black and white checks on one wall gradually diminished in size, giving the room an asymmetrical look that had a tendency to unbalance the people inside. There was a handrail on the far wall, but Rick wasn't about to take any unnecessary detours. The roller was straight ahead. Ten, maybe twelve steps, and they'd be out of here.

Lexie's uncertain gaze was fastened on the open door behind her. Someone had shoved her in here, she'd said. Well, that someone had obviously managed to reach the control panel. The lights were blazing, the roller was turning and Rick's distrust of Sherwood's killer was growing with every passing second.

He took Lexie firmly by the hand. "Keep your eyes on the tunnel," he cautioned her. "And no matter what happens, don't let go."

Prophetic words. He should have known better than to utter them. They hadn't taken more than three of those ten steps when a shot rang out, sending a bullet whizzing past his ear and the two of them diving for the nearest cover.

"Damn," he swore through clenched teeth. He should have seen this coming. The murderer had a gun. And it was being fired from the other end of the roller.

Their exit had been cut off.

Chapter Ten

A second explosion shattered the air in the checkered room. Lexie heard the bullet lodge itself in the wall behind her and tried to scrunch herself deeper in the corner. Rick was shielding her with his body, but there was precious little protection between him and the roller to their left. The legs of a disproportionate table that had been nailed to the floor were his only cover, legs that wouldn't be nearly wide enough if the murderer ever got a clear shot at him.

Another explosion rent the air, and this time Rick returned the fire. His bullet zinged off the roller's metallic rim, barely missing the black-gloved hand that jerked away at the last second.

Lexie lost count of the gunshots. Three more. Four. She couldn't tell who was squeezing the trigger. All she saw was Rick crouched behind the table, his forearms resting on the Formica top, his sights aimed squarely on the roller, his profile a mask of calm professionalism.

She was grateful for his stoic attitude, but she couldn't imagine how he maintained it. They were trapped, cut off from the door to the corridor as well as the rolling tunnel. At some point he was bound to run out of bullets, unless the majority of the shots had been fired by the murderer.

On that devout thought, she risked a glance at the cylindrical exit. The revolutions continued, metal rasping lightly across wood. She picked up on a hurried scrabbling sound, then nothing except a silence so profound that it was almost deafening.

Rick kept his gun pointed at the roller, his eyes trained on the purple shadows inside as the empty seconds ticked away. Finally he lowered his hands, pushing himself up and motioning for Lexie to stay put.

Breath held, she scrambled to her knees, but remained in the corner. There was nothing she could do unarmed to help, beyond keeping her eyes glued to the tunnel and her nerves steady.

With a gruff "Don't move" to her, Rick swung himself into the roller, and all Lexie could do was watch as he disappeared from sight.

She tried, she really did. But as the seconds ticked away and the stillness became a nerve-racking buzz in her ears, she knew she had to do something. Rick was out there with a killer. She couldn't just sit here and let him take all the risks.

The chamber's false perspective and decided lack of symmetry made her head spin. The longer she stared at the black and white checkers, the worse it got. Averting her eyes, she focused on the revolving cylinder. She hadn't heard any more gunshots, which was good. On the other hand, Rick hadn't returned yet....

An icy claw of terror closed about her heart, and she fought back of all the dire possibilities, all the things that could have happened to him. Moving warily, she inched over to the roller, took a deep breath and peered inside.

It was empty, and so was the space behind it. She didn't stop to judge the speed of the tube. She simply crawled through to the other side, not caring that she banged her elbow and shoulder in the process, and jumped to the floor and looked around.

She was in another corridor. It was dark and shadow filled, with a door at the far end and a metal panel on the left, and she could only hope it would conduct her out of this awful place.

The smell of green grass and damp earth greeted her when she eased the bolt back and gave it a tentative pull. It had to be the moors that stretched out before her, but the fog was too thick for her to be sure. "Marshmallow clouds," she murmured, huddling deeper into her jacket.

"Pea soup." A disembodied voice supplied the traditional expression, and whirling, Lexie ran toward the sound. She almost missed him, but Rick caught her easily, hauling her into his arms and bringing her firmly against his warm body.

For a long time she didn't move, so relieved to see him that she forgot why she'd been worried. His heartbeat was steady, soothing, and the heat of his skin soon drove the chill from her bones.

Slowly, insistently, the nightmare came back to her. He'd been chasing a killer! She pulled away just enough to stare up at his shadowed face. "Are you all right?" She ran her hands over his shoulders. "You didn't get hit, did you?"

A slow smile spread across his mouth. "No." Without relinquishing his hold on her, he drew a familiar-looking object from his jacket pocket. "I lost the shooter, but came across this right outside the fun house."

Lexie regarded the gray metal weapon he held, smaller than the Magnum he carried, but every bit as deadly. "The murderer's?" she assumed, her throat muscles tightening. She definitely should have let Rick shoot earlier.

A guarded "Maybe" was all Rick would concede. He shifted his gaze over her shoulder. "One thing I can tell you: I've seen it before."

"What? Where?"

"Charles found this same .38 caliber gun in a shoe box under Gwendolyn's bed the first time we searched her caravan."

"EVERYONE AT THE CARNIVAL had access to that gun," Lexie repeated, her expression steadfast. "For that matter almost anyone in the village could have gotten hold of it."

"Including Diana."

She glared at him. "Why do you keep saying that? Do you still think she's guilty?"

"I think what I've thought all along," he said as they made their way back to the caravan row. "I have strong doubts about her guilt, but I also don't think we can condemn Gwendolyn simply because the gun I found belongs to her. It's too neat, too easy."

"Why?" Lexie demanded. "Do you think the gun was dropped on purpose?"

"It's possible."

Looking away, she continued to walk. "That still doesn't rule out Gwendolyn. Maybe she deliberately used her own gun to shoot at us, then dropped it where she figured you'd find it, knowing that as soon as you did, you'd scratch her as a suspect."

Rick couldn't resist a grin. "No matter what the murderer's plan was, you have to admit it's working. We're more confused now than ever."

Ahead of them, the caravan row began to take shape. While his watchful eyes scoured the purling mist, Rick's mind traced every line of reasoning the murderer might have used tonight to its logical conclusion. There were any number of possibilities, too many to sift through, he realized, keeping his fingers firmly linked with Lexie's. The only sensible thing to do was start in the most obvious place and see where that led them.

"There aren't any lights on," Lexie noted as they approached the fortune-teller's trailer. She looked up at him. "Are you absolutely sure the gun belongs to Gwendolyn?"

"It's hers. I recognize the dent in the handle." He nudged her up the stairs. "Go on and knock. Unless—" his lips quirked "—you'd rather I picked the lock."

For an answer, she raised her hand to the door, giving the metallic surface a resolute tap. Rick saw a light flick on in the hall and spied Diana stumbling past the living room window, tying the belt of her blue chenille robe.

She pulled the door open to stare sleepy eyed at Lexie. "Hello," she said finally, her voice thick, her facial expression a little vacant. "I'm, uh . . ." She blinked. "I'm sorry, I seem to be having trouble waking up. Come in, please. Both of you. Er, did you want to talk to me about something, Lexie?"

"Not you, your roomie." It was Rick who furnished the answer. "Is she here?"

Diana looked bemused. "I think so." She pushed the tousled hair from her cheeks. "Would you like me to wake her?"

"Yes," Lexie said.

"In a minute," Rick amended, aware of the level dagger her eyes flung at him. From his pocket he pulled the .38. "Have you ever seen this gun?"

The lines of perplexity that creased her forehead seemed genuine enough. "I think so," she said. "I'm not sure, but it looks like the one Skelly gave to Gwendolyn after, uh, well, just after," she finished lamely.

Lexie captured her attention. "So you knew about it?"

"Yes." Diana frowned. "Is something wrong?"

Wisely, Rick backed off—physically if not in any other sense. Leaving Lexie to explain the situation, he made a polite show of drifting down the hall toward the bathroom.

Diana's reading lamp was on when he glanced into her room. The sheets were rumpled and there was a book turned upside down on the nightstand. About what he'd expected. He switched direction, staring at the other closed door. He considered knocking, then rejected the idea. If Gwendolyn was guilty he didn't want to give her any warnings. Besides, after he'd seen nine years with Scotland Yard, there wasn't a whole lot he hadn't seen.

With a stealth born of practice, he eased the latch back, cracking the door open just wide enough to step inside. A sliver of light spilled into the darkened room, illuminating a bed covered with magazines, stockings, crumpled napkins and various other items—everything except the fortune-teller herself.

Since he had no time for a comprehensive search, Rick contented himself with reaching under the bed and pulling out the shoe box Charles had found the previous week. It didn't surprise him to find the .38 missing. But that didn't necessarily mean Gwendolyn had dropped it. Lexie was right. Anybody could have known about the gun. Charles, Skelly, Fitz, even Victoria.

Shoving the box back where it belonged, Rick pushed himself to his feet and made a final assessing sweep of the room, pausing on the windowsill, on a strongbox that hadn't been there last week. The same strongbox Charles had mentioned, he wondered, flipping up the unlocked lid and examining the opaque crystal ball without much interest. It seemed likely, although it certainly wasn't being used to store the Saxony jewels.

After a detour to the bathroom, he rejoined the women. An imperceptible shake of his head signaled to Lexie that Gwendolyn was not in the caravan, a fact she might have relayed to Diana if the fortune-teller hadn't chosen that particular moment to come slamming through the front door.

Rick noted her clothing first—dark jeans, black, soft-soled shoes and a black hooded sweatshirt with a pouch at the front—and the calculating gleam in her slitted eyes second. Sliding his hands into his jacket pockets, he lounged negligently against the back of the chair where Lexie was seated and watched as Gwendolyn sauntered past them and on into the kitchen.

She was puffing and trying hard not to, he noticed. One leg of her jeans was torn at the bottom as though it had gotten snagged on something sharp, and her cheeks were deeply flushed, blotchier than her heavy-handed application of rose blusher could account for. She didn't say a word, despite being the center of attention, until she'd snatched a Pepsi from the fridge and banged the door shut with an insolent swing of her hip.

"Cozy," she observed after a prolonged appraisal of the threesome in her caravan. "A solicitor, a roustabout and an accused murderer. Quite the intriguing ménage à trois."

"You'd know all about such sordid arrangements, I'm sure," Lexie retorted sweetly.

It was obvious to Rick that the fortune-teller didn't appreciate being bested. Her lips thinned, her nostrils flared and her eyes all but spewed venom. He fully expected her to hiss and stalk from the room, but she surprised him by raising the soda can to her mouth and forcing a plastic smile. "I know about lots of things," she said placidly, but the nasty light still lurked in her eyes.

There was something else, too, Rick discerned, something hidden behind that virulent gleam. He couldn't quite read it, but he had no doubt it was there, a tiny glimmer that resembled the flashes of fear he'd seen in a thousand different faces over the years.

She flopped onto the sofa next to Diana who immediately sidled away. Waiting until she'd filled her mouth with soda, he opened with a mocking "You look winded, Gwendolyn. Don't tell me you've been running around the carnival grounds in the middle of the night?"

She swallowed loudly, covering her reaction well. "Would it be any of your business if I had?"

"Call it justifiable curiosity," he suggested, moving to sit on the arm of Lexie's chair. "Someone lured us into the fun house tonight."

"Interesting." She kept her voice even but a belligerent edge crept in. "I presume since you're telling me this, you believe I was that person."

"It occurred to us," Lexie replied while a nervous-looking Diana endeavored to put more space between herself and her poisonous co-worker. "Were you?"

Rick honestly thought Gwendolyn was going to lunge at her. With a snarl, she catapulted from her seat, eyes flashing dark fire. "You've a bloody lot of nerve to strut in here and start raking me over the coals. I told you before, Lexie, if it's answers you're after, I've given you all I intend to. If it's advice you're wanting, then you'll take the free helping I dished out before and leave this place while you're still able to make the choice."

"That sounds more like a threat than a piece of advice," Rick observed.

"And you sound more like ruddy John Law than a roustabout."

"Why?" Lexie challenged, fielding the accusation smoothly. "Because he's one of the very few people at this carnival willing to help me? Try getting shot at sometime, and see if you don't find yourself asking similar questions."

"Shot at?" The look of surprise that invaded Gwendolyn's face didn't extend to her eyes. Sweeping her frizzy hair over one shoulder, she shrugged. "Well, you can't say I didn't warn you. That's *warn*," she repeated, glowering at Rick, "as opposed to threaten. Not," she added coldly, her cold gaze embracing them all, "that I'm obliged to defend myself to any of you, but as I'm certain you're about to start pointing fingers, I'll tell you this much. I've been with a friend tonight. All night."

From his makeshift seat by the window, Rick caught sight of someone heading toward the caravan. "A friend?" he repeated, keeping his expression blank. "You mean Skelly?"

"Yes, I mean Skelly." Angrily, she flung an arm toward the caravan row. "Go on and ask him if you don't believe me."

A knock on the door interrupted her tirade, and Diana, eager to be out of the fortune-teller's range, hastened to answer it. "Uh, come in," Rick heard her murmur, and smiling complacently, he sat back to observe Gwendolyn's reaction to the arrival of her "friend"—one Leonard Skelton.

As he'd anticipated, her hands clenched into tight fists at her sides. Before she could alert Skelly to what was obviously a lie, Lexie jumped in to ask, "Excuse me, Mr. Skelton, but would you mind telling me where you've been for the past hour?"

The man had a bad poker face. He darted an awkward look at Gwendolyn who must have relayed some message with her eyes, then cleared his throat and nodded. "I've been with Gwendolyn ever since we closed."

Diana's brow furrowed slightly, but she said nothing.

"You've been together since ten o'clock?" Lexie sounded unconvinced.

Gwendolyn speared her with a vituperative glare. "That's what the man said—and what I say, too." Her tone dared them to contradict the word of two people. "Is there anything else you'd like to know?"

"One thing." Rick rose in a single fluid movement. "Maybe you can tell me what this was doing in the grass outside the fun house."

Skelly's gaunt cheeks paled while Gwendolyn's reddened. Her mouth was a grim, claret slash as she stared at the gun being held in front of her. She lifted hostile eyes. "Maybe I can't tell you a bloody thing, Rick."

"Can't or won't?" Lexie demanded, drawing a surly growl from deep in the woman's throat.

"You're the legal eagle," she snapped. "You figure it out. Skelly and me, we were together, and not you nor anyone else hereabouts can prove otherwise." With that, she offered Skelly a smile rich in meaning, grabbed her Pepsi and marched into her room, banging the door loudly behind her.

For a tall man, Skelly moved quickly. He was across the floor and out of the caravan before a single question could be directed at him. The logical one would have been, why had he come here so late if he and Gwendolyn had just spent the better part of two hours together?

As far as Rick was concerned, the answer was simple. They hadn't really been together. Not tonight and definitely not the night Wren Sherwood had died. The officers assigned to the case had established the latter by catching Gwendolyn off guard. She'd admitted to being alone in her caravan because she'd believed that Skelly was playing poker in the roustabouts' tent that evening. On the flip side, Skelly claimed to have changed his mind about gambling away his weekly pay in favor of listening to a BBC broadcast in his own trailer. The opportunity to kill Sherwood was something a number of people had. However, a lack of solid evidence against them and an abundance of the circumstantial kind against Diana had made the decision to arrest her inevitable.

Rick swung his hooded gaze to the accused woman as the door thumped shut behind Skelly. Her brows were still knitted. Obviously she was troubled about something. "What is it?" he queried softly, conscious that Lexie was trying to catch a glimpse of the fun house operator through the window. "Are they lying?"

"No." The denial came out swiftly, supplemented by a perplexed, "Rather, I don't know. It's just, I thought I heard Gwendolyn say she was going to bed earlier."

Lexie joined Rick in the middle of the floor, her Skelly-watching having been suspended by the fog. "So you're saying that Gwendolyn and Skelly haven't been together ever since closing time."

"Well, no, they couldn't have been. I didn't get here until ten-fifteen, a few minutes after Gwendolyn. She had her robe over her arm, and she was looking for a meat pie in the refrigerator. Skelly certainly wasn't around anywhere."

Diana's frown deepened, then cleared a little. "Oh, wait, maybe that's it. Gwendolyn ate the last pie yesterday. After I turned in, she must have gone out to get some more."

"From the food tent?" Rick asked.

"I should think so. She's done it before. We all have. She probably got Skelly to keep watch for her." The relief in Diana's voice was palpable. Rick supposed any explanation, even a weak one, was preferable to the thought that her roommate might be a murderer. "It must have been someone else who—" she shivered and rubbed her arms "—shot at you."

"With Gwendolyn's gun," Lexie said flatly. "Did everyone at the carnival know she kept it under her bed?"

Diana spread her fingers. "I guess there were some who knew. It's hard to be sure." She halted for a moment. "Do you think whoever shot at you might be the person who, um, killed Glen—Wren?"

"It seems like a good bet," Rick replied, watching Gwendolyn's bedroom door out of the corner of his eye.

"A good bet doesn't prove much, though, does it?" Diana said as she sank onto the couch.

Lexie went to sit beside her. "No, it doesn't. But it might make you feel better to learn that those two missing teacups we talked about a few days ago turned up in Wren's cupboard the night before last."

"Someone put them back?" At Lexie's nod, Diana glanced in the direction of the red trailer. "But that's silly, isn't it? Why bother? You said the police never even noticed the cups were missing." She shook her head in bewilderment. "I honestly don't understand what's happening at this carnival. First I get arrested for a murder I had no part in, then I received a threatening note, then you get shot at and now you tell me about two missing teacups that are no longer missing. The more I think about it, the more this whole thing doesn't make any sense."

"It will," Lexie promised, her delicate jaw set in a deter
mined line. "Eventually everything will fall into place."

From the end of the hall, Rick heard a small click, th
distinctive sound of a door being closed by a careful hand
and he knew Gwendolyn had been listening covertly to every
word they'd spoken. On the surface, things did seem to b
falling into place—and not in the fortune-teller's favor.

MIDNIGHT.

Rick wondered if he was tired and decided he probabl
was. He just tended to notice his own physical discomfor
less whenever Lexie was around.

They hadn't really spoken to each other after leaving th
carnival site, not so much because there wasn't anything t
say, but rather because there was nothing they *could* say a
this point that would get them anywhere. An easy silenc
continued to reign between them as he pushed open th
lobby door of the Pendragon Inn and followed her inside.

Against his better judgment, he let his eyes stray to th
slender curve of her hips, provocatively outlined by th
faded denim jeans. It was a mistake to look at her. The hea
surging through his lower limbs wasn't going to subside un
less he made a concerted effort to direct his thoughts awa
from Lexie and onto a more impersonal topic. Then again
that wasn't likely to happen with her mounting the stair
ahead of him.

"We should have stopped at the pub," he muttered whe
they reached the landing.

She smiled back at him. "Why? Do you need a drink?"

What he needed had nothing to do with alcohol. "I *wan*
a beer," he said, giving her door a firm inward shove. H
also wanted her, but that wasn't his choice alone to make.

The four-poster bed with its snowy white sheets an
goose-down pillows looked a little too inviting as Ric
crossed the carpet and reached for the phone on the night
stand. He'd promised Lexie at the carnival that he woul

heck his answering machine after walking her back to the
in. And once that task had been taken care of, he'd be well
dvised to check on Charles, if for no other reason than to
nake sure the unreliable sergeant was in his room.

With his back to the bed, he dialed the number of his
London flat, then sent a beep across the wire to retrieve any
nessages. He could hear Lexie rummaging through a cabi-
et behind him, but he knew better than to look at her
gain.

He tried the next best thing, focusing on the dangerous
spects of this case as opposed to her part in it. Even that
idn't work. Neither did concentrating on his messages. He
wore under his breath at the cheerful prattle of a rugby
eammate's girlfriend who chattered over the line, not car-
ig that she was talking to a machine.

"Any news?" Lexie asked from the other side of the
oom.

"A mate of mine is having a barbecue after the rugby
natch next Sunday," Rick relayed with a shrug. "I'm sup-
osed to bring charcoal."

"That's not exactly what I meant." She came around the
oot of the bed and into his line of vision, offering him an
ncapped green bottle. "It's apple cider," she said. "The
'endragons believe in stocking the rooms with whatever
ood and drink they think their guests might enjoy in the
niddle of the night. For a healthy price, of course," she
dded, grinning.

Her amused tone wiped away Rick's irritation. With a
huckle, he raised the bottle to his lips, letting the tepid ci-
er flow down his suddenly parched throat. He saw her cast
faintly wistful look at the blackened grate of the old stone
ireplace, then wander to the window that overlooked the
obbled lane behind the inn.

Fog swirled in eerie circles around the lead-rimmed glass,
locking out the view of Wexford Castle's crumbling tower
nd the few lights that continued to burn in the cottages at

the base of the hill. Rick's muscles tightened as he watche
Lexie in silhouette against the veil of mist. He felt the hea
that invaded his loins when she stretched her arms over he
head like an awakening feline and blew out a frustrate
breath as his machine kicked into yet another persona
message.

Giving her arms a final stretch, Lexie turned from th
window. "Wouldn't it be faster to phone Scotland Yard?
she teased.

"Probably." Rick took another drink of cider. "But the
I wouldn't have the pleasure of hearing that my cousir
Janis, is flying in from Amsterdam to see me."

"Does she live in a cave like your Alaskan relatives?"

"Actually, she lives on a boat," Rick said, listening as
new voice crackled across the line. "There's some infor
mation about O'Brien on here."

An expectant gleam lit her golden brown eyes, and sh
hastened across the floor to his side, not making a soun
until he finally dropped the receiver back in its cradle.

"Well?" she asked. "Is there a connection between Wre
Sherwood's partner and Victoria's nephew?"

Rick shook his head. "They're not sure yet. Apparentl
there's been some problem locating Danny Farraday's rec
ords."

"What about Aidan O'Brien? Is he dead?"

"Officially, yes. But the officer who ran the check for m
said the remains of the body found in the rubble wer
burned beyond recognition. Moreover, O'Brien had n
traceable medical or dental records. The bone structur
seemed to match, and there was a ring he'd been known t
wear on one of the fingers. He was identified pretty muc
on those two pieces of evidence."

Lexie stared at him, her nails biting into his arm as the fu
weight of what he'd told her began to sink in. The chance
were remote, but the possibility did exist.

Aidan O'Brien might still be alive!

Chapter Eleven

"Ghosts," Lexie murmured. "Now we have to consider the idea that a man who's supposed to be dead could have killed Wren Sherwood. I'd rather believe that Lord Storm and Algernon did it."

Rick shrugged, accepting the turn of events with an enviable passivity. "I don't think you would have liked their methods," he returned, eyeing the empty grate. "Do you want me to build a fire?"

A shiver that incorporated a number of emotions passed through Lexie's body. There were traces of fear and lingering guilt, determination and impatience, but those feelings paled next to the ones involving Rick—the ones she was neither inclined to nor able to resist.

Nodding, she rubbed her bare arms beneath the rolled-up sleeves of her cotton shirt. "I'd like that," she said and hoped he wouldn't decide to leave the minute the logs began to crackle. She didn't think he would, but he wasn't the easiest man in the world to read, and she was hardly the best judge of human nature. Unlike Rodney, about whom she definitely didn't want to think, Rick's steady blue eyes betrayed very little of his feelings, except on those rare occasions when he chose to let something out.

The Pendragons not only stocked the guest rooms with assorted foodstuffs, but also provided a stack of dried logs in an ancient coal scuttle beside the hearth. Lexie handed Rick several sticks of kindling, then wedged two of the smaller logs from the pile and leaned them against the stonework. For tonight at least, she found herself curiously unwilling to worry about all the things she couldn't change, the questions, both personal and professional, she couldn't answer. There had to be a better way to expend her energy.

"Tell me more about Algernon, Rick," she invited, sitting down cross-legged while he arranged the kindling strips.

He touched a match to the wood, rocking back on his heels as a line of orange flame raced along the underside of a slender twig. Amusement glittered in his eyes when he turned his head to smile at her. "You want to talk about a phantom?"

No, but it was a start. And she did like ghost stories on foggy nights. "I have no quarrel with the medieval kind. Why did Algernon do his conjuring in an old Roman fortress rather than up at Wexford Castle?"

"Because his magic was strongest there."

"Was there a reason for that?"

"Some say it had to do with a former occupant of the fortress, a sorcerer whose ideas of immortality were similar to Algernon's. It's claimed that when the sorcerer learned he was dying he found a way to transfer his soul into the foundations of the old ruin."

"And Algernon freed it?" Lexie guessed.

"Nothing quite that dramatic." Rick added the small logs to the burning kindling, then shed his jacket and sat down beside her, taking a long drink of his cider. "Algernon was an alchemist, not a wizard. He used the magical properties in the stones around him to feed his potions."

"Did he also use them to bring the fog down from the north?"

"Probably." A slow smile crept across Rick's lips, and he changed position, turning her slightly and fitting her against his warm body. With his head, he indicated the layers of white mist floating past her window. "As long as the fog didn't develop a green tinge, the villagers knew they were safe."

Leaning back, Lexie absorbed the enticing scent of his skin, the solid feel of his muscles. "And if it did?"

"Then they knew one of them would be spirited away to Algernon's workshop—which is a chapter of the story you don't want to hear on a night like this."

"Is there a more pleasant chapter you can tell me?" The question stemmed as much from a desire to hear his voice than it did from her affinity for ghostly tales. Rick possessed an innate sensuality and an ability to arouse her in ways she wouldn't have believed possible a week ago. Hearing his voice, feeling his breath on her temple, his fingers resting lightly on her waist—all those things added to her awareness of him, fanning the desires that smoldered so restlessly inside her.

"Love potions," he murmured, the words a lazy drawl in her ear. He stroked the hair from her cheek with his fingers, sliding his mouth along the side of her jaw to her earlobe, then down to the pulse that beat an erratic cadence just above her collarbone. "The villagers say that Lord Storm's fixation with immortality was spawned by an even deeper obsession."

A feverish tremor shuddered across her skin. Closing her eyes, she rested her head against the broad plane of his shoulder. "What was this obsession's name?"

She heard the thread of amusement in his voice. "The Duchess Madeleine de Beauvrier, a woman of extraordinary intelligence and beauty who wanted nothing that the barbaric lord had to offer." Deftly, Rick rearranged her in his arms, pushing aside the lavender cotton material of her shirt, exposing more of her skin to his roving lips.

A small sound of pleasure escaped from Lexie's throat as the hand on her waist began a provocative exploration of its own. "Maybe that's why Lord Storm set Algernon free," she suggested, although she found it increasingly difficult to concentrate on anything except the fervid cravings evoked by Rick's touch. "In exchange for a love potion he could use on Madeleine."

Rick lifted his mouth from the side of her neck, capturing her chin between his thumb and forefinger and smiling. "Maybe," he agreed. "But if that's the case, it didn't work. Madeleine de Beauvrier wanted no part of love. Her only lust was for money and the power that came from having it." Lowering his electric blue eyes, he inclined his head again, slowly this time, brushing her lips with a teasing gentleness that drove all thoughts of Algernon and his ancient companions from Lexie's mind.

She swayed against him, sliding her arms around his neck and pulling him closer, deepening the kiss he'd begun until the force of it made her fevered nerve ends tremble from a longing she couldn't control. Never, never, in all the time she'd known him had Rodney kissed her like this.

Rick's mouth opened hotly over hers, his tongue probing between her lips with an insistence that was as subtly forceful as it was intoxicating. His kisses were a drug to her senses, and she dug her fingers into the sinewy muscles of his shoulders, responding to him on every level both conscious and unconscious. She tasted the desire that ran as strong and unchecked in him as it did in her, felt the circle of his arms tighten around her. And she heard the low moan of protest that came from her throat when he eased his mouth away so their lips were barely touching.

"The fire's dying," he murmured, and for a startled moment Lexie wasn't sure what he was talking about. But when he half released her to stoke the flaming coals and toss three large logs onto the grate, she noticed the damp chill in the air, a detail she'd overlooked with Rick's body doing an all-too-effective job of warming her.

Once the fire was flaming again, he moved up behind her, gathering her close and grazing the soft skin of her cheek with his thumb. "I thought you might be leaving," she said, a little shocked by the strength of her desire, yet more resistant to the idea that the hunger burning inside her might not be satisfied.

Rick wanted her, she knew that, and there was no question in her mind that she wanted him. It was so simple, so basic—and perhaps not quite as complicated as she'd first thought.

Rick's breath fanned her skin in a featherlight caress as his lips brushed across her warm brow. "Do you want me to leave, Lexie?" he asked, waiting patiently for her response.

Turning slightly so she could see him better, she shook her head. "No, I don't." And wrapping her arms around his neck, she reached up to meet the mouth that came down to cover hers.

It was a long, devouring kiss, sensual and deeply arousing. With his tongue Rick explored all the soft, dark hollows of her mouth, taking his time while he familiarized himself with the more sensitive areas of her body. She worked at the buttons of his denim shirt, unfastening them one by one so she could run her fingers over his sleekly muscled chest. She felt the fierce yearning that gripped her as his hand strayed slowly from her waist to her rib cage and around her back to the hook of her bra.

Her breasts swelled beneath the lacy fabric, her nipples hardening in response to a touch that hadn't even been felt yet. He swallowed the moan she couldn't hold back and slid the cotton shirt from her shoulders. Her bra followed it to the floor, and then he was rolling smoothly to his feet, lifting her up in his arms and carrying her effortlessly to the bed.

He set her down on the sheets without removing his mouth from hers. In a hazy part of her mind she heard a click and knew he'd extinguished the glaring light of the bedside lamp, leaving only the warm orange glow from the fire to illuminate the room.

A whole new set of sensations shot through her as he stretched out beside her on the mattress and she realized the extent of his arousal. The hardened muscles of his body dug into her tender hip, but still he took his time, lifting his head for a moment and gazing down at her through the veil of his dark golden lashes.

He looked as if he wanted to say something; it was there in his eyes, a vaguely troubled gleam that came and went so quickly that she thought she might have imagined it.

"Are you all right?" she asked, unsure of the expression on his shadowed face. A horrible thought occurred to her, and she snatched her hands from his chest. "You're not married, are you?"

The corners of his mouth curved into a grin. "No. And I'm not almost engaged, either."

Lexie swallowed a moan of frustration. "Rick, I don't want to talk about Rodney."

He wouldn't look away. "Neither do I, but I'd like to know how you feel about him."

"I'm not . . ." She bit her lip. "I don't . . ."

"Are you still going to marry him?"

The question stung her pride. She tensed a little. "I wouldn't be here if I were."

"Well, one of us wouldn't be here," Rick said, his voice a seductive murmur. "Do you love the guy?"

She considered hitting him—or kissing him. It would have been a toss-up if his mouth hadn't been a mere two inches above hers, two inches she desperately wanted to eliminate. "No," she said, pulling his head lower. "I don't."

The admission seemed to further stimulate Rick, if that was possible. Lexie shivered as he slid his darkened gaze along the creamy smooth skin of her upper body, stopping on the rosy peaks of her breasts that swelled beneath his intensely compelling stare. A low groan rumbled deep in his throat, and he bent his head to tease the hardened nipple with his lips and teeth. She gasped out loud, unable to contain the sound as the ache inside her became a throbbing need. Arching toward him, she dug her fingers into his shoulders, savoring the lean strength of his body as his mouth opened over her breast and his tongue moved in hot, moist circles around the sensitive tip.

It was a delicious form of torture that she wished would never end. Her fingers curled into the thick layers of his hair, her hips moving against the hand that shifted to the button of her jeans. When he touched her, her skin burned, and all she wanted was to feel more of him. She heard the rasp of a zipper, and then he was drawing her jeans over her hips, discarding them easily along with her lacy bikini briefs.

His clothes followed hers to the floor. He shed them quickly with a graceful economy of movement. In the burnt orange glow of the fire she saw his beautiful male body, lean and supplely muscled without a spare ounce of flesh anywhere. For a long, breathless moment he hovered above her, his eyes absorbing the sight of her, memorizing the slender line of her ribs and waist, the flare of her hips and the sleek length of her legs.

"I feel like I've waited to make love to you forever," he murmured as he bent to trace the outline of her trembling lips with his tongue. Silently, Lexie echoed the cryptic remark. She'd had enough of forever. She didn't want to wait another minute.

She reached up to pull him closer still, letting her palms slide across his shoulders, and the sweat-dampened hair under his arm, then down his chest to the rigid muscles of his thighs.

The shudder that swept through him made her touch even bolder, her senses far more acute. And then it was her turn to shudder as his mouth came down on hers once more. His tongue investigated intimately all the sweet, moist corners while his hand made a fiery descent across her quivering stomach, and lower, until everything was blotted out except the ache that raged deep inside her, the cry that swelled in her throat and a need that was so overwhelming that it hurt.

With his knee, he spread her legs, fitting himself between them, letting her know that his desire was as strong as hers. She could hear his ragged breathing, but it was a distant sound that couldn't quite drown out the hot flow of blood that pounded in her ears. Every part of her came alive as his hands reached down to support her hips, her fingers closed around him.

The damp, foggy air beyond the window was a blur in Lexie's mind. A log popped, and there was music playing somewhere close by. Or was it in her head? She couldn't tell, didn't care. She was lost in a place she'd never been before, lost in Rick's touch, in the heat and the wonder and the passion that swept her along until she was crying out for him, arching herself up so she could feel all the sweat-slick contours of his body.

He paused above her, but only for a moment before his mouth caught hers, lifting her higher and higher as he entered her with a single thrust that robbed her of breath and elicited a convulsive response so intense that she knew there couldn't be anything more.

She was wrong. His drumming heartbeat was a match for hers. His muscles were taut, his flesh damp beneath her clenched hands. She reveled in the feel of him, in the earthy scent of his skin, in the softness of his hair and the rhythmic pulsations that built between them. Her mind was beyond rational thought. The world dissolved around her, fading away until everything and everyone ceased to exist and only their lovemaking was real.

She could have gone on forever, straining to grab that extra bit of pleasure, not wanting to miss any of it. She ran her fingers over Rick's satin-smooth back, pressing them into the rippling muscles as her eyes opened to stare into his. The impassioned expression on his face and the glittering intensity of his eyes said it all. She held him tightly, feeling his release and her own avid response. If she'd tried, she couldn't have held back the cry of pleasure that suddenly tumbled from her lips.

The darkness closed in slowly, drifting through her highly sensitized body like a languorous cloud. She wanted Rick to remain inside her for as long as possible, but that wasn't nearly long enough. She caught back the sigh that was half-bliss, half-regret as Rick eased himself from between her legs and rolled away, bringing her with him and smiling when the sigh slipped out, anyway.

It was a long time before either of them spoke. Rick had little choice. He felt as though his body had been shot with a huge bolt of lightning, and even that wasn't an apt description of his response to the woman in his arms. When he was capable of stringing two coherent thoughts together, maybe he'd come up with something. Until then he'd just enjoy the primitive emotions that continued to charge through him at a feverish pitch.

Beside him, he felt Lexie shift, and with a supreme effort he twisted onto his side, keeping her firmly pressed against him. "Don't move," he murmured, his lips grazing her forehead.

"I have to," she said softly, and he heard the reluctance in her wonderfully husky voice. "My arm's asleep."

Amusement rose inside him as he obligingly readjusted his hold on her. "Better?" he asked when she pillowed her head on his shoulder.

"Uh-huh." She slid her palm across the flat plane of his stomach, sending a renewed shaft of desire to his lower body and a fierce tremor over his skin.

He groaned at the reaction her touch evoked. "Frankenstein," he rasped, drawing a sharp breath as her fingers wandered along his inner thigh. "Are you trying to kill me?"

"No." Her mouth found the slamming pulse at the base of his throat. "And I'm not trying to create a monster, either. But I do think just about anything else would be fair."

Rick snapped his mouth shut, unable to utter another intelligible sound, unwilling to even try. His body came alive beneath the brazen exploration of her hands and lips. And he knew there was nothing on the planet that would ever top this moment—except maybe a thousand more just like it.

THERE COULD NOT be another night like this!

The murderer made the furious declaration over and over and over again, each time more violently than the one before. The episode in the fun house had been a stupid mistake. Problems loomed everywhere now, the biggest of them still being Lexie and Rick and what they were bound to learn about Aidan O'Brien.

The troublesome thoughts were ruthlessly shoved aside as the person thinking them crept to the place where the Saxony jewels were hidden. Sapphires, emeralds, rubies, amethysts, even a tazanite or two. Beautiful stones, all loose and sparkling despite the near absence of light.

They were safe. All was well so far. Mollified, the murderer returned them to their hiding spot and started back across the meadow. A dense curtain of fog still hung over the entire region. Rotten luck that it hadn't rolled in just a little sooner. Maybe then . . .

No! Nothing good could come of dwelling on the past. Issues had to be dealt with as they cropped up. Wren was a splendid example of that belief. He'd discovered the truth; he'd died. There could be no other way.

The murderer heard the clock in the village tower: 4:00 a.m. already, and still so much to be done. Gloved fingers closed convulsively around a small white envelope, and turning, the figure in black headed away from the meadow and the jewels and another very real problem that was only slightly less sticky than the one posed by Rick and Lexie.

The questions came as they always did when there was time to think. How close were they to the truth? Who was their strongest suspect? What about the gun? Had dropping it been a terrible mistake, or a stroke of genius?

A disgruntled breath rushed from the murderer's lungs. Silent, sneaker-shod feet approached the Pendragon Inn. No lights shone in the lobby, and the street door was unlocked. Lovely. Anyone could get in. Not a single condemning finger could be pointed.

The envelope crinkled as it was stuffed in the proper pigeonhole. This would help, but it was no permanent answer. It wouldn't stop them. In some ways it might even do more harm than good....

Eyes devoid of all emotion looked at the narrow staircase. Caught between a jewel-seeking copper and a truth-seeking solicitor—and God knew what other bothersome nuisances. That fabled Irish luck was in dire need of a helping hand, more than a simple message could provide. If they ever found out about Aidan O'Brien, it would all be over. Hence, the only possible solution: they couldn't be allowed to find another thing.

The black-gloved hand began to reach for the envelope, then stopped as a recognizable shape passed in front of the lobby window. The doorknob turned slowly, leaving no time for thought. The murderer made a lunge for the message, then swore in furious silence as it slipped away and floated to the carpet behind the counter.

There was no time to retrieve it, no time to do anything except duck into the lift and wait to see what happened next. Not that it would matter in the end. Like Rick and Lexie, this person, too, must be eliminated. And death was the only sure way to do that.

"MORNING, MATE."

Rick stepped from behind the door in his partner's room, reaching out to shut it while his level gaze swept over the scrawny legs visible below the hem of Charles's brown terry bathrobe.

The sergeant started violently at the unexpected greeting. "I say, Rick," he admonished somewhat shakily. "That's hardly cricket, is it? Popping out at me like a ruddy jack-in-the-box. At seven in the morning, no less."

"Six thirty-three," Rick corrected without looking at his watch. He knew exactly what time he'd been forced to drag himself from Lexie's bed, and he was no happier about it now than he had been twenty-eight minutes ago. His expression was bland as he ran his eyes down Charles's shower-wet body. Scraggly thin strands of hair hung over the man's forehead, his mustache was twitching like the one on a cartoon rabbit Rick had seen when he was a kid in Chicago, and his beady eyes kept darting to the nearly made bed. He knew what was coming, and in typical Gideon-esque fashion quickly affected a haughty air of indignation.

"Six thirty-three indeed," he scoffed, trying to look miffed. "The time is entirely irrelevant. While I'm loath to do so, I feel I must remind you that this is my room. You've no business walking in unannounced."

Rick ignored the peevish protest. "Why hasn't your bed been slept in?"

Charles's head went up. "It has," he replied stiffly. "I made it myself, before my shower."

"Did you iron the sheets while you were at it?"

"The sheets! What on earth are you talking about?"

Rick regarded him impassively. "The sheets you insisted Mrs. Pendragon change daily. They're clean, unwrinkled and unslept in. Where were you last night?"

"Now see here," Charles blustered. "You're not my nursemaid."

"No, I'm your boss. Were you at the carnival?"

"Certainly not." His partner seemed offended. "You told me not to go there at night."

"I told you that if you endangered my cover again I'd see to it that you were chained to a desk for the rest of your career." Leaning against the door, hands jammed in his jacket pockets, Rick smiled with false pleasantry. "I might anyway."

"Well, I hardly think that's fair, old chap," Charles pulled, tugging at the belt of his robe.

Rick shrugged. "Lots of things aren't fair, mate. I wasn't too happy about getting shot at in the fun house last night."

"Shot at?" Charles echoed in a slightly choked voice. "Last night?" He cleared his throat. "Er, I say, that is rather awkward, isn't it? I mean, people don't usually go around shooting at carnival workers."

"I doubt if it's an everyday occurrence."

"Yes, well, in that case, I suppose it would be, er, logical to assume that someone has tumbled to the fact that you are not a real roustabout."

"Sounds like a reasonable assumption."

"You're in danger."

"I know."

"That's all you have to say?" Charles flapped an agitated hand toward the meadow. "Surely you don't intend to go back there. Good Lord, man, if your cover's no longer intact you'll be a walking target. As I see it, you've no choice here. You must let me continue the search for the Saxony jewels on my own."

With an effort, Rick bit back a barbed retort that would have sounded very much like an accusation and settled for a mocking "Thanks for your concern, Charles, but I think I'll stay on the case."

Charles's lips thinned. "As you wish, Inspector." He raised a faintly imperious brow. "Now, if you'll excuse me, I must get dressed. I can't be traipsing around a carnival in my bathrobe."

Wheeling awkwardly, he marched to the closet, but for once his haughty expression failed him. Rick spied the underlying traces of guilt, the uncertainty that caused a deep furrow to form between the man's eyebrows and made him rub his fingers and thumb together in a harassed fashion.

Something was wrong, but what? Rick dragged the door closed behind him and turned for the stairwell. This case definitely wasn't getting any less complicated as time went by.

Lexie was seated on the top step when he approached. The temptation to scoop her up and carry her back to bed was almost too strong to resist. He was fighting the urge and starting to wonder why when she grinned and offered him the cup of coffee she must have wangled from Kate.

"Your mask of inscrutability is slipping, Rick," she teased, looking pleased with herself. "For once, I can actually read your mind."

"You think so, huh?" Chuckling, he reached down and pulled her to her feet. "Then you should be blushing."

"I've been doing that all night. Anything new with Charles?" Rick swallowed a mouthful of the hot coffee, grimacing at the bitter taste. "He's hiding something," he told her without inflection. "I don't know if it has any bearing on the stolen jewels, but after I told him about last night's shooting, he suggested I back off and let him take over the case."

Lexie frowned. "So either he's a good cop and he's trying to keep you from getting hurt or he's a bad cop who wants to remove you from the investigation, thereby giving himself a clear shot at the jewels." She glanced rather wistfully in the direction of her room, unaware of the expression on her face. But Rick saw it, and he smiled, pleased to know her thoughts so closely mirrored his own. Glad that there was no more Rodney Boggs between them. "Could he have killed Wren Sherwood?"

"I don't know," Rick admitted truthfully. "Charles isn't exactly what he appears to be, and he isn't the best partner

I've ever been assigned, but that doesn't necessarily mean he's gone bad.''

''And there's still the possibility that Aidan O'Brien might not have died in that fire.'' She looked up at him as he finished the vile coffee. ''Are you sure you should be going back to the carnival? You said yourself, the murderer probably knows you're working for Scotland Yard.''

''The murderer also knows that you're Diana's lawyer,'' he reminded her while they descended the stairs. ''However, I have a solution.'' He allowed a tiny smile to cross his lips at the wary light that entered her eyes, but didn't elaborate, certain she'd have a few choice words to say on the subject—which she did.

''If this solution involves one of us spending the day here while the other takes all the risks at the carnival, you can forget it,'' she said in a sweetly sarcastic voice. ''If I wanted a life fraught with boredom, I'd be in London right now, listening to, uh, one of Malcolm Sutcliffe's lectures on the importance of keeping a neat desk.''

Malcolm, or Rodney? ''At least you'd be safe.''

''You wouldn't say that if you knew some of our male legal assistants. What's your idea?''

He grinned at her droll tone, shoving the worst of his misgivings aside as he pushed open the front door. ''I have a lot of repair work to do this morning. You can stay with me and still ask all the questions you want to of the workers. After lunch, we should be able to do some more searching for the jewels.''

The air outside was cool and damp, tinged with the remnants of the previous night's fog and a light drizzle that fell from the overcast sky. Rick eyed the sullen clouds, then the distant carnival. A handful of names, faces and motives ran through his head, but it was difficult for him to concentrate on any of those things. He kept thinking about Lexie, about his feelings for her that seemed to grow stronger with every passing minute. What should have been simple wasn't. What probably shouldn't have happened had.

He loved her. God, he'd walked right into that one. And now he was in trouble. Emotional considerations aside, Rick was first, last and always a cop. Getting shot at might not be a routine occurrence, but it wasn't a novel experience, either. Few women could accept that. Fewer still could live with it.

He loved her... and he was a cop. How could two such wonderfully simple thoughts be so damned complicated?

"GOOD MORNING, Lexie." Smiling brightly, Victoria left Fitz's game booth and came to meet her at the end of the midway. "How goes the battle? Any luck with your investigation?"

Lexie was glad Rick was in sight, working on one of the other arcade booths. She didn't trust the gleam in the carnival owner's eyes. She also felt bad for searching the woman's caravan last night and couldn't help wondering if Victoria knew about it. "Things are looking up," she managed to answer without batting an eyelash.

The genial smile grew a bit strained. "That sounds most encouraging. Do you have anyone specific in mind as a suspect?"

"Oh, here now, Victoria," Fitz clucked in a lazy reproach. He leaned over his counter, eyes twinkling as he lit a stubby cigar. "Even a scoundrel like me knows better than to ask an indelicate question such as that. Right remiss in her duty Miss Lexie would be if she was to crow her findings to the world."

Victoria shot him a cold glare, then endeavored to soften it with a smile that had a somewhat sour aspect to it. "Perhaps I'm being impertinent," she said to Lexie. "Forgive me. It's just that I'm concerned about Diana. And I must say I'm none too pleased at the thought of harboring a murderer. Whoever did kill Wren Sherwood, I want him taken away and punished."

"Or her, as the case may be," Fitz added with a grin. "I expect a bloke as unsavory as our Wren got himself into more than a few tight spots with members of the opposite sex."

"You're right, of course," Victoria acknowledged stiffly. Zipping up her black jacket against the damp morning chill, she nodded at Lexie. "I'll be going, then. If there's anything I can do to help you, please don't hesitate to ask."

As the woman moved off, Lexie glanced unobtrusively at Fitz. His expression, as always, succeeded in being both artless and sly. She wished she could figure out how he did that, and more to the point, *why* he did it. What did this ex-pickpocket know about the people he worked with?

If there was one thing she'd learned about him, it was never to bother wasting time with a lot of carefully worded queries. He was too sharp to fall into any verbal traps. Her only hope of worming information from him lay in using a direct approach.

Once the carnival owner was gone, Lexie walked over to the ring-toss booth, a steady stream of questions drumming in her head. She asked the first one that came to mind. "Didn't you ever wonder about Wren, Fitz?"

His foxlike features took on a reflective cast. "Wondering isn't worth tuppence, Miss Lexie. Besides, a bloke of Wren Sherwood's persuasion wouldn't take kindly to being wondered about. No, I keep me nose in me own affairs and me speculations to meself."

Lexie didn't believe him. "All right, maybe you weren't openly curious about his past. That doesn't make you blind to what went on around you. You must have seen or heard something that will help Diana."

A cloud of gray-white smoke swirled about Fitz's head. "You've a mind to sort this through," he allowed, the glint in his half-closed eyes considering as he regarded her. "I'll grant, I've been doing a fair bit of thinking since last we spoke. Told you, I did, about the night Wren died, how he scuttled out of his booth like all the demons of perdition were on him. Muttering under his breath, he was, too, looking as peaked as if he'd caught himself a glimpse of a right fearsome spook.''

Lexie recalled the name Aidan spelled out on Wren's letter stand. "What did he say?" she prompted. "Do you remember?"

"Not right off, I didn't." He scratched his forehead underneath the brim of his battered derby. "But then I got to pondering his departure." A mischievous grin spread across Fitz's narrow face. "I reckon me curiosity's been sparked a mite ever since I struck off down the road to redemption. The recollection came to me this morning when I heard two young lads talking about Algernon. 'Ain't any such things as ghosts,' one of the tykes insists, and right then me memory takes me back to Wren's last words. 'Two years, and not a single ghost,' I hear him mumble. 'I should have known his would be the one to catch up with me.' That's the last I saw of him, Miss Lexie. Off he went into the night."

"And a little over an hour later, he was dead."

Fitz puffed calmly on his cigar stub. The light in his eyes was shrewd, perhaps a trifle ironic. "Looks like Wren's 'ghost' did a mite more than just catch up with him, doesn't it?"

"AIDAN O'BRIEN was not the only person Sherwood ever turned on, Lexie," Rick pointed out as they neared the Pendragon Inn late that afternoon. "Besides, I thought you didn't trust Fitz."

"I don't. But I still want to know whether Scotland Yard found a link between Aidan and Danny. If there is one, it might turn out that Victoria had an even stronger motive to kill Wren than the one we came up with yesterday."

The suggestion of a smile hovered on Rick's lips, but he said nothing. Lexie wasn't surprised by his skeptical attitude; she had plenty of doubts about the possibility of Aidan O'Brien's being alive. And she wasn't completely convinced that Victoria was the type of person who would go off on a bloody vendetta, either. Still, someone had shot Wren, and despite another lengthy search today, she and Rick had found no trace of the Saxony jewels. Right now, the only belief she could really cling to was that the murderer must have been in possession of those stolen jewels, and sometimes she found herself questioning the validity of that assumption.

She walked into the lobby ahead of Rick, grateful for the coal fire that took the chill out of the preautumn air. Thoughts of the night she'd spent with the man behind her were still fresh in her mind and just a little too tantalizing to ignore. A reminiscent smile curved her lips. Maybe she shouldn't try. After all, it was teatime. They were both entitled to a break.

"Rick, I . . ." she began, then stopped as Kate, the pretty blond woman employed by the Pendragons, waved at her from behind the small reception desk.

"Hello, Lexie, Rick." She greeted them in her usual cheerful fashion. "Your timing's impeccable. I was about to go off duty, and I really didn't want to leave this in Mrs. Pendragon's hands." From the pocket of her skirt she removed a crumpled white envelope with Lexie's name typed on the outside. "I'm so sorry, I can't tell you when this was delivered. Robbie found it after lunch. It must have slipped out of your key slot and gotten wedged between the heater and the wall. I do hope it's nothing urgent."

Forcing her lips into an oblique semblance of a smile, Lexie took the envelope. "I'm sure it isn't," she replied, feeling Rick tense beside her. His expression revealed nothing, and after issuing another apology, Kate moved off in the direction of the dining room.

"Do you want me to open it?" Rick asked as Lexie continued to stare at the sealed flap.

"No." Shaking herself from her momentary trance, she tore off one end and pulled out the folded piece of paper.

Shadows created by the lapping flames behind her fell across the typewritten words, making their meaning seem doubly forbidding. Steeling herself not to flinch, she read the baneful message:

THIS IS YOUR LAST WARNING.
LEAVE THE CARNIVAL, OR DIE....

Chapter Twelve

More than anything, Lexie wanted to scream. Not because she was scared—it was easy enough to be bold with Rick standing next to her, studying the note—but out of sheer futility and anger. Who was this lunatic, and what was his or her ultimate plan?

"The type looks the same in this note as it did on the ones you and Diana received," Rick said, sounding uncharacteristically surly. "We'll have to compare them, but I think the spacing might be different."

Lexie stared at his grim features. "Is that significant?"

He stuffed the message back in the envelope and jammed it into his pocket. "Details are always significant. You know that, Lexie."

"It's what I used to tell myself—until I got mixed up in this case." She shuddered and started for the stairwell. "Do you realize how many details we've managed to accumulate that add up to absolutely nothing? At least if they do, we can't figure out the answer. I'm a lawyer, and you're an officer of the law. Wouldn't you think between the two of us, we'd be able to come up with—"

The question broke off as Rick halted suddenly and snapped his head up. A second later he was grabbing her and pushing her into the shadows alongside the stairs. "Quiet," he cautioned, although it was hardly necessary. Much as she would have liked it, Lexie knew he wouldn't be inclined to drag her into a darkened corner on a whim.

Since she didn't dare ask him what was going on, she risked a glance over his shoulder—and felt her eyes widen at what, or rather whom, she saw. It was Charles Gideon, and he was moving furtively past the stairs, checking over his shoulder with every careful step he took.

He must have used the lift, but of course he always did, didn't he? She'd just grown so accustomed to the creaking cables that she hadn't noticed the noise this time.

For a moment he paused, half turning to glance behind him, and Lexie suppressed the surprised gasp that leaped into her throat. He was carrying an odd-shaped bundle, paper wrapped and securely tucked under one scrawny arm. She clutched a handful of Rick's jacket, straining to determine Charles's destination as he scuttled past them. Though she quickly lost sight of him, her instincts told her the little squeak she subsequently detected didn't come from the front door.

"He's gone into the basement," Rick said in a low voice. Reaching back, he took her hand. "Come on. I don't want to lose him."

Lexie glanced around the deserted lobby, unsure why her skin felt so clammy and cold. Maybe she was more leery of Charles Gideon than she'd originally suspected.

The unlit cellar smelled dank and musty, like a medieval grotto. There was one tiny window that Lexie could see. Situated below the ceiling beams, it was coated with a thick layer of grime. Like the walls, the stairs were constructed of stone, worn smooth in the center and badly eroded around the edges, the result of hard use and neglect. Stringy cobwebs, heavy with dust, hung loosely from the rafters. A stack of unmarked crates stood to her left next to a bolted wooden door that couldn't have been more than four and a half feet high.

There were many such doors in England, particularly in those buildings dating back to the fifteenth and sixteenth centuries. Lexie supposed there were also many old cellars like this one, replete with hidden alcoves, narrow passageways and sooty, straw-filled chambers that could have told a thousand fascinating tales.

As they descended the stairs, she noticed the rusted metal remnants of something that had once been a wall sconce. It would have been nice if it were still intact and holding a candlestick. The muddy glass let in virtually no light. The basement was dark and airless and full of foreign shadows.

The steady plop of raindrops hitting the cobbles beyond the window was a soothing sound, but insufficient to calm her jumping nerves. Seconds passed slowly, stretching to minutes. Lexie took her cue from Rick and kept silent as they prowled the stale-smelling rooms, opening every door that wasn't locked, rusted shut or just too swollen with moisture to budge. Charles was nowhere to be found, not even in the wine cellar, which Rick checked twice.

To her relief, Lexie discovered a handful of fat candle stubs and a box of matches on one of the shelves. After touching a flame to two of the blackened wicks, she drew her first easy breath. It was amazing what a little light could do. Once the candles were burning, she had no trouble mustering the courage to poke around the basement on her own.

"He must have gone up this back stairway and into the lane," Rick said from the rear of the wine cellar. "Obviously he didn't want to be seen leaving the inn."

Lexie squeezed past a heavy claw-footed chair that resembled a plundered throne, sparing only a brief glance at the shredded brocade and unraveled corner tassels. The bulk of her attention was centered on a stunted door about four feet high that appeared newer than the others. "Rick, did you see this?" she called out, bracing herself and tugging on the handle. "It must be the..."

She didn't get a chance to finish. A blast of down-pouring air extinguished the candle's flame just as she ducked beneath the door's wooden frame. At the same time, she caught her foot on a ledge that jutted out sharply from the threshold. Before her equilibrium could restore itself, she was tumbling into the narrow chute, unable to stop her forward momentum since there no longer seemed to be any floor underneath her.

The sensation of falling lasted for only an instant. She landed hard on her hands and knees, absorbing the impact with her muscles, somehow managing not to hit her head on the wall in front of her.

"Lexie?"

She thought she heard Rick shout her name, but she couldn't be sure. Her mind was still reeling from the fall and the sudden darkness that threw a blanket of sinister shadows over her. For a startled moment she thought the largest of those shadows moved; however, when she twisted her head around she saw nothing in the doorway except a vague outline of the chair she'd noticed earlier.

"I'm here," she replied when Rick called to her again.

"Where's here?" He sounded closer.

Sitting back on her heels, she looked up. "In the elevator shaft, I think." A familiar clacking noise reached her ears, and she grinned, rubbing the dirt off her scraped palms. "I take that back. I'm definitely in the elevator shaft."

"Now why didn't I guess that?" His lazy drawl came from the open door, and Lexie turned to find him crouched down, his forearms resting on one bent knee. "Last night you fell into Skelly's workshop. Today it's the lift shaft. Are you sure you're not hurt?"

"I'm fine. I just dropped my candle." She took the stub he handed to her before he hopped into the shaft himself. "What makes you think I was in Skelly's workshop last night?"

"Because I was in there this morning while you were talking to Diana. So were the three skeletons you told me about."

"And Skelly? Was he around anywhere?"

"Nope." Rick circled her waist with his hands, lifting her to her feet. "For some strange reason, he's been avoiding me lately."

Lexie opened her mouth to dispute the wryly humorous remark, then clamped it shut again when she heard the chair's ball-and-claw feet scrape harshly against the stone floor. Her first thought was that Charles had been in the cellar the whole time. Her second had to do with the shadow she'd dismissed from her mind a few moments ago. And her third was that the door had begun to move.

"Rick!" she screamed, but it was too late. She heard the screech of unoiled hinges followed by a mighty slam that was instantly absorbed by the damp wooden frame.

Just as it had in the fun house, everything took place within the space of two or three seconds: the blunt flash of movement, the blackened silhouette, the bang of the door, the bolt being jammed into place, Rick's automatic reaction and her own. They flung themselves at the solid planking to no avail. All they received for their joint effort was a dull thud from the other side—a hand or perhaps a foot testing the thickness of the wood.

It was too much. Lexie stared at the door in disbelief, her temper snapping at the sight of it. She pounded on the heavy planks with her fists, angry beyond words or rational thought or even tears. She was almost too furious to notice when Rick trapped her flailing wrists in his hands and dragged her back against him, holding her tightly despite her incensed struggles.

"Let me go!" she shouted, trying to squirm from his pinning grasp.

"You're upset," he said simply. "I'll let you go when you calm down."

"I don't want to calm down, and why shouldn't I be upset?" She kicked the weighty door with her foot, venting her rage on it rather than on her human captor. "I've been threatened with notes, and boulders, vans, footsteps in the fog, window messages, reflections of skeletons, hand-crafted skeletons, crystal ball predictions, bullets and now I'm locked in an elevator shaft. Yes, I'm upset. I admit it. Now let me go!"

"Why? So you can bloody your fists on the door?"

"They're my fists." She tried again to twist free of his grip, but he was much too strong for her. And, as she quickly discovered, the more she struggled the more friction she created between them—the kind of friction that caused a very different emotion than anger to surge through her bloodstream. The unconscious grinding of her hips against his thighs, the feel of his arms around her, the fervid memories of last night, the sensations that gripped her now—she let all those things shoot through her, let the strength of her rage stoke each one until the fire inside her had nothing to do with fury or frustration.

He must have noticed the changes. His fingers slackened their hold on her wrists, sliding across her breasts as he slowly turned her to face him. She felt his breath on her lips, saw the glitter of desire in his eyes.

It was a bizarre reaction to a bizarre situation. They were trapped in an elevator shaft, and suddenly, irrationally, all Lexie could think of was how much she wanted him. How much she loved him. And how very much she wanted him to know both those things.

"Are you calm now?" he murmured, grazing her cheekbone with his thumb.

"Not at all," she said. And tipping her head back, she pulled him down, letting her mouth open invitingly beneath his.

THE RASHNESS OF HER ACTION galvanized Rick. He couldn't think of anything except the bold exploration of her tongue and hands, the feel of her body swaying against his and the heated response he had no desire to stave off.

He should have made an effort, he knew that much, but dammit, the relationships—the real relationships—in his life had been few and far between. He loved Lexie, and he suspected she loved him. If he couldn't handle an emotional involvement with a woman and still be an effective cop, then he had no business working at the Yard, and even less business intruding in Lexie's life—both of which he flatly refused to believe.

Against his better judgment, he deepened the kiss, adjusting his hold on her, fitting his body to hers.

He heard it first in the back of his mind: a series of clicks he should have recognized but managed to ignore. Or rather he wanted to ignore them. The longer they persisted, the more the strange noises encroached on his thoughts, building in volume until he could no longer block them out.

He dragged his mouth from Lexie's with a low growl of protest for the interruption, his eyes lifting instinctively to the source of the irritating sound. It took only a split second for his brain to register what was happening, not much more than that for his reflexes to kick in. The curse in his throat became an imperative "Get down" as he thrust Lexie against the wall and shoved her to her knees.

"Oh, my God—!" She breathed the exclamation in a barely audible whisper, then ducked even lower as a horrible creaking filled the air.

The solid black mass of the elevator car was rolling down the narrow shaft, its descent labored and sluggish—relentless. It kept coming, sinking lower and lower on its time-worn runners and ancient cables. Teeth clenched, Rick watched the advancing monster, feeling Lexie move beside him as she pressed her back flat against the wall.

"Stay down," he told her.

"I am down." She managed a quick glance at his face. "I love you, Rick," she murmured. "I want you to know that."

"I love you, too," he said, tightening his arm around her.

Anything else he might have wanted to add, any final words he might have wanted to utter, died in his throat. The car was less than two meters above them now and still dropping.

There was nothing he could do to stop it.

IT WAS DONE....

Eyes closed, the murderer relaxed, welcoming the fierce sense of relief that came from disposing of an enormous problem. Lexie and Rick were dead; they must be by now. Crushed beneath the heavy lift at the Pendragon Inn.

In a way, it was sad that such a gory scene had had to take place without benefit of an audience. Unfortunately, it would have been too risky to linger. Anyone could have wandered into that cellar. And witnesses were something no killer could afford to have.

"Well, now, don't we look relaxed. Hard day?" A woman's all-too-familiar voice scraped across the murderer's nerve ends like sandpaper. "Let me guess." The voice grew blatantly mocking. "You've been running after Lexie and her carny friend again, haven't you?"

Eyes cracked open, the murderer shrugged. "Have I?"

"Oh, you needn't bother denying it. You see, I followed you last night—all the way to the fun house. I know you knocked Wren off, and to be perfectly frank, I think he probably had it coming."

"I'll bet you do."

"I hear he was a killer without a conscience. All he ever cared about was himself."

"And Diana."

Lips compressed, the woman muttered a grudging, "Yes, I expect you're right." Shaking the moody lapse aside she took a seat. "Tell me, was it worth it?"

The murderer's smile was serene. "I haven't the faintest idea what you're talking about."

"You killed him," the woman repeated, waving an airy hand. "If you don't want to come right out and admit it, fine, but don't insult my intelligence by playing silly games. I didn't come here to trap you. I could have done it before now, I'm sure. I only want you to know that I know what you've done."

"Oh, I've no doubt you want much more than that."

She moved her shoulders. "Probably not as much as you think, but yes, now that you mention it, I wouldn't object if you were to slip me a shiny bauble or two. A couple of emeralds perhaps. I've always been partial to green."

She tilted her head to one side, eyes narrowing in contemplation. "I really don't understand you," she said, dropping all pretense. "You knew I came to see Wren in his caravan the night he died, didn't you?"

"I knew."

"Then why did you—"

"You weren't the only one who was in his caravan that night," the murderer interrupted, growing impatient.

There was a lengthy pause before the woman inquired, "Why did you do it? Was it for the jewels?"

It seemed pointless to deny the truth. In a few hours it would all be over anyway. "Partly," the murderer admitted, making a gesture of disinterest. "Most of all, I wanted to repay an old debt, even the score, you might say."

"So you recognized Wren right off."

"Yes."

"And it was always your intention to kill him."

The murderer laughed. "None of your business." A shrewd brow was raised. "As a matter of interest, you wouldn't be taping this conversation, would you?"

Not a flicker of guilt crossed the woman's crafty features. "No tapes, no traps, no tricks," she promised. "All I want is a few sparkling gems, and I'll be on my way. Surely that's a fair deal."

"I'm sure we can work something out."

"When?"

"Tonight. I'll come to your caravan."

"Like you came to Wren's?" The woman snorted her derision. "We'll meet someplace a bit more public, if it's all the same to you."

"As you wish."

Standing, the woman shook her head. "You really are cool about all this," she noted gruffly. "Tell me just one more thing. What have you done with Lexie and Rick?"

The murderer's gaze didn't falter. "I've removed them from the picture."

"I see." Lips quirking, she murmured a sly "I don't suppose you'd be willing to tell me who you really are and what kind of score you had to settle with Wren."

"Let's just say that Wren Sherwood was killed by a ghost from his past," the murderer replied, masking a smug grin. "The spirit of his former partner, Aidan O'Brien."

TWO METERS . . . one and a half . . .

The elevator car continued its onerous descent. Lexie had stopped breathing a long time ago. She didn't want to think but she couldn't help it. The clacking sounds intensified, growing louder, closer. They were going to die. In a matter of seconds the heavy metal base would bear down on them. . . .

Directly above her head—no more than a meter away—she heard the clacking stop with an abruptness so unexpected, so unbelievable that she actually considered the possibility that she might be dead. Nothing moved in the narrow shaft. Not her, not Rick, not the lift.

For several tension-filled seconds time truly did seem to stand still. Then suddenly, the mechanism gave an unwieldy jerk. A moment later she heard the cables begin to creak. The clacking sounds started up again, and she pressed herself into Rick's strong body, darting the swiftest of glances at the cumbersome mass of metal and machinery poised over them.

No, not poised, her shocked mind corrected. The car was climbing, rolling up now rather than down. Moving away from them. They weren't going to die, after all!

If she could have summoned even a particle of energy, she would have jumped up and flung her arms around Rick. Since she couldn't, she settled for letting her head drop onto his shoulder and her body go completely limp against him. . He said something she didn't hear and wrapped his arms around her while her thoughts spun into a semblance of order.

One recollection was very clear to her. He'd said he loved her. She knew she loved him. Where that would lead, she wasn't sure, but she wanted to find out. First things first, though. They still had to get back into the cellar.

Raising her head, she asked, "Do you have your file with you?"

He released her, climbing to his feet and pulling her with him. "No, and it wouldn't help if I did. This door has a bolt, not a lock." He eyed the lift, hanging like a motionless behemoth above them. "We were lucky. This is probably just an access door for repair work. I imagine the car only comes down so far then stops and reverses automatically unless it's keyed into place."

"Wren Sherwood's murderer probably didn't know that," Lexie declared in disgust. "Whoever locked us in here intended to kill us."

An indistinct smile curved Rick's mouth. He cupped her neck with his palm, kissing her soundly. "Too bad the plan didn't work."

"Well, we didn't get crushed," she acknowledged as h crouched to inspect the door. "But we're still stuck in her while the murderer wanders around out there." She tugge on one of the lift's worn metal runners. It was bolted fast to the wall. "If by some miracle we get out of this place be fore we're middle-aged, you should call Scotland Yar again. They might have found more information on Dann Farraday. And even if they haven't, we can still searc Skelly's caravan. I finally got one of the ticket sellers wh likes to spend time with one of his trailer mates to confid in me. She says there's usually no one around between 7:3 and 8:30 p.m. Not that I'm especially eager to hunt throug an ex-undertaker's personal effects, but you have to adm he's been acting awfully strangely—unless, of course, h behavior is considered normal in morticians' circles, i which case—" A quiet chuckle from Rick brought her e rant ramblings to a halt. "What's so funny?"

He leaned against the door, reaching for her. "Nothin I'm just—" his fingers threaded through her silky, brow hair "—enjoying myself."

"You're warped, Rick. In case you haven't noticed, we' trapped in an elevator shaft."

"And plotting our strategy even so," he said, rubbing hi lips lightly over hers.

Lexie's response was forestalled by the muffled but u mistakable sound of voices from another part of the cella It couldn't be Wren's murderer, she reasoned on a spurt c hope. For one thing, this particular murderer, as far as sh knew, had no partner. For another, these people wer laughing.

She glanced up at Rick who'd been listening intently t both voices. Her gaze had scarcely lighted on his face whe he muttered something that didn't sound overly flatterin and gave the door a forceful whack with his fist.

"Open up," he ordered, and the voices immediatel ceased. "In here," he said after a protracted silence, b

Lexie noticed his hand stayed close to the waistband of his jeans as he added a dry, "Sometime today, Charles."

Once the agitated whispers and odd scuffling noises passed, a peculiar hush fell over the basement. At a nod from Rick, Lexie blew out the candle, just as the massive bolt was edged aside.

The door opened slowly, tentatively, swinging back to reveal the astonished face of Sergeant Charles Gideon and a rather contrite-looking Kate.

"I SAY, RICK, I feel bloody awful about this," Charles insisted. "Shirking my duty and all. But, well, it just happened. Kate and myself and the bard of Avon. Would you believe we've been reading *Romeo and Juliet*?"

Rick had a feeling he'd believe almost anything at that moment. Charles and Kate? Together? He bit back a smile and glanced at Lexie, who looked as bemused as he felt. They were in the dining room at the inn, deserted now that afternoon tea had been served, listening to Charles's semi-repentant explanation of his strange behavior these past few days. To say the least, it was an unexpected tale.

"It's really all my fault," Kate inserted softly, returning from the kitchen to set a tray of biscuits and tea on the table. "My schedule here is so very unpredictable." She blushed a little. "We've had to steal whatever time we could between shifts. I'm dreadfully sorry if our relationship has caused Charles to be derelict in his duty."

Lexie stared at the man across from her, obviously not convinced. "I saw you creeping down the hall the night of the thunderstorm with a big bundle under your arm. What was in it?"

Even abashed, Charles managed to affect a lofty posture. "Soiled clothing," he stated succinctly. "I took rather an ungainly spill in the mud on my way to Kate's flat."

"And today?" Rick asked. "What was in that package you were clutching this afternoon?"

"Duck." Charles's voice was tart. "From a restaurant I should not recommend to anyone with a weak stomach."

Lexie sat back in her chair. "Why did you sneak out through the cellar?"

For once, Charles didn't shrink from the question. "I thought by using the rear exit that perhaps no one would notice my comings and goings."

"No one being me," Rick assumed, knowing he should be angry, yet unable to dredge up more than a faint glimmer of annoyance. Charles was guilty of neglecting his assigned duty; he was not a killer. That narrowed the field by one—but only one, Rick reflected, slanting a disinterested glance at the delinquent Scotland Yard sergeant and a much more determined look at the woman he loved.

They still had to find the Saxony jewels. And the person who'd murdered Wren Sherwood.

Chapter Thirteen

Lexie knew she should feel slimy and nefarious as she climbed through the large bedroom window and into Skelly's caravan, but she didn't. Maybe almost being mashed by an elevator changed a person's perspective on such ignoble acts, or maybe she'd simply reached the point where she could justify any shady deed that stood a chance of netting them a murderer.

Scotland Yard certainly wasn't providing many answers. As of fifteen minutes ago when Rick had checked his phone messages, the only thing his friend had been able to tell him was that Danny Farraday's records were still unavailable— or perhaps more correctly lost in some arcane computer shuffle.

Cautiously Lexie climbed across the sill and jumped to the floor, assessing the shabby furniture around her while Rick hoisted himself over the ledge. "I wonder if this is Skelly's room?" she mused. Her doubtful eyes strayed to the long single bed. "I half expected him to sleep in a coffin."

Rick's lips twitched. "You'd better hope he doesn't. I don't carry silver bullets."

"Wooden stakes," she corrected, inching open the closet door.

"Whatever. This is his room. I recognize his pet python."

Lexie spun from the closet to find Rick calmly rummaging through a dresser drawer under scrutiny of a huge coiled snake. How had she missed the beady-eyed reptile? "Is it—" she swallowed weakly "—real?"

"Harry?" The snake's head moved as Rick shut the drawer. "Of course."

Her fingers curled around the edge of the door. "I hate snakes," she stated, teeth gritted, eyes fixed on the sluggish creature. "How could you have let me come through that window first knowing there was a python in here? What if I'd stepped on it?"

"That would have been some step." Rick's grin was anything but apologetic. "I saw him sitting on top of the dresser before I opened the window."

Still grinding her teeth, Lexie turned back to the closet, not trusting herself to say another word, not trusting that fork-tongued, skin-shedding, slithering mass of coils behind her, either. She continued to cast covert glances over her shoulder as she pushed aside hangers and rearranged boxes on the shelf.

"You don't suppose there could be a connection between Skelly and Aidan O'Brien, do you?" she asked, taking another quick look at Harry.

Rick kicked the dresser drawer closed with his foot. "I'll suppose just about anything at this point. If my mate at the Yard doesn't turn up Danny Farraday's records by tomorrow morning, I'll have him start working on Skelly's."

"Wouldn't his background have been checked already?"

"You mean after Wren Sherwood was killed?" Flipping up the drab brown coverlet, Rick peered under the bed. "I doubt it. Remember, all the evidence pointed straight at Diana. The arresting officers didn't know about any disappearing teacups, and I'm sure they never saw Fitz's Scrabble board with Aidan's name spelled out on Sherwood's side. There wouldn't have been any reason to do a background check on any of these people. Besides—" he drew out a light gray case "—much as I hate to admit it, altering personal records isn't a particularly hard thing to do."

"That's not what I wanted to hear," Lexie muttered. But she knew it was true. She'd heard about cases of fraud where false identities went unchallenged for years, sometimes scores of years. It wasn't an encouraging thought.

A fierce sense of determination set in as she knelt down beside Rick and unlatched the case he'd discovered. "No jewels," she announced, removing the lid. "Just an old electric typewriter."

His brows came together in a frown. "What kind?"

"I can't tell. The name's worn off. Does it matter?" she asked, then remembered. "The notes! They were all typed!" Her eyes roamed over the machine, finally landing on the cartridge. With her fingers, she hunted for the release button. "I know these things come out," she mumbled impatiently. "Why aren't any of the levers marked?"

Beneath her questing hands, the typewriter started to purr. Actually, it was more like a rattle. A moment later, Rick inserted the note Lexie had received that afternoon and hit a few of the keys.

"Is the type the same?"

He nodded. "The type is, but something's different."

She located a new button and pushed. The ribbon cartridge immediately popped free. "Got it," she exclaimed in triumph. Careful not to smear the carbon all over herself, she extracted the ribbon from the casing and kept pulling until she found what she was looking for.

"This kind of ribbon can only be used once," she told him, "unlike the nylon ones that can be used over and over again. Each time a key is hit, the carbon is punched directly onto the paper, making it possible to read what's been typed from the tape." Shuddering, she pointed to the words in front of them. "Leave the carnival, or else . . ." she quoted.

"Get rid of your attorney, or else..." Rick indicated the spot where Diana's note was visible. "Two out of three messages came from this machine. Interesting."

Lexie reexamined the entire cartridge, but found no sign of the note she'd gotten early that day. "Why would he use a different typewriter for the third note?" she wondered aloud. "This one isn't broken, and there's still plenty of fresh ribbon."

"There was," Rick said, scooping up the mass of carbon tape and shoving it under the bed. "As for this other note, I think it's time we stopped guessing and starting pinning a few people down. Beginning with our not-so-friendly fun house operator."

"If we can find him. One of many things I've learned during my five days here is that Skelly spends an inordinate amount of time away from his own exhibit."

"And a great deal of it in Gwendolyn's company." Smiling, Rick inclined his head toward the open window. "Shall we go?"

"To have a chat with a fortune-teller?" Lexie grimaced. "I can hardly wait."

"SKELLY? Why, no, I haven't seen him. You might try the fun house. Or possibly the pub. I do let my employees take the occasional night off...."

Victoria's rather hurried words stayed with Lexie long after the carnival owner uttered them. She'd looked anxious, as though she'd had neither the time nor the desire to talk. But at least she'd been available for comment. Gwendolyn seemed to have disappeared.

"You know, if Skelly is the murderer, I don't imagine he'll be expecting to see us," Lexie remarked as she went through the door of the Rose and Crown.

"Not alive, at any rate." Rick scanned the unfamiliar faces in the pub. "Do you see anyone from the carnival?"

"A couple. I think that's Fitz over by the cider press, playing Scrabble with one of his cronies." She took a second look around. "I don't see Skelly, though, do you?"

"No, but he could still show up."

"And he could be back at the fun house, hanging out with a rubber bat or some other creepy puppet he's created. Just because he has a guy filling in for him doesn't mean he isn't there."

Rick's grin was tolerantly amused. "I checked the place, Lexie. Trust me, he isn't there."

"Well, he isn't here, either. And even if he does come, he'll take off again the moment he spots us."

"In which case, we'll have to choose our ambush site wisely."

She couldn't hold back a smile. "You have a pat rebuttal for everything, don't you?"

"I try." He steered her toward a small table to the right of the dart board, but didn't sit down. "I want to talk to Fitz for a few minutes. I'll order us a drink on my way back."

Lexie chose a chair facing the door. "What should I do if I see Skelly?"

Rick's lips quirked. "Duck under the table—what else?"

"Why did I ask?" she said with a sigh.

Leaning forward, she cupped her chin in her hands and surveyed the Friday-night crowd. Some of the people she recognized from her previous visit, but Burt Drury, the man with the pointy white whiskers, wasn't among them—a circumstance that seemed to be the predominant topic of conversation with his friends.

Resolutely, Lexie blocked out their heated grumbles and turned her mind to the typewriter tape she and Rick had found in Skelly's caravan. He'd obviously used it to write two of the threatening notes; it only made sense that he'd also been responsible for the third. So why hadn't the words been visible on the carbon ribbon?

"She's as evil as Old Scratch himself." One of the louder grumbles cut in on Lexie's thoughts. "Mark me, none but the devil would let such a fiend tell his fortune. Stepping on a dog's sore paw, indeed. She should be boiled in oil, she should."

Lexie resisted the urge to nod her agreement. These men had to be talking about Gwendolyn, just as they'd been doing the last time she'd come here. It appeared the disagreeable fortune-teller was not especially popular with the pub's patrons.

She was popular with Skelly, though. Was it possible that Gwendolyn had borrowed the man's typewriter to compose those notes? Everyone apparently knew she'd had an affair with Wren. Three months was ample opportunity to discover a person's real identity.

Of course, anybody at the carnival could have learned about Wren's felonious past—if in fact his crimes really had been in the past. After looking through Victoria's accounting books, Lexie suspected the man hadn't exactly been leading an upstanding life these last two years.

The myriad possibilities began to whirl through her head again. Clues and details that seemed to lead nowhere, but had to mean something. Two teacups, a dropped gun, notes, warnings, Scrabble letters that spelled Aidan . . .

In all but the last instance, it was the fortune-teller's name that sprang to mind. And yet, there was no real proof against her, nothing except a lot of nagging doubts and suspicions.

"Drove all the way to Tavistock, Burt did." Another coarse growl near the dart board diverted Lexie's attention. "This would be the second trip to the vet's he's made since that carnival witch stomped on Gordon's sore paw. First was the day that jewel thief got himself shot. Left before tea, they did. Poor old Burt. He and his hound missed all the fuss. Told him about it, I did, when he came home next morning, but it just wasn't the same."

The man's playing partner snorted. "Too bad it wasn't the fortune-teller who took the bullet. Now that would have been a right fair bit of justice."

Gwendolyn again. Lexie dragged her attention away from the vinegary old men and tried to concentrate on her investigation. Her eyes flicked absently to the table where Fitz had been sitting a moment ago. He was gone. So was Rick, she noticed with a small frown. Well, that was just wonderful. Skelly could walk through the front door any second now. The way her luck had been going lately, he'd probably haul her out into the lane and—

The lane!

The words sliced through her jumbled thoughts with a stroke so sudden, so intense that she almost forgot to breathe. She snatched herself upright in her chair. Out in the lane!

An icy chill crawled across every inch of her skin, the muscles in her throat constricting as disbelief slowly changed to dread. Her temples began to pound. Oh, Lord, it all made sense. Horrible, evil sense.

A frozen feeling of calm settled over her. Her response was swift, instinctive, her mind alert, stripped of all the confusion that had previously impaired her thoughts.

She shoved her chair back roughly, searching the crowded pub for Rick, not finding him. Where was he? A feeling of desperation rose inside her. Desperation and terror. She couldn't be wrong about this. Everything fitted. Finally, she knew who had killed Wren Sherwood.

With one last unavailing look for Rick, Lexie made her decision. Battling the barbs of fear that attacked her nervous system, she made her way along the wall to the door and slipped out into the cool night mist. Her eyes focused automatically on the lights of the distant carnival. Somehow, without looking at her watch, she was aware of the time: 9:15, forty-five minutes until closing.

Shoulders squared, she started for the glittering lights. There was only one thing she could do. Before it was too late, she had to find the murderer.

THE FIRST THING Rick did when he came out of the washroom was look at the chair where Lexie had been sitting moments before. It was empty. He glanced back in the direction of the rest rooms, then crossed to the table where Fitz and one of his carny cohorts had been playing Scrabble for the past half-hour. Although the wily informant wasn't in his seat, the other man was still watching the door as Rick had requested.

"Fitz nipped 'round to the tobacco shop," the barker everyone called Chimmy explained. "I been keeping a lookout, but I've not seen Skelly." He swallowed the last of his ale. "Now that you're back, I'll get me another pint. Maybe it'll improve my vocabulary for the next game."

Chimmy was gone before Rick could ask him about Lexie, but since it seemed unlikely that she would have strayed much farther than the ladies' room, he straddled Fitz's chair, switching his thoughts to the less palatable subject of murder.

Frowning in contemplation, he rearranged the letters before him, just as Wren had apparently done the night he'd died. Fitz claimed that Sherwood had left his booth midgame. Why? Had he spied Aidan O'Brien? Could the man still be alive? Or had Fitz been lying? About the name, about everything? No one had ever accused P. J. Fitzwilly of being a fool. He was shrewd, discerning and extremely clever.

He was also taking his sweet time at the tobacco shop, Rick reflected, lifting his brooding gaze to the door. How the hell hard could it be to buy a package of cigars? And where was Lexie?

His patience ebbing slightly, Rick shoved the letters away and started to rise. He stopped suddenly halfway to his feet, his attention riveted by something he'd missed earlier.

It hit him with the same violent impact as a blow to the stomach. Aidan... Aidan O'Brien! That was it! How could he have overlooked something so obvious? There *was* a connection after all. A lethal connection.

Swearing through his teeth, he shouldered his way across the floor, only vaguely aware of the low-lying mist that slunk about his legs when he reached the street. He spotted Charles coming toward him, and without a moment's hesitation moved to cut him off.

"Come now, Rick!" The sergeant launched a feeble protest while endeavoring to maneuver out of range. "Not you, too."

"Not me, too, what?" Rick didn't slow down. Reaching out, he grabbed his partner's arm, dragging him along to the edge of town.

Charles squirmed. "I say, where are we going? For heaven's sake, my dear chap, I just left the carnival. Surely you're not about to make me go back."

Rick glanced at the man. "You just left?" he repeated, his muscles tightening painfully. "Did you see Lexie?"

"If you can call it that. She charged past me like a bloody thoroughbred, just as you almost did when you came flying out of the pub."

"Where was she?"

"In the arcade."

"Which direction was she going?"

"East. Steady on, Inspector," Charles fussed, slipping on the wet grass. "I really must protest this breakneck pace you've set. I'm hardly dressed for an Olympic sprint." He stumbled again, but this time it was because he'd bumped into Rick's back. "Oh, what's this, then?" His arms flailed wildly as he fought for balance. "I'm not a blooming yo-yo."

Stifling a snarl, Rick whirled the man around and gave him a shove back toward the village. Dragging Charles through the carnival was no solution. It would make matters worse, if that was possible.

"Find Constable Chance," he ordered, checking his gun. "Tell him to bring his men and meet me outside the carnival gates."

"Constable Chance!" Charles drew himself erect. "What on earth for?"

"To catch a murderer," Rick told him darkly, jamming the gun into the waistband of his jeans. "A very clever murderer."

IT WAS DARK, hideously dark. And damp. A gossamer mist had crept in from the moors, seeping over the meadow like a filmy layer of white cobwebs that rose no higher than Lexie's knees, lending a strangely supernatural air to the still-active carnival.

A chill rushed across her skin. God, everything felt so creepy. It was as though she'd stepped into some kind of fantasia that existed in the clouds. Even the calliope music sounded wrong, off-key by half a note.

People floated past her on the midway, drifting vaporously toward the gates. They all had vacant expressions on their faces. Like mannequins, she reflected, then shook herself. This was no time to be entertaining nightmarish thoughts. The real horror was still out there. She had to find and confront it, preferably before the carnival closed.

An array of brightly colored lights blinked at her; voices warbled from behind megaphones. All the sights and sounds and smells should have been so familiar, but instead they seemed foreign, barely recognizable to her disturbed senses. She climbed noiselessly over the lines outside the equipment tent, telling herself she might be wrong, yet knowing it was a forlorn hope. Too many of the pieces fitted and there was simply no way to justify the two conflicting statements that continued to race through her head.

A throaty grunt from the rear of the tent alerted Lexie to an unknown presence. Deeply grateful for the wealth of sound behind her, she ducked into the shadows and risked a cautious glance around the edge of the canvas. Her eyes locked instantly on the woman who emerged from the pool of darkness.

It was Gwendolyn, and she wasn't alone, Lexie realized with a combined jolt of uneasy antagonism. There was someone else lurking in the pitchy region of the awning. Someone with whom the fortune-teller was calmly conversing. A black-clad figure who had to be Wren Sherwood's murderer. Although Lexie couldn't imagine how Gwendolyn fitted into the picture, she got no sense of a long-standing partnership between these two people. Snakes, she thought cynically, tended to do their nastiest work alone.

Tapping a flashlight experimentally in one gloved palm, the sanguine figure emerged from the shadows, teeth flashing wolfishly in the pearly light, confirming Lexie's suspicions. "Time to leave," came the bloodless announcement. "You will of course stay five steps ahead of me."

Gwendolyn's lips curled, but she didn't demur. "Where are we going?"

"To a place I know." The murderer motioned her forward. "A legendary realm."

Lexie's gaze rose to the crumbling tower of Wexford Castle. But it was so far away, and they were walking. She glanced over her shoulder at the outline of Algernon's workshop. That made more sense, yet the twosome appeared to be moving in the opposite direction.

She had to follow them. She didn't want to, but what else could she do?

The question hung in her mind along with a host of other pernicious thoughts and vengeful possibilities. She refused to examine any of them. Instead, she crept around the side of the tent, hugging the shadowy canvas walls, determined not to lose the pair in front of her.

They looked to be riding the gauzy mist as they struck out for the caravan row single file, with the murderer several paces behind the fortune-teller, keen eyes combing the area ahead, seldom bothering to glance back.

Nevertheless, Lexie made a point of clinging to whatever dark spaces she could find. Her lungs ached from not breathing and she was sweating lightly by the time she'd trailed them to Wren Sherwood's caravan.

"Keep going," the murderer intoned when Gwendolyn would have halted.

Lexie immediately flattened herself against the side of the trailer as the fortune-teller unexpectedly twisted around on the broken ground. "In there?" She sounded incredulous. "What kind of a fool do you take me for?"

One gloved finger slid along the caravan's grimy outer wall, so close that Lexie could hear the rasp of wool across the pitted paint. She forced herself not to inch backward.

"A greedy one," the murderer answered. "Now, I suggest you do as I say."

The threat was silky but unmistakable. For the first time Gwendolyn actually seemed nervous. Eyes darting about, she half turned and continued trudging forward—right into the sparse stand of trees where the intruder who'd been in Wren's trailer had vanished three nights ago.

By slipping from trunk to trunk, Lexie was able to keep the pair in sight. When they stopped next to a malformed stump, she quickly crouched, her nails biting into the papery bark of a sapling ash.

Heart thumping, she strained to see through the deepening murk, simultaneously fascinated and infuriated as the murderer tugged a thick clump of bracken away from the stump's base. With a flourish three weathered strips of wood were removed and quickly hidden from sight beneath a sprawling patch of briars.

"What's this?" Gwendolyn demanded harshly, but Lexie didn't need to hear the figure's response to understand. She'd already drawn the imaginary line in her head. A line that ran from the tower of Wexford Castle to the old Roman fortress on the outer rim of the meadow.

The murderer had discovered the tunnel that led to Algernon's workshop! Suddenly, everything about Wren Sherwood's death fell neatly into place.

No, not quite everything, Lexie amended, cursing herself silently. She'd taken her eyes off the tunnel entrance just long enough to look up at the castle. In doing so, she'd lost track of her quarry.

Or had she?

A tiny click mere inches behind her was succeeded by the feel of something cold and steely being pressed against her nape. A layer of ice formed over her heart, spreading through her body, numbing her terror as the murderer's smug voice crooned in her ear.

"So, Lexie, it looks like you got what you came for, after all. You found Wren Sherwood's killer." The voice dropped to a satiny whisper. "How unfortunate that no one will ever find you."

Chapter Fourteen

Shifting the gun to the small of Lexie's back, the murderer shoved her forward, down a set of crudely formed stone steps and into the moldy tunnel where Gwendolyn was nervously pacing.

"Pull the bracken over the opening, and keep your questions to yourself," the fortune-teller was instructed in a tone that brooked no argument. "As for you—" the metal barrel dug into Lexie's spinal column "—I'm not even going to ask how you escaped from that lift shaft. All I want to know is how you figured out the truth."

A thousand spiky shards of anger unleashed themselves in Lexie's brain. She wanted to scream, to fight and kick and punch, to lock this lying trot away for thirty lifetimes. "You made a mistake," she replied, holding fast to her feelings of spite, fighting the tremors that would have betrayed her terror.

"You lead, Gwendolyn," the murderer ordered, and in the glow of the fortune-teller's flashlight Lexie glimpsed a white-lipped look of fear that hadn't been as pronounced earlier. "We'll follow. First Lexie, then me."

A sharp jab from the gun accompanied the serene statement, heightening the bitter sense of treachery that Lexie had so far refused to dwell on. Swallowing hard, she took a step forward, willing herself not to flinch as the remnants of a sticky spiderweb glued itself to her cheek.

"Now stop and turn around. I want to see you."

Until that moment Lexie had managed to avoid a face-to-face confrontation. Somehow it made things easier. She could almost convince herself that this was all a hideous nightmare.

"Turn or I'll shoot you."

Lexie fortified her defences, swinging around in a burst of rage and fright, unsure which emotion was stronger—until she saw the murderer's expression: placid amusement stamped upon features that could have been carved from a block of ice.

A feeling of panic gripped her, clawing at her stomach, threatening to undermine her defiant stance. This person, this killer was devoid of compassion and undoubtedly every other charitable emotion. A wintry gleam shone from deep within a pair of burning eyes. Ice on fire, Lexie thought dismally, trembling at the sight. Not crazy eyes. Not really. Just cold and calculating and temporarily brightened by her reaction.

"How did you know?" the murderer inquired with a reptilian smile that seemed even more grotesque in the mutable glow of the flashlight.

Lexie edged backward, conscious of Gwendolyn hovering uneasily by the lichen-infested tunnel wall. "I learned that Burt Drury and his dog were in Tavistock the night Wren Sherwood was shot," she choked.

"Burt and his dog?" The murderer frowned. "How could that possibly have...?" The question trailed off, dissolving into a chuckle and then a reckless peal of laughter that was instantly sucked away by the rank earth around them. "How meticulous of you," the figure applauded, still chortling. "You actually picked up on a mistake as insignificant as that, and yet you overlooked the most obvious one of all. The name."

Lexie licked her dry lips. "Whose name?"

"Mine." The teeth looked pointed now in the opalescent light, not unlike fangs. "Mine and Aidan O'Brien's. One and the same, Lexie, if you'd only taken the time to think it through."

One and the same. Aidan O'Brien and— "Oh, my God," Lexie breathed as the letters dropped woodenly into place in her benumbed brain. "It's an anagram. Your name and his. Aidan O'Brien." She squeezed her eyes closed. "And Diana Beroni."

AIDAN O'BRIEN. Diana Beroni. It was so simple. A child could have seen it. Or a Scrabble player, in Wren Sherwood's case.

"Pardon me, ladies, if I may be so bold." Gwendolyn sounded anything but bold to Lexie's still-reeling mind. "Aren't we forgetting someone?"

Diana's eyes took on a rancorous light. "Who?"

"Lexie's shadow."

"Ah, yes, the Scotland Yard inspector." She laughed, her hostility fading. "Don't look so shocked, Gwendolyn. Surely you suspected Rick was no carny. Not that it matters," she added, moving closer and rubbing the tip of the gun barrel up and down Lexie's arm. "Lawyer-client privilege and all that. You didn't tell him a thing, did you?" she crooned in a low taunt.

Lexie held her body rigid. This woman was pond scum. "I—no," she responded in a restrained voice, trying desperately to think. There had to be something she could say. "I don't— Diana, why are you doing all this?"

"All what?"

"The death threats, the elevator at the inn. Why try to kill me? It doesn't make any sense. As your lawyer, I couldn't have turned you in."

With a shrug, Diana shoved her forward. "Walk," she ordered Gwendolyn. Then to Lexie, she murmured mocking, "Maybe you couldn't have turned me in, but Rick could have. Besides, who would suspect an accused murderer of trying to kill her attorney? I rather thought I was being clever. You must admit, everyone looked guilty for a while. Everyone except me." Her smile was deceptively sweet. "Now move while you still can."

The tunnel smelled of decaying animal and plant matter, though Lexie found it hard to care. The gun Diana held was lodged at the base of her spine, and there was absolutely no doubt in her mind that the weapon would be used. On her and likely Gwendolyn, as well.

Thankfully, it was only a short distance to the crawlway that opened into the bowels of the old Roman fortress. Here, in Algernon's workshop, the walls were constructed mainly of stone, crumbling badly in a few spots, but still relatively intact. Two of the five dark passageways that branched off from the main room appeared to be blocked with a mixture of dirt and rock and rotted wood, and the staircase leading down from the level above was little more than a pile of broken rocks. However, the air was noticeably less fetid than it had been in the tunnel, the more persistent whorls of fog that floated along the ravaged ceiling visible proof that the meadow wasn't impossibly far away.

If Diana's attention could be diverted, Lexie knew she might yet have a chance to escape.

On that devout prayer she scraped up every gram of courage she possessed and turned to look at the woman who was leaning against one of the sturdier sections of the wall with a frighteningly self-assured smile on her lips. "Why did you do it?" she queried softly, masking her fear with a gargantuan effort.

Leaving her flashlight burning, Diana set it down on a pile of rubble next to a fragmented archway and glanced at her watch. "Twenty minutes until closing," she announced, then laughed. "Sit, Gwendolyn," she bade the edgy for-

tune-teller. "Over there on the stairs. I'm going to tell yo‹
a short story."

"But Lexie isn't—"

"I said sit!" Her velvet whisper contained a warning mor‹
potent than any shouted command. Lexie's entire body wer‹
clammy as she regarded the woman's distantly amused fa‹
cial cast.

Diana ran her fingers lovingly over her gun as she peere‹
idly into the adjoining chamber. "To begin with, I didn'‹
actually plan to kill Wren. I only wanted the Saxony jewels.‹
Her eyes glittered. "The ones Wren murdered my ste‹
brother, Aidan, to obtain."

Lexie had risked taking a couple of steps away from th‹
staircase, but she stopped in her tracks at the embittere‹
statement. "Aidan O'Brien was your stepbrother?"

"My mother married Aidan's father." Diana moved he‹
shoulders, frowning slightly as a small stone clattere‹
somewhere deep in the ruin. "They're all dead now. But I'‹
still very much alive, and I wanted Wren to pay. It starte‹
off well. A perfect scheme, you might say. Wren had nev‹
seen me, didn't even know I existed. I had only to loca‹
him, which was time-consuming but not particularly diff‹
cult. You see, Aidan told me all sorts of juicy little thin‹
about his sleazy partner, including his fondness for carn‹
vals. So I started searching, and eventually I tracked hi‹
down. From there it was simply a matter of getting myse‹
hired—an easy enough feat since I am a dancer—an‹
worming my way into Wren's thoroughly repulsive affe‹
tions. It took me five long months, but I finally got him ‹
confide in me about the jewels, and on the eve of his deat‹
no less."

Lexie thought she heard another pebble clatter along o‹
of the walls, though no one else seemed to notice it. Car‹
fully, covertly, she sidled toward the nearest passageway. ‹
was probably asking too much for a bolt of lightning ‹
strike Diana dead where she stood. No, escaping from th‹

place would require skill, timing and a huge dose of luck. "Why did you use an anagram of Aidan's name?" she asked.

"Because I wanted to beat Wren at his own game," Diana's tone was frigid. "I was going to take the jewels and leave a gloating letter in my wake. A flagrant taunt he would never have forgotten—or bested. Unfortunately, things didn't work out that way."

"He unscrambled the anagram, didn't he?" Lexie guessed, recalling the Scrabble board in Fitz's game booth.

"Quite by accident, yes. Nevertheless—" she waved the gun toward the carnival "—always the arrogant fool, he made the mistake of coming into the dance tent while I was onstage. One look at his face and I knew he'd figured it out. Oh, he tried to stay in the shadows, but I saw him. And I realized he'd kill me the first chance he got." She moved to lean against a precariously tilted section of the wall. "Since I wasn't about to allow that, I snuck into his caravan on my break and took his gun. Then I went back to the dance tent and finished my show."

In the distance Lexie heard a burst of calliope music and realized the carnival was still open. Unobtrusively she traced the beam of Diana's flashlight. If mist could seep into the fortress, light could surely filter out. It was a meager hope, but she clung to it. Drawing a deep breath, she asked, "What about your walk on the moors that night?"

Diana's teeth flashed again, reminding her of vampire fangs. "Obviously I didn't take my usual walk, as you so shrewdly perceived."

"But you must have left the carnival. There are witnesses who saw you go."

"Oh, I left, all right. I just didn't make it to the moors—or to the lane by the pub where I would normally have stopped to pet Burt Drury's dog." As casually as if she were ticking off items on a grocery list, she flipped open the bullet chamber on her gun and began counting. "You know

that really was a brilliant piece of detective work you did. It
never occurred to me that old Burt and his dog might no[
have been at the pub that fateful night." She slapped the
loaded chamber back into place, cocking the hammer at the
precise instant Lexie curled her fingers around the edge o[
the entranceway to the corridor. Without so much as [
sideways glance, she smiled and aimed the barrel at Lexie'[
hand, murmuring a cheerful, "One more step, and your arm
will end at your wrist. Now, where was I?"

Clamping down on her terror, Lexie pried her hand from
the cornerstone. "You were telling us about your walk."

"Oh, yes." Diana's smile widened, leaving the impres[
sion that she thoroughly enjoyed watching people squirm.

"Guttersnipe," Lexie muttered bitterly. Maybe God
would be merciful and make the gun explode in her smug
face when she pulled the trigger.

"Did you say something?" Diana inquired sweetly.

"No. Go on. What about your walk?"

Diana's eyes glittered. "Yes, well, naturally, I made [
pretense of leaving the grounds. Then I ducked down her[
into Algernon's work shop. You see, I discovered the tun[
nel about ten days before I shot Wren. Quite by accident, [
might add. It came in rather handy that night. I was able t[
surface in the woods, sneak into Wren's caravan, pull th[
trigger, run back through the tunnel, alter my usual route t[
compensate for lost time, return to the carnival as I alway[
did and find my lover's body."

Keep her talking, a small voice in Lexie's brain in[
structed, though she wasn't sure what good it would do[
"Why did you pick up the gun and fire it again?" she quer[
ied, while behind her, Gwendolyn began to stir in he[
makeshift seat.

"Because I wasn't sure about the powder residue." Dian[
pushed herself restlessly from the wall, surveying the packe[
dirt of the ceiling. "I didn't have a chance to put on a pai[
of gloves when I shot Wren, but I thought it wouldn't ma[

ter. I knew I could wipe away my fingerprints. It wasn't until I'd left the caravan that I remembered something about gunpowder, how it penetrates pores and material. Since I couldn't wash it off, and since I knew the police would test me for residual traces, I had to think of another plan fast." She sauntered toward the stairs, her pale features so waxy that they didn't look real. "I decided to take a blind shot at the person who responded to my exceptionally well-acted screams. Admittedly, that strategy was risky, but I really had no other choice."

With a dancer's grace she knelt beside the staircase, removed a loose stone and extracted a sack of what appeared to be trash. Keeping the gun pointed at Lexie she delved among crumpled wrappers, soggy napkins and paper cups to remove a stained and tired cigar box. "Unappealing but effective," she said, grimacing at the unpleasant odor of spoiled garbage. A spark of amusement passed through her dark eyes and she dropped her gaze to her watch. "Time marches on. If there's anything else you want me to explain, you'd better ask now. As the saying goes: I've a train to catch."

It was Gwendolyn who spoke up, fists clenched, eyes blazing with accusation as she said, "You never intended to share any part of your swag, did you?"

The amusement became a tranquil smile. "No."

"You set me up. With the jewels. With everything."

"Mmm, well, I had a bit of help to that end," Diana admitted, kicking the garbage away. "Skelly, your devoted guard dog, was an effective, albeit unwitting, ally. Unless I'm mistaken, he actually thought it was you who murdered Wren."

"Me! That's bloody ridiculous."

"Personally, I felt it was bloody marvelous," Diana countered indifferently. "Until your nitwit friend started botching things. I'm afraid, however, that's a story I have no time to tell."

From a point beyond the central chamber, Lexie detected a subdued sound that could have been a spray of loose earth showering down from the ceiling. Diana heard it, too, and immediately swung her gun toward the corridor.

"Who's there?" she snapped, her serenity evaporating. Her moods, it seemed, could shift very quickly. When no response issued from the shadowy passage, she impaled Lexie with a deadly glare. "Rick?" She called his name as she jammed the cigar box inside her zippered jacket.

"Algernon!" A burst of coarse condemning laughter spilled from Gwendolyn's throat. "It's Algernon. It's your turn to pay, Diana."

"Oh, shut up," Diana spat. With the swiftness of an angry cobra, she bridged the small gap to grab Lexie's arm and twist it around behind her back. Angrily she shoved the gun under Lexie's chin, partly cutting off her air supply. "I'm not in the mood for games. Whoever's here, you'll either show yourself now, or I'll kill both these women right in front of you."

Pain shot along her arm to her shoulder, but Lexie managed to choke out a frantic "There's no one here, Diana. You're imagining things."

The words had no sooner left her mouth when the entire rear wall seemed to come alive. Her arm was jerked higher on her back. Shadows swam dizzily before her eyes, mingling with a blotchy darkness that all but consumed her as a fresh bolt of pain streaked through her body. Diana's nails bit into her skin, drawing blood. The gun was lodged against her windpipe and for a horrible moment, she was certain the whole chamber was going to shake apart.

Lexie was only distantly aware of Gwendolyn's cries of retribution and something about Algernon. Her mind, her surroundings, everything became a blur. She tasted the powdery fine dust that suddenly pervaded the moist air, and despite the punishment being inflicted on her arm, found herself watching in shock as the foundations of the wall before her collapsed, not all at once but slow motion, stone by stone, until there was nothing left to support the weight of the heavy structure.

In her ear she heard Diana's displeased reaction. Between the roar of cascading rocks and the disbelief that momentarily gripped the woman behind her, Lexie recognized that this would undoubtedly be her one and only chance to escape. She didn't waste a second. Unable to breathe properly with the dust billowing around her, she tried the first thing that came to mind and brought her free elbow back, directing it into Diana's ribs. She felt the sickening crunch of a bone breaking, then almost choked on the scream that was torn from her lungs as her arm was very nearly ripped out of its socket.

Diana's fingers were incredibly strong, like talons, and she somehow maintained a stranglehold on the gun. But she was also off balance, fighting hard not to pitch backward. Muscles straining, Lexie seized the opportunity, working herself around and easing the pressure on her shoulder, concurrently knocking the gun away with her unbound fist.

A shot exploded inside the ruin, but she disregarded it, wrenching her trapped arm loose instead—and stripping both Diana and herself of their tenuous balance in the process. Through the churning mass of dust and fog, she saw the woman stumble headfirst into the newly formed mound of broken stones. She might very well have plunged into it herself if something hadn't checked her fall.

She felt the strong forearm that spanned her waist preventing the harmful spill. Again the breath was snatched from her lungs, but this time she had trouble getting it back. Even knowing that it was Rick who'd caught her from behind didn't help. A string of profane squawks rent the air as Gwendolyn made a desperate rush for the tunnel entrance in response to the nebulous apparition that arose from the pile of rubble.

It looked like a phoenix rising from the ashes, or more aptly Algernon rising from the depths of his workshop. But that simply wasn't possible. Was it?

Instinctively Lexie slammed herself back into Rick's solid body, struggling to rationalize the bizarre sight.

Mixed in with Gwendolyn's crass curses, she heard Algernon's name and at length became conscious of the fact that Rick was calmly staring down at a rather groggy Diana, not seeming the least bit interested in any phantoms.

"Come back here, you cheeky little scrubber."

The instant the apparition spoke, Lexie recognized his voice. Unless Algernon had spent some time on the streets of London, the awakening ghost was none other than P. J. Fitzwilly.

Weak with relief, she sagged against Rick, who hooked an arm about her shoulders to keep her on her feet. "Are you all right?" he asked, taking his eyes but not his gun off Diana's sprawled form.

"As always," she lied. "How did you know where we were?"

"Fitz was coming out of the tobacco shop near the pub when you started along the path for the carnival." Rick nodded at the wiry little man now unconcernedly lighting a cigar while one sturdy elbow kept Gwendolyn securely pinned to the fortress wall. "He followed you, then sent one of the other carnies up to the village to find me."

Lexie stared at the heap of shattered stone. "Did you bring the wall down, too, Fitz?"

His dark eyes sparkled. "Don't know as I should answer that one, Miss Lexie, there being a Scotland Yard inspector present and all. Could be some who'd liken toppling such a wall to painting a mustache on a picture of the Queen. Let's all agree that old Algernon wanted in on the fun and games and leave it at that."

Fun and games? Lexie could have disputed the term; however, a murderous glower from Diana had her quelling the impulse. Her arm ached from shoulder to wrist, and she was still grappling with an assortment of conflicting emotions, the most prevalent being lawyer-client privilege versus the bitter sense of betrayal. Diana Beroni—or whatever her real name was—deserved to be thrown in prison for the rest of her natural life. Vindictive or not, Lexie couldn't help hoping that when all was said and done the presiding magistrate would come across with a life sentence, then turn around and toss the key to Diana's cell in the Thames.

Removing his arm from Lexie's shoulders, Rick crouched in front of Aidan O'Brien's scheming stepsister, a lazy smile curving his lips as he regarded her icy features. "Taken up smoking, have you, Diana? Or can I assume that box sticking out of your jacket is something other than a container for cheap cigars?"

"Go to hell!" she spat, but Rick merely shrugged and deftly plucked the box away before she could rake him with her claws.

"Sorry, lady," he drawled, handing the long-lost Saxony jewels to Lexie. "The only person going to hell tonight is you."

"DIANA'S A MURDERER, Charles is a lousy police officer, Skelly's a fool, Victoria has disgustingly bad judgment, Gwendolyn is slimy and corrupt, and you, Fitz, are a wonderful human being." Lexie hoisted herself onto one of the painted carousel horses, sitting sideways across its motionless back and resting her shoulder against the pole. "How's that for an accurate summation?"

Grinning, Fitz flipped a series of switches inside the round's central column. Within seconds the ride sprang to life, running more smoothly than it had for days now. "Meself, I fancy the last part," he confided. "As for the rest—" he took a short puff on his cigar "—well, I've always found it in me own best interests to forgive and forget."

"Forget that Diana's a killer? Fitz, she tried to drop an elevator on Rick and me."

"Don't you think you're forgetting something here, Miss Lexie?" Fitz queried gently.

"Forgetting what? That she tried to set someone else up to pay for her crimes? That she shot a man? Granted, he was a creep, but she had no right to shoot him."

"Before he could shoot her," Fitz inserted. Then he gave his head a sorrowful shake. "No, she's a bad apple, right enough, I'll not deny that. But inside—" he tapped his forehead "—she's all twisted up, she is."

"You think she's crazy?" Lexie didn't buy that explanation for a minute.

"Hungry." Fitz supplied a more appropriate term. "It was revenge she wanted."

"She got it."

"Aye, that she did, but at a cost so dear, she couldn't see her way clear to pay. And that's when the twisting got a hold on her."

"You mean she could justify anything she felt she had to do after she murdered Wren Sherwood?"

Nodding, Fitz puffed on his cigar. "'Once the killing starts...'" he quoted. "The road to redemption will be a mite bumpy for that one, I'm afraid."

And rightly so, Lexie thought, though she didn't admit as much to Fitz. Her feelings of spite were too new to allow for objectivity. In time she would probably soften, but for the present she was glad to be unofficially off the case and away from the Scotland Yard detectives who had arrived on the scene within an hour of her ex-client's arrest. Or was it rearrest?

"Will your legal firm be representing Diana?" Fitz inquired, the canny light in his eyes indicating he already knew the answer.

Lexie gave him one in any event. "No. I spoke to Malcolm Sutcliffe an hour ago. Once he woke up and recovered from his shock, he immediately agreed that the firm of Bardsley, Sutcliffe and Townsend could no longer be handling the legal affairs of Ms. Diana Beroni, or whatever her name is."

"Fiona Flynn of Dungarven, Ireland."

Lexie's eyes narrowed. "How do you know that?"

"I heard the coppers conversing." A foxy grin appeared on Fitz's narrow face. "It seems Fiona Flynn changed her name to Diana Beroni two years ago. All lawful and above-board it was, too. Just in case Wren got a notion to check her records, she wanted him to find no ties between her and her late stepbrother."

"So she used an anagram of Aidan's name instead." Lexie shifted position on the bobbing horse. "That wasn't particularly smart."

"Maybe not, but it almost worked." The indolent comment floated over Lexie's shoulder, and twisting around in her seat, she spied Rick smiling lazily at her, not looking anywhere near as exhausted as he should have at three in the morning. In fact, he seemed positively refreshed. With one lithe move he rounded the horse, deftly circling her waist and unseating her. "I might also add that if she hadn't used an anagram of O'Brien's name, the Saxony jewels would still be missing, and in all likelihood we'd still be searching for Wren Sherwood."

"Who would still be alive," Lexie was quick to counter.

"True," Rick conceded. "However, minus the jewels, it's a good bet he would have either hunted Diana down and killed her or planned another heist to make up for what he'd lost, murdering God knows how many people in the process."

"Then again, he might have chosen to follow my shining example and sworn off a life of crime for the rest of his earthly days," Fitz suggested. Chuckling, he gave them a wink and politely touched his derby. "I believe I'll be on me way now, Miss Lexie, Inspector. I reckon I've got this story about as straight as I ever will.''

Lexie watched the spry little man hop nimbly from the merry-go-round, wishing she felt as satisfied as he obviously did. She still had half a hundred unanswered questions whizzing through her head.

"Did you say something?" Rick asked, and with a mildly surprised start, she realized he'd steered her over to one of the ornately carved booths and drawn her onto his lap.

She was tired, she decided, biting back a smile. Tired but still alive, and well on the way to getting her second wind. Wrapping her arms around his neck, she replied, "Maybe I did. There's a lot of things I don't understand yet."

Rick shifted to sit lengthwise in the booth, rearranging her so that her head was leaning back against his shoulder. "Okay, fire away."

She thought for a minute, then asked, "When did you figure out the anagram?"

"Right after you figured out that Diana's account of her walk couldn't possibly have been true."

"What about the other people?"

"You mean Skelly and Gwendolyn?"

"For a start."

She felt his lips move against her hair, against her ear. "I'll give you the condensed version of that tale. To begin with, Diana was right: Skelly did think Gwendolyn killed Wren Sherwood. He saw her go into Sherwood's caravan at 9:40 p.m. and come out again at 9:55. Evidently he was curious about the visit, but he didn't have time to follow Gwendolyn over to her tent. He had to close the fun house. Once he'd done that, he went back to his caravan and brooded for a while. Then he heard Diana scream."

"Was it Skelly who stole the teacups?"

"Uh-huh. He swiped them before the police arrived, cleaned them up and locked them away for safekeeping."

"So who put them back?"

"By his own admission, Skelly wanted to, but he couldn't manage to break into the trailer to do it. In the end, it was Diana who wound up returning them to Sherwood's caravan. The way I understand it, Skelly didn't think anyone had noticed the cups were missing. He felt if he could get them back where they belonged, everything would be fine."

Lexie frowned. "Yes, but Diana saw the teacups on the counter when she 'discovered' Wren's body."

"And she very shrewdly made a point of letting you in on that little secret," Rick remarked, threading his fingers through her hair. His breath was warm on her cheek. "When the police photos revealed nothing on the counters, she made it seem obvious that someone else had indeed been in the caravan the night of the murder. And by stealing the cups from Skelly and returning them to the cupboard, she further convinced you of her innocence."

A shiver that had nothing to do with fear skated along Lexie's spine. "I think I'm more confused now than ever. I assume what you're saying is that Skelly stole the cups to protect Gwendolyn because he truly believed she'd killed Wren. Then when he didn't put them back, Diana decided to do it for him. Which must mean she knew what Skelly was up to right from the start."

"Oh, she knew," Rick confirmed, pushing the collar of her sweater aside so he could nuzzle her shoulder. "And she used the knowledge to her advantage. For a time everything Skelly did was beneficial to her cause. He tried to warn you off up at Wexford Castle. He also wrote the death threat on the window of Sherwood's trailer, followed you from the restaurant, lured you into the house of mirrors, used a cloth drawing of a skeleton to scare you, and we already knew he wrote threatening notes to both you and Diana."

Not unexpectedly, Lexie found it more and more difficult to concentrate. But she had to know it all. "Who wrote the third note?" she asked, her voice husky as Rick's mouth found the hollow of her collarbone.

"Diana. On a similar typewriter but with a differen
pitch. That's why the letters matched and the spacin
didn't."

"What about the gun she dropped outside the fun house
Did she do it on purpose?"

"Uh-huh."

"To further frame Gwendolyn?"

"Or anyone else we might have suspected at that point."
He lifted his head for a moment, turning her slightly on hi
lap, pushing the hair away from her neck. "One thing I'
say about Diana: she's very perceptive. After we chased he
out of Wren's caravan the night she put the cups back, sh
realized I had to be working for Scotland Yard. A littl
skulking behind the scenes verified that suspicion, so sh
took her plan a step further and reasoned that since she'
been arrested for Sherwood's murder, I must have searche
Gwendolyn's trailer thoroughly, looking for the Saxon
jewels."

"She assumed you would have unearthed Gwendolyn'
gun in the process and figured that as soon as we found i
outside the fun house, we would head straight for the for
tune-teller's living quarters."

"Where a sleepy Diana would be waiting in her robe
looking entirely innocent and doubtless rejoicing in an
other unexpected dose of good fortune."

"What do you mean?"

Rick grinned. "Somewhere along the line, somethin
Diana said or did must have tipped Gwendolyn off. Sh
followed her new roommate to the fun house that night, bu
lost her on the way back."

"So that's why Gwendolyn came bursting in." In spite of
herself, Lexie couldn't resist a satisfied smile. "She mus
have been shocked to find Diana already back and decke
out in her bathrobe and slippers. Is there anyone who didn't
inadvertently help her?"

"Only Wren," Rick said with a shrug, tugging at the hem of her sweater. "And Fitz. Diana spent a great deal of time trailing around after him. The day we found Aidan's name spelled out on Wren's side of Fitz's Scrabble board, she finally realized what had tipped him off to her identity. She knew it would only be a matter of time before one of us unscrambled the letters, so she decided to wait for her chance and kill us."

Shivering, Lexie pushed all thoughts of the descending lift aside as Rick's hands slid teasingly over her stomach. "Uh, what about Gwendolyn? I know she was blackmailing Diana for a portion of the Saxony jewels, but are there going to be any charges laid against her?"

"Obstruction of justice. I imagine her lawyer will be able to swing a deal in return for her testimony at Diana's trial."

"And Victoria?"

"As we suspected, Wren was skimming. She found out, intended to confront him, then heard Diana scream. With Wren dead and her own problem solved, she didn't want to risk saying anything to the investigating officers for fear of incriminating herself." Turning Lexie in his arms, Rick pulled her up higher until she was looking into his eyes. "All clear now, Counselor?"

"Clear enough, Inspector."

He brushed the hair from her cheek, his fingers warm and wonderfully gentle. "No more problems?"

"No... Yes." She groaned and pressed her forehead against his shoulder. Rodney. She had to go back to London and talk to Rodney. To tell him— What? That she'd changed her mind? That a safe, secure life-style was no longer what she wanted?

"He'll never believe me," she moaned against Rick's jacket.

"Is he British?"

"Who?"

"Rodney?"

She raised her head. "How did you know who I meant?"

Rick's grin was blithe. "Lucky guess. Is he?"

"Very."

"Then he'll believe you. And he'll understand."

A reluctant smile tugged at her lips as Rick's mouth began making a thorough investigation of her throat. "Is that the voice of experience talking?"

"Only in a relative sense." His lazy words were muffled against her skin, but Lexie wasn't about to let him pull away. "Some of my ancestors were Druids. I'll tell you about them on our wedding night."

She ran her fingers through his silky hair. "Do that and it'll be the shortest wedding night in history."

He stopped kissing her long enough to run his thumb across her full lower lip. "Does that mean you'll marry me?"

"I'll take it under advisement," she said, shifting her weight on top of him, delighting in the strength of his arousal.

His blue eyes glittered in the carousel lights. "Is that a yes?"

Smiling, she lowered her mouth to his. "That's a very definite yes, Inspector."

UUNDER A FULL PARADE of stars, P. J. Fitzwilly strolled toward the carnival tent where he slept. He was almost there when he noticed the official stragglers lurking outside Algernon's workshop. Removing the stub of his cigar from his mouth, he sauntered over to the old ruin, making no attempt to sidestep Charles Gideon who turned suddenly and smacked right into him.

"I say, I am sor— Oh, it's you." The sergeant's faintly contemptuous sneer took in Fitz's rumpled countenance. "Fitzwilly, isn't it?"

"At your service, Sergeant," Fitz responded with a cheerful nod of his head.

"Indeed." Charles's pinched nostrils flared slightly. "I understand you aided Inspector Matheson in the apprehension of Diana Beroni. I expect he was most grateful."

Fitz popped the cigar back in his mouth and shoved his hands in his jacket pockets. "I've no need for gratitude, Sergeant. Rick's my mate. And mates are always glad to help their own."

"Yes, quite right." Charles didn't understand a word he'd said, but Fitz didn't really care. Rick knew. That's what mattered. "Well, I shall say good-night to you, then, Fitz-willy."

"Good night to you, Sergeant Gideon." Out of the corner of his eyes, Fitz saw the man start to move away. His darting gaze bounced off the distant carousel, then came to rest on the fortress ruin before him. Taking a slow puff on his cigar, he called out a soft "A moment, Sergeant, if you please."

"Yes? What is it?"

Again the impatient, faintly derogatory tone. Fitz shrugged it aside, holding out his hand to the starchy detective. "I believe you dropped these."

For a moment Charles gaped at the objects. "How did I— How did you—" he spluttered, then clamped his mouth shut. "I see you haven't lost your touch."

Fitz grinned. "Only me criminal tendencies, Sergeant. Only me criminal tendencies."

Charles grabbed his watch and wallet from Fitz's outstretched hand. "Picking pockets, bringing down walls." He stopped and swung his gaze to Algernon's workshop. "Exactly how did you bring down that wall? You never did explain yourself."

"No," Fitz agreed, "I never did." His twinkling eyes fell on the ancient fortress. Touching the brim of his derby, he winked at the stone foundations. "Thanks, mate," he murmured.

And with a polite nod at Charles, he strolled off into the darkness, whistling around the stub of his cigar.

Indulge a Little
Give a Lot

A LITTLE SELF-INDULGENCE CAN DO
A WORLD OF GOOD!

Last fall readers indulged themselves with fine romance and free gifts during the Harlequin®/Silhouette® "Indulge A Little—Give A Lot" promotion. For every specially marked book purchased, 5¢ was donated by Harlequin/Silhouette to Big Brothers/Big Sisters Programs and Services in the United States and Canada. We are pleased to announce that your participation in this unique promotion resulted in a total contribution of *$100,000.*

*

Watch for details on Harlequin® and Silhouette®'s next exciting promotion in September.

HARLEQUIN
American Romance®

THE LOVES OF A CENTURY...

Join American Romance in a nostalgic look back at the Twentieth Century—at the lives and loves of American men and women from the turn-of-the-century to the dawn of the year 2000.

Journey through the decades from the dance halls of the 1900s to the discos of the seventies ... from Glenn Miller to the Beatles ... from Valentino to Newman ... from corset to miniskirt ... from beau to Significant Other.

Relive the moments ... recapture the memories.

Look for the CENTURY OF AMERICAN ROMANCE series starting next month in Harlequin American Romance. In one of the four American Romance titles appearing each month, for the next twelve months, we'll take you back to a decade of the Twentieth Century, where you'll relive the years and rekindle the romance of days gone by.

Don't miss a day of the CENTURY OF AMERICAN ROMANCE.

A CENTURY OF
AMERICAN ROMANCE
1900's

The women...the men...the passions...
the memories....

Harlequin Superromance®

A June title
not to be missed....

Superromance author Judith Duncan has created her
most powerfully emotional novel yet, a book about
love too strong to forget and hate too painful to
remember....

Risen from the ashes of her past like a phoenix,
Sydney Foster knew too well the price of wisdom,
especially that gained in the underbelly of the city.
She'd sworn she'd never go back, but in order to
embrace a future with the man she loved, she had to
return to the streets...and settle an old score.

Once in a long while, you read a book that affects you
so strongly, you're never the same again. Harlequin is
proud to present such a book, STREETS OF FIRE by
Judith Duncan (Superromance #407). Her book merits
Harlequin's AWARD OF EXCELLENCE for June 1990,
conferred each month to one specially selected title.

S407-1